Weathermen

Weathermen

Robert C. Moore, Jr.

Writers Club Press
San Jose New York Lincoln Shanghai

Weathermen

Writers Club Press
an imprint of iUniverse.com, Inc.

For information address:
iUniverse.com, Inc.
5220 S 16th, Ste. 200
Lincoln, NE 68512
www.iuniverse.com

ISBN: 0-595-19629-2

Printed in the United States of America

Dedication

To Stephanie, after twenty years my best friend, and my parents and family for love and support. And to the Weathermen, for inspiration.

Acknowledgements

Thanks are due to Ron Jacob, author of 'The Way the Wind Blew' for very helpful technical and editorial comments. Thanks also to Framingham Public Library and Wellesley College Library for assistance in tracking down the government report on the Weathermen. Thanks to friends and colleagues for encouragement in pursuing this odd topic. What a long, strange trip it's been.

Any errors, technical or grammatical, are the author's fault.

1969

"*I met a gin-soaked bar-room queen in Mem-phis,*" Mick oozed from the radio. Carl played air guitar from behind the wheel of the stolen 64 Plymouth Valiant. Tom rolled his eyes; he didn't like the Stones, all he seemed to like were the folk singers and the protest songs.

"I can only take so much Joan Baez, man," Carl apologized as the guitar riff made the radio speaker buzz. Carl was stocky, Tom decidedly lean. It was May but it felt like August, the temperature a humid eighty-five degrees. Both were twenty years old, bearded, their hair to their shoulders, dressed in jeans and sneakers and sheathed in sweat, some from the heat but mostly from nerves. "*I met-a-di-vor-cee in New-York-City…*"

Across the parking lot, dotted with cars, only a third full, was a branch of the Bank of Ohio, a small brick building with big glass windows and, if Tom and Carl's observations were correct, they were due for a pickup. "What time is it?" Tom whispered for the third time since they'd parked. Carl held up his wrist and Tom read the watch. "Damn pigs," Tom said, "it's four-fifty, we've watched this place for three frigging days and they always," he pounded the dash with the heel of his right hand, "always get here at four-twenty-five. Where the fuck are they?" he asked.

Carl turned off the radio; Mick was getting on his nerves.

They waited, car idling, the sun low in the west over a flat horizon. "We can't stay here, man," Tom said, looking left, then right, then over his shoulder and out the back window, "someone will remember us."

Carl nodded, looking through the side and rear view mirrors. "All we need is for some flunky cop to run a check on the license plate. Where the fuck are they?" he wondered. He reached under the seat and retrieved his handgun, a .44 magnum, blue steel, and again felt exhilarated and terrified at the weight of it.

Tom's nerves fretted tighter at sight of the gun. "What we should say, when we start it," he rehearsed, "this is a political act to support the resistance against American imperialism. Did David say we should say 'Weatherman' or not? I don't remember." Carl shook his head. Tom retrieved his smaller, nickel-plated .22 pistol, nervously stroking the grip. "We should've practiced with these," he said, thinking of it for the first time.

"Don't worry, man," Carl tried to ease his friend's nerves, "if it goes down right, we won't even need to shoot these." The guns were David's idea. David, their cell leader back at Hawthorne College, who had asked for volunteers to raise money.

"If," Tom said. "Should we get out of here and pick some other place?"

Carl shook his head; his friend was losing his nerve. "We don't have time to find another place. David told us to be back by tomorrow. They're going to have the demonstration at the Springfield Armory and they need the money for bail and lawyers." Tom nodded. "Next time don't volunteer," Carl added.

"Someone had to," Tom said softly. It was easy to be a Weatherman and sit on your ass during meetings, argue through the night about how best to attack the fascist state and why they had to destroy the army and the police. It was easy to demonstrate, to insult the cops, it was even fun. But the revolution wasn't coming through sit-ins, wasn't going to happen by fools surrounding the Pentagon and trying to levitate it. "This money is being seized in the name of the people to support the revolution against

U.S. Imperialism," Tom recited. "Dumont always says you have to be clear whether it's a political act or a crime. We aren't criminals."

"Bullets and blood will be the mortar of the revolution," that was what their history professor said. Professor Peter Dumont was fresh from his doctoral studies in Buffalo, where SDS was very active. Until Tom and Carl had dropped out to devote all their time to Weatherman and violent revolution, Dumont had been their inspiration, their catalyst. "Wonder if Dumont ever robbed an armored car," Tom wondered, and Carl laughed.

"Not likely," he said. "Too cushy a job. Dumont's okay, but he's all talk."

And then the sun's beams reflected off the nearly flat windshield of the armored car as it turned off Rt. 20. "Go," Tom said in a low, urgent voice. Carl was already turning the wheel. The armored car's motor growled as it slowed and navigated the parking lot, and Tom and Carl followed it in the Plymouth until it came to a stop at the curb in front of the bank, pulling up close behind. "Now," Tom said, and they opened their doors, guns aimed at the guard who was coming out of the passenger door. "You!" Tom yelled.

The guard, in his fifties, a fellow with short gray hair under his cap, turned to see a longhaired hippie with a pistol. Trying for his side arm, the hippie ran up to him and held the gun to his stomach. "Don't try it," said the hippie. "Open the back, now." The guard had been trained and periodically retrained on how to respond in a robbery.

"Calm down, kid," the guard said, disgust leavened by a healthy fear of a gun barrel. "I don't have the key to the back—" but the hippie had already seen the keys and the guard reluctantly opened the back door. Carl got in the truck.

Tom pulled the guard's gun from his belt and threw it under the Valiant, then ordered the guard ahead of him. "Everybody just lay down," Tom said, dimly aware of his heart pounding. Sweat was trickling down his face. There was a second guard inside, and a driver, and everyone had their weapons on the ground; none of them seemed keen on risking a bullet for the company. He got in the truck. They sorted through a pile of canvas bags, each full of money, looking for a larger bag to put them all in, and then someone's scream pierced the air. A woman and child came around the corner and saw the guns and understood instantly. She screamed again, a long, loud one, as though she was in personal danger. "Shut up!" Tom yelled. Then she grabbed her young daughter and dragged her away.

"Jesus Christ, what a set of lungs," Carl said.

"Police!" It came from the street, and Tom looked out the back to see a cop running from a work detail on the highway. "Drop your weapons," he yelled. He was a husky guy, but he was moving fast.

"All these pigs look like pigs," Tom joked nervously, but no one laughed.

"Here," Carl said, handing him three of the deposit bags, "we'll just have to make a couple trips."

"Police!" The cop was in the middle of the parking lot now. Tom stood on the back bumper, waving his handgun in case the stupid pig didn't realize he was charging armed men. Then, to his own surprise, he squeezed off a shot, at a forty-five degree angle well over anyone's head. The cop dove behind a parked car, and Tom felt the adrenaline rush. "It works," he said, climbing down the tailgate to put the bags in the car.

"Drop your weapons!" As Tom climbed back into the armored car a bullet zipped close by his ear. Tom spun, pointed his pistol and pulled the trigger and he and Carl heard the gun jam. Tom glanced at Carl, panicking; Carl, dropping three canvas bags, jumped in front of Tom and raised his pistol. The cop fired and Carl fired; the sounds blended into one, from inside the truck an ear-splitting roar. A ricochet off the truck door accounted for the cop's bullet. The cop said nothing, staggered and fired again, the shot bouncing off the Valiant. "Just stop!" Carl screamed, and squeezed off more shots. The guards were hugging the floor tightly. The cop took another step, and Carl fired until the trigger clicked. Then the cop fell. "Fuck!" Carl cursed. He dropped the gun, picked up two more bags, and he and Tom abandoned the truck to shove their haul into the back seat. "You saved my life," Tom said. Carl nodded, fumbling with the keys. "Get us out of here," Tom said, his eyes on the dead cop, dark puddles of blood welling out from under him. "Oh Christ," he moaned.

Carl squealed the tires taking off, the security guards were on their radios, and the cop was lying still on the pavement behind them. "Oh fuck!" he screamed, "FUCK FUCK FUCK!" The plaza disappeared behind them.

"Turn here," Tom said, and Carl made a left turn onto a tree-lined residential street. "Keep your speed down. We can get away if we don't attract attention." Tom seemed calm now, and he guided Carl through a residential subdivision they'd explored yesterday, back onto another highway, and as the sun's last rays threw long shadows on the highway, they made it to the Interstate.

"Better start cutting open those bags," Carl suggested, calm now. "We can stop and throw out the bags, and get rid of that evidence."

Evidence of armed robbery, Tom thought, which is now the least of our troubles. Half an hour later he cut through the last canvas bag, collected the haul and counted it. "You know how much we got?" he asked, allowing himself a modest smile. His heart was pounding, but this time it was just excitement.

Carl shrugged. "Five thousand?" Tom shook his head. "Fifteen? Fifty?"

Tom flourished a paper-tagged bundle of hundred-dollar bills. "This little bundle is just ten thousand. We have six hundred and fifty thousand," he said, enunciating each syllable. "Six hundred and fifty thousand. I didn't know there was that much money in the whole fucking state."

That evening the Valiant was a burned wreck on the outskirts of Erie, Pennsylvania, and the Weathermen got on a Greyhound. The robbery made news in Ohio and western Pennsylvania, less so as they traveled east. "No mention of us being Weathermen," Tom said, reading the headline through the glass of the vending machine while they waited for the next bus in New York City. "We forgot to tell them," Carl said. Tom bought the paper. The story was below the fold, with poor composite pictures of the two, and details about the dead policeman. Tom carefully tore the story out and threw the paper away. "He had a kid," he said once on the bus ride.

It seemed safer not to call ahead to alert David but when they reached the off-campus house that they and ten others called home, he was overjoyed with the money and unfazed by the consequences. "You shot a pig?" he said, sounding amused. "Hey, one less pig. This, this is fucking magnificent," he squeezed a bundle of bills. "I'm going to report in." He went into his bedroom and was on the phone for half an hour. Tom had a Coke and Carl had a beer, as they watched the Assistant Attorney General call for, "harsh measures to suppress these ideological criminals."

"Think he means us?" Carl asked. He was half-asleep, not having slept well on the bus. In his closed eyes he discovered a permanent image in his memory, of a police officer lying in a pool of his own blood, an image that would never fade.

When David came out he was subdued. "Okay, you guys fucked up."

"How? You were glad we killed the pig," Carl said.

"You didn't make a political statement, which is bad, because now we just look like thieves. What's worse for you two is you left a gun, covered with finger prints," David said. "And there were witnesses."

"It's our first time," Tom said miserably. "The cop kept coming. At least the guards followed directions."

David, his own hair in a braid down to the middle of his back, his t-shirt sporting a clenched black fist, shook his head in dismay. "I just talked to my cell leader. You guys need to leave the country for a little while."

"Leave the country?" Carl looked scared.

"It's okay, man, it's okay," said Tom. "We can go to Canada. Toronto is really cool, Montreal is okay."

"No," said David. "Not just leave the country. Leave the continent. I'm sorry, I should've," he left the sentence dangling. After an awkward moment he said, "if it helps, you've made a huge contribution to the cause. But you've got to stay out of the country for six months," David ordered. He gave Tom a scrap of paper. "In six months call this number and ask for Ruby Tuesday. If it's safe to come home, Ruby is in the shower and will return your call. If it isn't, Ruby is out, we don't know when she'll be back. Understand?"

Two evenings later, with borrowed passports, they flew out of Logan, feeling uncomfortable in their brush cuts, clean-shaven, in business suits, with round trip tickets to Gatwick they wouldn't complete. They had a suitcase apiece, one with clothes, the other containing some of the money. It would be years before they returned to Amerika.

Old Acquaintances

On a wall in my office in the Department of History at Hawthorne College was a framed poster from Woodstock, the original Woodstock, thirty plus years ago. I have it there because my niche in academia here is the Sixties, and it's the most clearly Sixties piece in my office, which is otherwise littered with papers and a collection of books. Some of the books I bought and read years ago, and don't now remember what they said, but I shelve them because titles like TEN DAYS IN OCTOBER and BAY OF PIGS should be seen in my office. Most of the books I've read, but the best read one, a well-thumbed copy of 'Best Stock Market Buys' doesn't reflect nearly so well on my academic rigor.

The poster gets lots of attention, some of it curiosity, some shy homage, some contemptuous, mostly silent. At some point in the early nineties I looked at it, on a sunny day when being inside seemed unnatural, and it looked silly and embarrassing, like a photograph of me then would look now, long bushy sideburns and haircut and a shirt with long pointed collar. But the photo is, again, a clear announcement to anyone entering that I either love the music or old posters or perhaps am a scholar of the era.

One of my devoted students, the ungifted Art, went to the third Woodstock and got a poster from it, framed. "Isn't it cool?" Art asked me, having brought it in just to compare to mine. Art was typical of my students; he was not bright, and he'll never get what he thinks is his dream job of teaching college history, but his adoration of my knowledge and mementos was groveling, so he made a good groupie. He wanted to be the first great comic historian, and wrote horribly long papers in which he struggled to make his points through jokes. He never got better than a 'B' from me so I didn't understand why he didn't just drop out and try to get on staff at the National Lampoon, or maybe Mad Magazine.

But I'm forgetting my story: Art brought in this slick, lithographed poster from Woodstock III that he'd spent thirty-five bucks for, another forty for a nice frame, and held it next to my Woodstock poster. My poster was also framed, but you could see the creases, the thumbtack holes, and the abuse the poster endured until it was preserved. I let him tell me about the music, bands like Phish that I'd heard of but was not familiar with, and otherwise tried to be a pleasant listener. Ultimately, though, I shut him down. "It's nice," I said charitably, "but it's not Woodstock, y'know?" Art was such a respectful follower that he smiled sadly and nodded his acceptance that his experience as a radical will always pale next to mine.

Here's my point: I bought my poster, too. In 1981, in an antique shop in New York City, and I paid over a hundred dollars for it (that included the frame). I didn't tell Art that I didn't actually attend Woodstock. That's a detail I omitted when teaching my American Radical History course. Where was I during Woodstock? That's a question none of my mediocre students ever thought to ask me.

And on that notable day when I put Art in his place, that fact was getting more and more depressing, and my niche at Hawthorne College had grown uncomfortable and less tenable. Hawthorne College sits on a hill in the middle of Framingham, which is a cozy twenty-some miles from Boston. It's a minor part of a good state university system, though our students come from nearby and usually stay nearby when they finish. I don't expect any of my students will ever become great academics. If they do, they certainly won't credit me with inspiring them.

Besides a decent teaching job and our campus, which is a nice wooded community on a hilltop, the other gift Hawthorne College gave me was the opportunity to meet my future mate, Linda Falcone, who managed the college bookstore. We met there in 1984. I was trying to order a title for my class and Linda was struggling to explain to me why books began going 'Out of Print' just twelve months after being published. I was very pleased to find an attractive woman who also had a graduate degree in American History, and who was making so much less than I was that I seemed to be the success story. At the time these events began, Linda and I had been 'dating' for about fifteen years. I called it 'dating'. She had begun a few months ago to call it 'our relationship'.

My faculty status at Hawthorne College was Associate Professor of History, with a concentration in American Radical History. I went from graduate student at Buffalo to lecturer at Hawthorne without so much as a trip around the country doing drugs in a multi-colored van, so my exposure to radicalism was pretty academic, or as Winfield Sinclair, our department chair called such stuff, "pretty thin gruel". Winfield never actually questioned the depth of my experience, and he voted for my tenure, so I assumed he at least accepted me. Since then I've learned how far out of the way most academics will walk to avoid a confrontation, and Winfield was ultimately no different, just crustier. I know he wished my background was more genuine, but I had the academic credentials, and Hawthorne couldn't afford a true radical.

I taught five classes each semester; included in that were the survey courses, the History of America and the History of Europe, at which all the faculty take their turns. I also taught American Radical History, one version each for undergraduate History majors and the other for our modest graduate department. I also had five graduate students doing 'directed readings' with me. That meant individual meetings once every two weeks, during which time we discussed the books I'd assigned to them. Actually, I'd been letting them pick the books, which was kind of a no-no, but they didn't turn me in. I just got tired of hearing another generation, three decades removed from the Sixties, trying to understand Soul on Ice or Steal This Book, when they had so much more fun reading The Anarchist Cookbook.

Art was one of my undergraduate advisees. He wanted me to get him into the graduate program, guide him to a graduate degree, and get him a teaching job there so he could stay close to his girlfriend and his mother. If only he was interested in computers.

I guess I'd say that I was depressed that day. The depression had begun half an hour before. I had come from my annual review with Winfield. He was always polite, treated us respectfully whether we deserved it or not, and our raises were usually adequate.

"Good morning, Peter," Winfield greeted me that morning, rising from behind his desk, coming across the poorly carpeted floor to give me his hearty handshake. "How are you today?"

"Pretty well, Winfield," I returned his handshake, trying to equal but not exceed the grip. "Sorry about the Patriots last night." Winfield was a devoted Patriots fan, and I had exercised my sole bit of political acumen in checking the score before my meeting.

A wonderful thing about Winfield was that he knew I didn't know squat about football, and that I was stretching to remember that New England's team was the Patriots, and he showed appreciation for my pitiful little gift. "That's the way it goes," he dismissed it, to our mutual relief. "How's that book coming?"

A brief history of my scholarly publications: I was hired fresh out of graduate school. Though doctoral theses' are supposed to be original works, mine involved editing—not writing, editing—a book of essays by Abby Hoffman, Bernardine Dohrn, Timothy Leary, and Eldridge Cleaver, to name a few. Since my thesis qualified, at the time, as current events, the University Press published it. VOICES FROM THE SIXTIES sold about forty-eight copies, of which I knew the owners of seventeen. That was my first book. I'd been writing my second book more or less ever since. "I'm still reading for it," I said, "probably this summer I'll have a solid outline and probably a good chapter or two." Winfield asked me about my next book at every odd review. Then I remembered, he'd asked the previous year. He wasn't supposed to ask again so soon. That's when I began to sweat. Ordinarily, Winfield would talk a few minutes about national conferences we should attend, about reading he'd done lately, to draw out details on what I've read lately, and he worked down to how the state had ripped the budget to shreds, and soon after I learned how much shred I got.

"You might remember," Winfield started, turning sideways in his desk chair, giving off that Einstein-ish profile he cultivated, "the governor promised a twenty percent cut in the university budget whilst running for re-election. Last week, when he won reelection I had my fears. Yesterday, I met with Tony," our diminutive nickname for Dr. Anthony Carballho, the President of the College, "and learned that the governor actually intends to deliver on a promise this year, probably because it hurts others and not him." Oh boy, I remember thinking, this is way off the usual script.

"We've got twenty faculty in the Department of History, counting adjuncts," Winfield went on. "I've been told to prepare to lose five seats at the end of the semester." I felt sweat trickle from all my pores. "You've been in the Department for thirty years, Peter, and you've done good work for us, and I am trying very hard to make sure that when the dust settles in June, the people who have kept this Department going are rewarded." I think about then was when my armpits soaked through. Luckily I was enough of a dandy to wear a tweed jacket, which was insulating me for better and worse. Winfield was still talking, "you know the old rule, Peter, 'publish or perish.'" He heaved the appropriate hearty sigh as he said; "you need to get some words on paper, perhaps a rough draft of your first chapter that you can publish as an article, review paper perhaps. I'm not talking about a major paper, just a fresh publication on your c.v. Do you think that's viable?"

I wanted to say, "Jesus Christ, Winfield, is this a school or some sort of factory where they toss out the old guys when they can't heft an I-Beam?" What I actually said? "Sure," I said, trying to sound positive, "I can do an article." Name the topic, I almost said.

Winfield faced me again, and had his apologetic face on, usually reserved for the presentation of the raise. "Our increases have been postponed until the end of the term, sort of all-or-nothing. If you keep your job, you get a raise." The air was dead and I forgot to inhale. "I'm sorry to deliver this kind of news, Peter. Every member of the faculty will be hearing this same information, in every department." He glanced out his window, then looked at me. "Let me give you a little edge," he added in a lower tone, and from his shirt pocket he pulled out a slip of paper. "This is the name of the editor of a new journal. I spoke with him at the New England Modern History meeting," which I should have attended, but Winfield was too kind to mention that, "and I've told him our department may have a burst of pro-lif-icity this term." He handed me the name. A few minutes and another handshake later, I was out in the hall, my armpits chilly and wet.

So that was why I was depressed. Art's groveling had helped to lift my spirits.

That day was also my annual Opening Night, except that it took place at 1:35 in the afternoon. Every time I taught American Radical History I did my 'Weatherman' talk. By way of preparation, I customarily skimmed my 'Weatherman' folder before the lecture. After Art left my office I pulled the folder. It was a thick file. It bulged with newspaper clippings from the late sixties and the seventies, from the New York Times, the Chicago Trib, the Herald, the Boston Globe and others I have ordered through our library. My earliest clippings were from the Buffalo student newspaper. Gently sifting through my clippings, I refreshed my memory before my coming lecture.

When I was finishing my education in 1968 at SUNY Buffalo, the Students for a Democratic Society came to the student union and held a rally in our auditorium. It was late April. Martin Luther King, Jr. had been shot three weeks prior. Every American ghetto was in flames, and we were, so it appeared, losing the war in Vietnam that General Westmoreland had just persuaded the country we were winning. I was one of several hundred resident students attending the SDS rally, sitting in the upper balcony, the cheap seats. Jerry Rubin was the main speaker at the podium, and he had long hair and was screaming some of his speech, and since there was a microphone almost in his mouth his words burst from the speakers more angry and incoherent than he was.

"We are here to STOP THE WAR!" Burst of static, "-fucking GENOCIDE!" The crowd began applauding, yelling out their approval as Jerry blasted Johnson, Humphrey, and the military-industrialist complex. "One-Two-Three-Four-We-DON'T WANT-YOUR-FUCKING-WAR! Stop the War! STOP THE DRAFT!" After that the crowd erupted and wouldn't quiet. Jerry tried, in vain, to make a few more profane points, then shrugged and joined the chant that had taken over, "1-2-3-4-WE-DON'T-WANT-YOUR-FUCKING-WAR!" You couldn't hear anything but the chant. I had had a few years of draft anxiety before the numbered lottery system made every draft-age male a selfish coward. You were delirious with joy if your number was 320, or tried not to piss your pants if your birthday came up as number four; the anger and fear were very real and SDS signed up a lot of kids that night.

I joined the line to sign a petition demanding the end of the war. "Join the cause!" urged a very sexy girl. She had an olive complexion and long brown hair, tied back in an orange scarf. She was also very buxom and was wearing a shirt with low neckline and no bra. I don't think SDS was blind to her appeal in signing up young men. There was a line in front of her table. I took the form and talked the SDS talk for as long as she would listen, all the while studying her cleavage, but I never did sign up.

Thirty years later, in my pendaflex folder, I still had a handout advertising the rally. It had gotten creased at some point, marring the capital letters

'SDS', but it was still legible, just frail. I remembered that night in Buffalo, and where I was two years later when I heard about Kent State, the National Guard insisting the students were armed (I was in Framingham watching 'Beach Blanket Bingo' instead of correcting papers).

But others were fighting the fight. Demonstrations at Columbia, at Washington State, at UCLA, at Ann Arbor, at Berkeley. Kids burning their draft cards, throwing pig's blood at the draft offices in Ottumwa, Iowa. Break-ins at draft boards across the country to destroy files. Even the UB Student Union was occupied; I had news prints of blurry photographs shot by the student photographer of a phalanx of angry cops bursting through a barricade of chairs blocking the glass entrance doors to reclaim the building and club any kids they could reach. Other photos: students set up first aid stations in the nearby dormitories, a girl puts a chunk of ice to her swollen eye, a couple bathes their eyes in a water fountain to wash away the tear gas. Good pictures.

Good thing all that was covered by dedicated journalism students. While it was happening some friends of the moment and I were barhopping. In 1965, just as SDS was gearing up, I learned from my advisor that the History Department wanted to anoint some students as Modern American Radical History scholars, with juicy assistantships, subsidized scholarly radicals. That was when I realized the overcrowded field of Colonial American History was overcrowded. So I made the change and started to collect my clippings, but I was never an activist, just an archivist.

Among all my memorabilia I also had a few videos, mostly cribbed from television specials. PBS did a good series on the Vietnam War and I taped the episodes on the Tet Offensive, the fall of Saigon and on Kent State. Most of my material I got from Armies of the Night, Fire In the Lake, Steal This Book, Soul on Ice, Dispatches and bits from books and novels written by soldiers and journalists who'd actually survived Vietnam.

I read everything about Vietnam. I had to, because I didn't go to Vietnam. I pulled a wonderfully low number and stayed in college and grappled my way into graduate school. When, in 1974, the draft stopped completely (college deferments having long since been respected) I was on the low rung of the greasy pole of academic advancement, a lecturer at Hawthorne facing my tenure review. So I didn't go to Vietnam, and I didn't go to Woodstock, and I didn't attend the March on Washington, or any civil rights marches, and I didn't join SDS or even bandage clubbed activists on campus. Pursuing the 'truth' on the Weathermen was the Holy Grail of which I made my career.

I first developed my course in 1977 as a lecturer, looking for a niche course that no one else could or wanted to do, and in 1977 the Sixties and the War were as dead as were the poor bastards on the Wall. During my first year teaching this stuff I barely kept enough students to keep the class running. That meant I had to be a popular teacher, i.e. entertaining, and not a real tough grader. I could do that; in fact I excelled at it. I put together a series of lectures and presentations, including some slides and some taped music, and I 'did' the Sixties. I hustled up some bell-bottomed jeans, a headband, and bought a long brown wig to 'play hippie' for the first lecture of the course.

"Hey, man, this will be the grooviest semester you've ever had, man, and I'm talking mind-blowing stuff," I would begin, sitting sometimes on the edge of my desk in a lotus position, my fingers in 'peace' signs, and as I recall it now I'm mortified by the memories. "I'm going to tell you about the Sixties. There were drugs, there was free love, there was great music, there was revolution, and there was a lot of protest. Be cool, hang out, and learn some fun shit." It was crude showmanship, and academia at its most banal and shameful, but it got me to Assistant Professor when the Department of History was being put on bread and water.

I regained some dignity as time progressed. When I made Assistant Professor I threw out the wig and the bell-bottoms and benched my rip-off of 'Hippie-Dippie Weatherman'. I don't look like George Carlin. Actually, as I get older, people tell me I look like Richard Dreyfuss, but I've never seen the resemblance. In 1981 I started beginning the course with a film clip, a one-hour video that encapsulated my entire course, perhaps too neatly. By then the students had come to expect videos and were as embarrassed to see my 'hippie skit' as I was doing it.

And on the day that I learned my future depended on another publication, I was due to introduce the 'Weatherman' chapter. In my first years I spoke of the underground in reverential terms. "These were the true radicals, the ones that literally played with fire. They stopped the Vietnam War," I preached. "They took to the streets. They threatened civil war."

My introduction had become harsher as the years passed, and history judged the veterans more kindly and, consequently, the protestors less kindly. I changed my introduction to the Weathermen to be harsher, more cutting, and no longer reverential. Looking back, I wish I had stuck to being either reverential or critical.

The classroom was a bare, sterile room with highly polished floors, walls so bare even graffiti would be welcome, hard, uncomfortable desks, and a blackboard. I rarely used the blackboard, and I barely used the desk in the front right corner, from which I could look into the hallway. The only reason the teacher's desk sits up there is because one doesn't want the students looking into the hallway. I was a few minutes early, as was my norm, and so were my current undergraduate groupies. Art was there, he of the framed Woodstock III poster. Next to him was the well-groomed and high-maintenance brunette bombshell of the year, Elaine Dunning. She transferred in from Amherst College, and none of us could figure out why, but we rarely had pretty girls in the department so the faculty, which is 65% male, didn't complain. Sometimes these pretty girls increased department enrollment.

Next to Elaine was the sociological opposite end of the spectrum, Judith Rosen, who was a purebred leftist. She wouldn't touch makeup, she wouldn't eat meat, and she sometimes acted as a moral compass when discussions got heated, as long as True North was True Left.

During a class spent discussing the McCarthy Hearings, one of my shyest students, Dan Crothers, ventured the opinion that, "there were a lot of Communists in sensitive places, and they were a threat to national security. The Rosenbergs—" and that's about all he got out.

"Are you fucking stupid?" Judith asked, turning to look at simple Dan. She looked like someone had dragged fingernails across the blackboard. She went on to tear apart McCarthy and praise the Rosenbergs, with a burst about nuclear proliferation and mutual-assured-destruction, and to complain that the current generation was illiterate and stupid. Dan tried to get in a few points, but he was badly outmatched. I let it happen, because Judith was bright and I hoped she'd eventually be my brightest advisee, and I was tired of Winfield getting all the bright ones.

The other ten students were picking up my course because it sounded more interesting than the competition—The Work Force in 19th Century Victorian Literature—and because I had a reputation as an easy grader. It was true, I didn't require much from my students, but that's because I didn't give them much. If I was still an active scholar, still reading and writing and going to conferences to swap thoughts with other scholars, and was injecting fresh material into my courses, I would have been more demanding. But a student who took my course in 1984 could give his notes to his nephew in 1998. The answers on the multiple-guess questions were almost exactly the same.

This laziness tripped me up at times. Students like Judith were active scholars, and did read current literature avidly, and once asked me, "what does it say about your generation that Tom Hayden is now in Congress?"

I'd forgotten about Hayden. "He is?" I looked at her, shaken from my usual lecture delivery. "I mean, yes, of course he is." Since most of our students were still reasonably respectful and polite, I blathered for a few minutes about "selling-out and going straight and how you can't fight the revolution forever" without saying why, and she didn't ask me any more questions.

I wasn't proud of being a lazy teacher. I wanted to be a retired teacher, but I was about ten years away from that. My only motivation in returning to scholarship would be either getting laid with someone like Elaine Dunning, who others speculated would go for the brainy sort, or if I wanted to get a job in a more prestigious college. I would have needed to publish a book, and probably a real book. One in which I actually did 90% of the writing. And Winfield had just pulled me up short.

"Good afternoon," I began the introduction. "Today we begin looking at the activism of the Sixties, and today I'm going to begin with the Students for a Democratic Society, and their violent off-spring, the Weathermen." I flipped open my folder and there was my script, just like I first typed it for my doctoral thesis over thirty years ago. "In 1960 a group of students protesting civil rights and the growing war in South Vietnam began the Students for a Democratic Society in Ann Arbor with the Port Huron Statement. The statement called for the forging of an alliance between blacks and whites, students mostly, and of peace groups and a broad range of liberal media and organizations like the ACLU, to bring about a liberal realignment of the Democratic Party." I paused. "They were nothing if not ambitious. But the world was slow to change. In 1965, SDS organized their first march to Washington to protest the Vietnam War. Though civil rights were a part of their agenda, their real fuel was anti-war sentiment. By December, 1966, SDS announced that draft resistance was its top priority." I paused again.

I had some slides, of the monks in Vietnam who immolated themselves to protest the war in 1963, and of students in long hair holding up anti-war signs. "In 1967, at its Ann Arbor conference, SDS moved further to the left and called for a revolution to create a new working class, without being clear what would differentiate the new one from the old one." That was a snide shot that usually got the desired snickers from the more flip students. "In 1968 a lot happened. In January, the Vietnamese Communists launched the Tet Offensive, which was militarily impressive and psychologically brilliant. In our country the Civil Rights movement was attacked, and in April, Martin Luther King was assassinated. A few months later, after winning the California primary, Bobby Kennedy, considered King's spiritual successor, was also assassinated. In April and May, SDS seized Columbia University. Leader Mark Rudd would become a leader of the Weathermen." I had some slides, including a shot of Rudd smoking one of the Dean's cigars in his leather chair. That always got a few laughs and hoots.

"During the Democratic Convention in August, 1968, the SDS tried to march to the convention and the Chicago cops beat the hell out of them. It was police brutality, captured on film, and it helped bring this country as close to civil war as we've come since 1861." That was largely histrionic, but I did want them to appreciate the forces at work. "In March, 1969, at an SDS meeting in Texas, a faction created the Revolutionary Youth Movement. Two months later the RYM fractured, into three main groups, the Maoist Progressive Party, a militant Puerto Rican separatist group called the Young Lords, and the Black Panthers." Once upon a time I used to interject my own memories from that time, until the day sometime in the Eighties when I realized that I was starting to create a fictional Peter Dumont who had actually stood at the ramparts, bandaged the wounded, screamed epithets at the cops, etc. I stopped adding anything personal.

"What spun the 'Weathermen' off from this 'melting pot' was the desire of the Maoists to incite socialist revolution in this country. They weren't settling for ending the Vietnam War; they wanted to start a new one, here. The Panthers and the Lords weren't ready for that yet. The 'Weathermen' were the Maoists that couldn't wait."

It was smart to pause at this point to let them scribble notes on the genealogy of the Weathermen. Sometimes I was asked to spell 'Maoists' or "is it Weather-man or men? "What distinguished the Weathermen from SDS was their call to violence. The Weathermen announced they would fight the Army, the corporations, any institution of the country. They vowed to disrupt the very fabric of American life."

"Between October 9th and the 11th, 1969, the Weathermen made their first public show. They converged on Chicago, site of the 1968 Democratic Convention, to exact vengeance on the Chicago police for beating the SDS demonstrators. They were loosely organized in that none of them knew how many of their brethren would make the trip. Those who recalled how ruthlessly the Chicago police opposed the demonstrators called it suicide. But 1969 would be different, if only because those returning were no longer novices. They removed their jewelry. They braided their long hair or tied it into ponytails and tucked it in shirts or under hats. Most wore Army surplus or bicycle helmets, many had armed themselves with clubs, baseball bats, and lengths of pipe. And everyone had a damp piece of cloth to prolong their resistance to tear gas."

I paused for dramatic effect and spoke louder and in a slightly deeper voice. "They were staging the riot to end all riots. In 1968, as SDS, they had had numbers but were novices. This was next year. This was their turn. They anticipated their anger and dubbed the event the Days of Rage. There was one rude surprise awaiting them. Instead of assembling in the thousands, or tens of thousands, or more, they found their numbers were only several hundred."

Dan smirked. He was a right wing Republican at heart. "What happened then was stupid," I picked up the pace. "Undersized, they proceeded with a plan conjured with a vision of thousands. They tore through downtown Chicago, smashing shop windows. They attacked the police, who were better armed, in better condition, and mentally more than ready. This time the police didn't respond with tear gas, but with shotguns. The police, by and large, won. There was some property damage, some police took licks before clubbing the protesters, one officer was permanently paralyzed." I paused again, but not for drama. It's a conservative world now and if I spoke about that paralyzed officer lightly I'd hear about it. "But the Chicago police did a pretty fair job of pounding the Weathermen into bandages and jail." That got rewarding smirks from Elaine, and from Art, who knew how to kiss up. Nothing from Judith. Damn. "Limping out of Chicago as fast as bail could be arranged, the Weathermen then analyzed their failure almost as viciously as the Chicago cops had beaten them."

"More than anything the Days of Rage proved that the Weathermen were badly organized, badly pissed off at society, and perhaps most important, a factor seen in the most feared terrorist organizations today, the Weathermen were capable of suicidal action when needed. The anger that propelled them, with bike helmets and clubs, maybe forty of them, to charge a line of armed cops to battle a society they found corrupt, caught a lot of attention. They spurred the FBI to levels of covert activity unknown outside of wartime."

"In 1970, to quote the British as we kicked them out of the New World, 'the world turned upside down,'" I paused, and my brighter students looked up at me from their note taking, their eyes curious. "In 1970 there was Kent State, there was a fatal error in a bomb-making factory in a Greenwich Village townhouse, and Nixon extended the war into Cambodia. The Greenwich explosion killed four Weathermen and sent most of the others into hiding. Kent State traumatized the antiwar movement, and when Nixon extended the war, it appeared that all the marching, all the demonstrating, all the protesting had been for naught," I said. "Ironically, in 1972, Nixon did begin to pull the troops out. By 1974 we were out of Vietnam."

I was winding down. "In so far as stopping the war, the war ended, but it almost seems coincidental. In so far as igniting socialist revolution?" I shrugged, and got a couple of chuckles. "With the war over, the student movement lost its motivation, and the Weathermen imploded." A last dramatic pause. "Some have since called them failed revolutionaries. Were they? That's one of the questions we'll examine in the next few weeks."

That was it. That was the intellectual high-water mark of my best course. That day was Friday, October 12th, and I didn't know it yet but it was to be the last time I delivered that lecture. I talked about some of the materials I had assigned for reading, none of it recent, most from a revisionist book that proceeded from the title THE LITTLE ENGINE THAT COULDN'T and discussed how the Weathermen had squandered their opportunities. The phrase 'Failed revolutionary' had to show up at least once in the test essays of students hoping for the 'A'.

"Questions?" There were almost never questions. "No? Okay, have a good weekend," I gave the benediction and they politely rushed out. That's when I noticed two people in the doorway of the classroom, a man and a woman. I think they had been there for a while, though I don't remember from when. They weren't my students, so I assumed they'd heard about my 'Weatherman' lecture and wanted to hear it.

Wanted to hear my lecture?

"Professor Dumont?" asked the woman, in a voice oddly female but with deeper and stronger timbre. "We'd appreciate a minute of your time."

"Do you have a question about the Weathermen?" I asked, flattered.

"Actually, it's about your book," said the man. My book? My book was thirty years old. It was twenty-five years out-of-print. Finding a copy of my book would have required an extensive search of used bookstores, which was an outlay of more energy that it deserved. I wanted to ask where they'd found a copy, but the man said, "you quoted from it several times and while I'm sure you have a better idea than I of what's in it, I have a question on Bernardine Dohrn, page seventy-two." I didn't remember what Weatherman was on page seventy-two; it had been four years since I last looked at my book. That put me on the defensive. I was intimidated by people who knew my book better than I did.

"Well, if you've got a copy with you—"

"Oh," he said, "sorry. It's in, uh, the car."

"Well, if you'd care to follow me to my office, I've got a copy of it there," I answered agreeably. I was stunned, to think that people in the community ever read my book and had a response. They followed me out of the lecture center. The warmth of the sun hit us as we left the building, and then we passed a battered van parked in a handicapped spot. "That's really irrespon—"

A cloth, probably a handkerchief, was pressed over my mouth and nose and the fumes of ether poured into my lungs and clouded my brain.

As I surfaced from the ether I saw that I was in my own living room in my modest house two blocks from the campus. I was strapped into a kitchen chair with a combination of nylon rope and duct tape. My abductors were making macaroni and cheese from a package, my macaroni and cheese. "Hi, Professor, " the woman said, glancing at me as she stirred the macaroni in the pot. "You up?"

I looked around; my TV and stereo were in place. My head was pounding.

She looked into my eyes and nodded. "He's up. Ready for de-briefing?" she asked me with a half-smile.

"Who are you? Why did you do this?" I was still groggy from the ether and feeling a little nauseous from the headache. I was comforted to be in my own home, but there was a reasonable edge of terror there, too.

"He doesn't remember us," she said to the man.

"I'm Carl Krajewski," said the man.

"I'm Rose Thomas," said the woman. "You knew me as Thomas Rose."

"Carl Krajewski? Tom Rose?" It wasn't hard for me remember Tom and Carl, as they had left Hawthorne in 1969, dropping out of my American Radical History course to join the Weathermen and briefly put old Hawthorne on the map. Tom had seemed overwrought. He argued passionately about civil rights, about the sexual revolution, argued too passionately, I remember thinking at the time. Like he cared too much.

"Rose," she corrected me.

Carl Krajewski and Tom Rose had both been on the FBI's Most Wanted List for months after killing a police officer in 1969 during an armored car robbery in Conneaut, Ohio, that netted them a cool $650,000. They were suspected [wrongly] in the bombing of the draft board's records in Erie, Pennsylvania, a month later. And they might have thrown a homemade hand grenade at the Army Recruiting Center in Buffalo. Buffalo being the busiest border crossing point to Canada, after no sightings for a year the FBI assumed the two were hiding in Canada. Except that their informants in the Toronto University community never saw them either.

Reaching Sweden by a circuitous route, Carl and Tom each underwent cosmetic surgery. Carl chose to alter his facial appearance just enough to permit eventual return to America with a phony ID. Tom went a step further, a series of operations that changed his gender, returning to the United States as Rose Thomas. Carl and Thomas had been students of mine thirty years ago, and had listened to the radical harangue of a lecturer hoping to make assistant professor. Carl and Thomas went beyond my academic gymnastics, well beyond. "Dear God," was my response. "Why are you here?"

Not answering, Rose stirred the macaroni as Carl found my colander to drain it. "Why change your sex?" I asked.

"Well, you wouldn't know this about me," Rose said, "but I was in therapy for the three years I was at Hawthorne. After the armored car job we had to hide somewhere, and the dollar was strong against the kroner. Once we got to Sweden, I did another six months of therapy and the clinic in Stockholm agreed with me that I'd be happier as a woman. And we were right."

"And then we came back," Carl said, by way of over-simplification. They'd lived 'underground', meaning under false names and false identification, for the past thirty years. And after living lives of careful anonymity, Carl and Rose had reached middle age and, "we want to leave a legacy." A legacy?

"See, Abbie killed himself and Jerry sold out," Carl explained. "Most of them became just like their parents. We spent six months as revolutionaries, five years hiding, and changing our identities in Europe, and got homesick. We came back in 1975, and thanks to the surgery and the paperwork, no feds have ever found us."

Rose got up to turn off the pot and drain the water from the cooked noodles. I looked at them and they didn't look stoned or mentally deranged. "A legacy?"

"Yea," said Carl. "In '74 most of us realized that with the war over we needed to refocus our energy," he continued by way of an answer. The Prairie Fire Collective was the belated peaceful return to life of the activists, peacefully agitating for freedom for American political prisoners, Leonard Peltier, from Wounded Knee, and members of the FALN, Puerto Rican freedom fighters. The hard-core, the ones who were hooked on violence, they joined with black activists who were also beyond reconciliation with society and created the May 19th Coalition—named for the coincidental birthdays of Malcolm X and Ho Chi Minh. The May 19th Coalition attempted an armored car heist in Nyack, New York in 1981. It turned into a bloody shoot-out, roundly condemned by everyone as non-political but a potentially lucrative haul for murderous thieves. It also exposed so many of the remaining underground members of the Weather Underground that police believed they'd captured almost all of them. "Except for JoAnne Chesimard, they captured the ones that didn't just surrender," Carl said, his voice now sad and tired, "but there's still us. Sort of revolutionaries emeritus."

"What have you been doing?" I asked. "As revolutionaries emeritus?"

Carl nodded to Rose, who was getting out some bowls. "Rose has been a beautician. Mostly I've worked as a mechanic."

I was nodding a lot. My mind flitted from one astounding point to another. "Did the money from the armored car job all go to the operations?"

"Not at all," Rose said, setting the food and the bowls on the table. Carl dug in. "We left over four hundred thousand of it to supply the Weathermen. It was for bail bonds, lawyers, just supplying the movement. As for the rest, my procedures were the most expensive, but between us we used up about a hundred thousand getting remade and buying top quality forged passports and drivers licenses. Then we spent some time in Europe, living inconspicuously but not in poverty. We still have about fifty thousand in a Swiss bank account in case we need to leave the country."

Weathermen with a Swiss bank account. "So you've just been living the quiet suburban life here ever since?"

"Oh, no, we've been socially active," Carl said. "We were heavily into anti-nuclear demonstrations. We also did a lot of work for Amnesty International. Lots of the grunt work, stuffing envelopes and canvassing for donations. We were out in California for a few years and we worked on Jerry Brown's first presidential campaign, manning phone banks, handing out flyers, all sorts of stuff."

"Did anyone in those organizations know your true identities?"

Both shook their heads. "The only ones who know who we are are us." Rose indicated the three of us. "My parents disowned me after I made the FBI Top Ten. Carl's father died while we were abroad and he talks and writes to his mother but they haven't had a face to face meeting since we went underground." Rose touched Carl's hand in a feminine, comforting way, as he looked a bit distant. She caught my glance. "And if your next question is 'are we lovers' the answer would be 'no'. Carl prefers short brunettes. And I'm not very interested in sex."

"That's a departure from Weatherman ideology," I said. "Should I also assume you've both sworn off LSD?" Both of them looked at me like I'd just farted.

"No more LSD," Carl said, in a world-weary voice.

I must have also been licking my lips. "Let me get some water for you," Rose said. "You're a little dehydrated." She put a glass to my lips and I realized how cotton-dry my mouth was as I gulped.

"So," I got my breath back, "you were talking about leaving a legacy?"

Carl answered, "I always wanted to have a family but I couldn't subject a wife and children to living like we have. Rose may have had some fleshy nodules shifted around but she's not going to have a child. We both want to leave something permanent behind. Something more enduring than reputations as what you called 'failed revolutionaries.'"

I blushed. "That's not at all what I'm saying in the lecture," I lied. I certainly never intended that line to be heard by its subjects. This was a meeting I'd always dreaded. "I'm sorry," was the best I could come up with. "Time changes our perspectives," I offered, unconvincingly.

"We don't think we're failures, Professor Dumont," Rose answered affirmatively, "and we thought, since you first opened our eyes to the lies of our government, that you would help us in this last act. Help us leave a legacy."

Help them? I tried to look poker-faced, but what showed through first, and was seen, was fear. Rose saw it and half-smiled; had she anticipated my cowardice? "Wouldn't you like that?" she asked in a teasing voice, "it would only improve your opinion of us. And it would make that lecture a real show-stopper."

Looking at a framed Grateful Dead poster on my wall that Linda had given me two years ago, I answered dryly, "what I said then should be viewed in context. There wasn't an academic worth a damn that didn't preach revolution." That, for what it's worth, was true. "If you were hoping guilt would induce me to assist you, I have to tell you, you need other leverage. Besides," I suggested, "aren't there other aging revolutionaries who would welcome the chance to be in a legacy?"

"I tried some old contacts," Carl said, disappointment in his voice. "A lot of them surfaced years ago and don't want more trouble." Since 1975 there had been a steady trickle of Weathermen surfacing to face their charges. Many found their charges were either reduced or forgotten, and some only endured probation and are now taxpayers and voters.

"But our charges weren't for starting a riot or resisting arrest or clubbing a cop at a rally. We aren't expecting to hear that all is forgiven," Rose said, ending that discussion abruptly. There was a dead cop in Ohio.

"So, to cap a career of revolution, murder and theft you two want a legacy? Isn't that already your legacy?" I asked, amazed at my own bravura.

"The problem we face is that history is being written by others," she looked at me, "and they are calling us, how did I hear it? 'Failed revolutionaries'?" I broke eye contact with her. "If the Days of Rage are being reduced to students rabid for a fistfight with cops, I want to try once more to show this society how hypocritical, how exploitative, and how selfish it is," she said with a steely edge to her voice. Carl touched her arm, as if to calm her. "Since you prefer to avoid a rendezvous with history, we will oblige, Dumont," she said in a calmer voice, "but we had hoped you might respect at least the memory of your political convictions. I thought you would. You certainly indulge in a scathing critique of our convictions."

The sting of her words faded slowly. "Sorry," I said in a very soft voice, still wondering about escape.

Rose frowned. Clearly, she'd hoped to goad me into enlisting. I'd folded, and there was nothing further to discuss.

They went into the living room to talk. My arms ached, and my fingers were numb, the cord having cut off circulation. I heard their voices, Carl's earnest, Rose's sounding critical. Which one was in charge? One minute it seemed Rose, then Carl. Did anyone see my abduction? Unlikely, or I'd like to think the police would have come calling. Shit, I thought, I fire up two undergraduates in the sixties and now it comes back to haunt me. "Professor," Carl called out as they returned to the kitchen, "we've been discussing what to do with you." They chose that phrase to scare the piss out of me, and it worked; I needed to piss. "Frankly, we were hoping you'd join forces with us, and since you haven't we have to work around you." 'Working around' sounded a little better than 'bury you' or 'dump you'. Rose was thumbing through a small notebook, perhaps an address book. Carl noticed my hands writhing for some comfort, and he knelt behind me and loosened the tightest cord. "Sorry about that," he apologized, "I've worn handcuffs. Trust me, this cord is better."

Rose called out, "found it." Carl sighed in relief. What the hell was going on? They mumbled together for a few more seconds, then Carl turned to speak to me again. "We're going to have to keep you tied up a little longer. You have an answering machine?" I nodded towards the phone. He played my message, a generic 'I'm not here, sorry, please leave your name'. "Okay, good. I'm going to cut this cord," he indicated the one that held me to the chair, "and we're going to go into your bedroom. You've got a master bathroom, I noticed, so you're just going to spend tomorrow in bed," he explained, trying to be nonchalant. "We will probably run up your phone bill a little."

"No problem. Write me a check from that Swiss bank account," I said, surprising both of us with my cheek.

He loosened my bonds enough to let me stand, and then he followed me into my bedroom. He glanced around, found my bedroom phone extension, found its wall plug and disconnected the phone. Pulling my shades down, he did a quick look around, looking for what I don't know, as I had never stocked my bedroom with an eye to escaping kidnapping. "Okay," he said, like he was showing me my room in a cheap hotel, "well, hope you like your room. You'll be in it for a while."

"How about cutting me loose?" I asked.

"Are you familiar with standard protocol in these matters?" Carl asked, with a hint of a smile. "We've invaded your home and kidnapped you. We asked you to join us and you declined. That means we need to keep you under control and out of our way. That means leaving you tied up."

So the way to get untied was to join them. My hands were numb and the shooting pains starting to travel up my arms felt likely to cripple me.

And I was getting curious. "Guys?" I hailed Carl as he was leaving, and Rose appeared as well. "I have two appointments with students tomorrow. Neither one of them will be traumatized if I don't show, and my planned visit to the library wouldn't have caught anyone's attention anyway."

"Any girl friends?" Rose asked.

I darkened a little. "Well, for your information, yesterday my office answering machine had a message from my," I felt a little old for the word, "girl friend, and her mother is on her deathbed for the second time this year so she is out of town for the next two days. In other words, I could lay low for a day and not raise alarms. And let's say I'm willing to permit this home invasion, and my own kidnapping, for old time's sake. What sort of crime am I on the verge of aiding and abetting?"

"I thought you didn't want any part of it?" She was poker-faced.

"I don't. Necessarily," I hedged. But then I realized, I did. See, I was belatedly appreciating that two old Weathermen were planning something, and my career crises could get solved if I could learn their plans. There'd been nothing new written on the Weathermen since 1981, as they haven't done anything but surrender. I just wanted to know what was being planned. I had a gut instinct it would come to nothing. "What are you planning?" I asked, trying not to sound like the little brother whining to play with the big boys.

Carl and Rose exchanged glances. "It's not an idle conversation you're asking for," Rose said. "We are planning a criminal activity," she said, with emphasis. "If I tell you what we have planned, and then we don't tie you up, you are criminally liable. I got the impression out there that you didn't want to help. You in or out?"

"In. Cut this cord, will you? Ohhh. That's much better."

Without signing any agreement to help them, I slept in my bed that night, untied, and they slept in the guestroom. I didn't attempt to escape or call 911. The next morning, when I awoke at dawn, I suspected that just going to sleep had made me a felon. I didn't know what making them breakfast represented.

I hadn't actually slept that much. I'd felt a swell of excitement that wouldn't fade and kept my adrenaline flowing. I felt like a young lecturer again, living in rented rooms in group houses filled with other young, impoverished academics, arguing earnestly about Civil Rights, the Brave New Society, but mostly about The War. Wondering if Hawthorne would offer me a continuation of my contract, wondering if I'd get tenured or if I'd have to crank out the resumes and struggle for transportation to make it to an interview at Des Moines Community College. I'd actually had a very easy time, as I said. But the bohemian days, without serious responsibilities, without car payments or mortgages, and having just one credit card with a $500 limit, made life very flexible and open-ended. At the time it seemed frightening because I never had enough money to comfortably get to the next paycheck, but lying in bed at dawn with two of the more elderly Most Wanted in the next room made it seem a pleasant time. And it kept me from sleeping.

I had planned to go for groceries after the lecture yesterday when they kidnapped me, so the larder was especially bare. My traditional food-gathering involves lots of macaroni and cheese, some frozen vegetables that had a fifty-fifty chance of living, some chicken, some frozen dinners, some cheap cuts of steak, and an unhealthy pile of junk food. Having reached my fiftieth birthday I decided I could have a bag of potato chips for lunch if I wanted. And I prefer cinnamon pop-tarts for breakfast, but I'd run out. So for breakfast that morning I had to chip ice off the packages in the back of the freezer. I found three bricks of broccoli and a package of waffles.

Rose had a healthy appetite; she cleaned me out of Eggos. On her last waffle, Carl having limited himself to two slices of toast and most of a pot of coffee, I caught her off-guard. "Rose," I began nonchalantly, "are you and Carl still angry?"

With a mouthful of waffle she could only give me a started look. Carl answered, "angry? Speaking for myself, I don't think 'angry' is the right word. Committed. I'm still committed."

Rose swallowed. "I'd agree with that. We were angry in 1969. We were scared in 1969. But that fear died, and then the anger faded. But nothing has actually changed. The powers-that-be are still in power. We could have another Vietnam."

"I..." I hedged, "would argue that."

And we were off. Some memorable moments from that morning's debate:

"The reason SDS collapsed was the failure of the Panthers to show solidarity with us!" Carl insisted over his second pot of coffee.

"What made you think they would?" I argued. "You were the children of wealthy whites. You were the system the Panthers were attacking. They knew the FBI had infiltrated you. At least sympathize with how it must have looked. Their targets had turned, faced them, and asked them to join in overthrowing the system. Wouldn't you be at least a little suspicious?"

"We had shown what our politics were," Rose said, "we cared as much about exploited blacks as how the Vietnamese were being butchered!"

"Neither of whom had any membership in the Weathermen. You never saw yourselves as others did, did you?"

Carl got up for more coffee. "What do you mean?"

"You were, almost without exception, the children of privilege, remember?" It had been an inside joke of the Weathermen that membership was limited to those with parents pulling down salaries in the current equivalent of at least six figures. Carl and Rose tolerated the statement. "It's 1968," I narrated for them. "The blacks have just had their non-violent civil rights drive shot to pieces, literally. The Black Panthers rise to resist violently, not unlike how you all spun off of SDS. But the blacks were being drafted for infantry duty in Vietnam like cattle being shoved through the stockyard pens. You guys," I blushed a moment, for Rose had once been qualified for the draft, "were in no danger of military conscription—"

"—that's bullshit!" they chorused, anticipating my next point.

"And," I prevailed, "if you weren't draft eligible it was impossible to put yourselves in the shoes of those being drafted! If you were born white and wealthy and enjoyed a college deferment you just couldn't appreciate the lives of minimally educated blacks, mostly poor," I retorted with an aged chestnut in one gusting breath of air, to make sure they didn't interrupt me. Left me gasping a little for breath.

We argued all morning, with more coffee. Carl went for cinnamon rolls. "We repudiated our families and upbringing," Rose said, "we lived poor. We understood the life of the exploited blacks because we went to live like them. We went without food. We'd spend money on weapons and on mimeographing pamphlets before buying food!"

"Living in dirt is not unusual for college students," I blandly replied. "And there's a huge difference between voluntarily and involuntarily slumming it. No Weatherman ever died on a hunger strike." We debated into the afternoon, and had Rose and Carl's arguments been recorded it could have been a re-enactment from the kitchens of college-based communes from Columbia to Ann Arbor to the University of Washington. It was a thirty-year old argument still unsettled. But at the end we looked at each other, and we all felt younger.

"This has been interesting," I said, after we'd all been relatively quiet for a few minutes, finishing off the rolls. "Since I haven't turned you in, I guess you can maybe start trusting me a little? Like, what are you planning?"

Carl went out to his van and brought in an Army duffel bag. That caught my attention. He retrieved from a side pocket a AAA-Trip-Tik, a well-detailed road map of New York, Pennsylvania, Maryland, and the District of Columbia. Rose, meanwhile, retrieved a news clipping from her purse. "Have you seen this?" she asked, and handed it to me. It was a short piece from the Boston Globe about the planned unveiling at the Pentagon of a statue of General William Westmoreland, commander of forces in Vietnam in 1967-68 and architect of the military build-up. "This is our target," Rose said in a subdued voice. "They seem to think that thirty years is a long enough time lag for Americans to forget what this bastard did. We plan to blow it up."

"How?" I asked. "I assume you've learned some better techniques?

New York City—Greenwich Village—March 15, 1970. Pushing past a crowd of curious onlookers, climbing over a pile of dirty snow, the detective flashed his shield at the officer guarding a corner of the crime scene. A tony brownstone had been gutted by fire, ignited by an explosion termed 'suspicous'. "Detective?" asked the coroner as the detective peered about inside the blackened shell, "got something." In a plastic evidence bag, the coroner displayed the blackened knuckle and tip of a finger. In hours the fragment was matched from prints taken during the Days of Rage to Diana Oughton, one of the Weathermen. The people in the house were putting together the component parts of a bomb and they did something wrong.

"We made mistakes. We learned, the hard way," Rose conceded. Carl reached into his duffel bag and retrieved a military identification card for a Joseph Ventry. The photo of Carl was a few years old; he'd lost some hair since then. He held it up, looking like the cat that ate the canary.

"I joined the Air Force Reserves," he said proudly. "It was really for the money, and because I really wanted to work on jets." And, I knew, because his father had been an Air Force officer. Carl looked at his ID. "It's ironic, I know, but if I hadn't been planning so intently to bomb the ROTC office I would have been knocking on the door to get a scholarship." Carl's only brother, Steven, died in a helicopter crash in 1967, training in Louisiana for service in Vietnam.

I never knew whether Carl's choice of violent rebellion against Vietnam grew more from his brother's death or the disapproval he knew he'd get from his father, Major Ernest Krajewski, USAF, whom he blamed for his brother's death. I never thought of Carl as being truly morally outraged about Vietnam. Instead of taking it as a cultural affront, he took it personally. As though, if his father could somehow apologize to Carl, accept the responsibility Carl assigned him for luring Steve into the Air Force and his death, then Carl would have worn the uniform as well.

Rose looked pensive, this being probably the only part of Carl she couldn't understand. "If they had looked twice at him, we were out the door, out of the country," Rose added.

"But they took me, and trained me in aircraft maintenance," Carl finished. The room seemed to get hot. Reaching into the duffel bag again, he retrieved a copy of a magazine. "I am, in fact, cleared to flight test this." He handed me a battered copy of AVIATION WEEK, and pointed to a picture of the Bell AH-64, known popularly as the Cobra gunship helicopter. "That is what we will use to destroy Westmoreland's statue." I was looking at the glossy photo of the helicopter, certainly a dangerous looking machine, and the story of the Westmoreland statue. The room got hotter. I mouthed the word 'how'. "Specifically," Carl answered, "there's a laser-guided missile used on tanks called the TOW, if I get the time, or the Sidewinder missiles. Whichever I can unload the easiest."

They were serious. They had a target, they had a method, and they were motivated. My composure crumbled. "You'll never get close," I said. "That's the nation's capital. I can't even image how the Pentagon defends itself against terrorism but I'm sure they've thought of this!"

"Professor," Rose intervened, "we're neither stupid nor suicidal. Although we're prepared for the possibility of dying, Carl and I have put some planning into this." I shook my head like a wind-up toy, saying, 'no way, no way'. "We're not asking you to join us in the helicopter!" she said with irritation. "You'll be completely out of the shooting."

That sounded better, but I was far from comforted. "So what do you need me for?"

"We're working that out."

A Plan of Sorts

Looking back, I guess the smart move would have been to tiptoe to the nearest phone, call the police, and let them chase these sorry revolutionaries out of my house. But, as I've noted, they'd touched a part of me long dormant and, once wakened, I couldn't let them go on alone. I've always been susceptible to a sense of missing the party, either because I wasn't aware the party was happening or because my innately cautious, careful self recoiled in fear at the doorway. This time I was awake, aware, and too damn old to surrender to fear.

Before going to bed, I dug out my journal clippings on the Weathermen again. My manila folder on PERSONALITIES bulged with old news. Names flashed at me from yellowed text. Mark Rudd, a founder of Weatherman, and one of the first to surrender to the authorities, in 1977. Susan Stern was a Seattle activist for women's rights; she joined Weatherman only to be thrown out for her failure to purge herself of such bourgeois mentalities as monogamy, then went on trial as one of the Seattle Seven. She served a short sentence, then wrote a blistering autobiography that exposed the Weather Underground's powerful self-contempt. Bernardine Dohrn, who boldly put her name at the bottom of many of Weatherman's inflammatory communiqués; she surfaced in 1980, completed her law degree and is now a successful member of the middle class. Kathy Boudin, who escaped the townhouse explosion, went on to heft a rifle at the Nyack shoot-out, and is now doing hard time. They'd bombed ROTC offices, draft boards, anything that represented the US Military. They declared war on the police. They waved a Viet Cong flag when they occupied the ROTC facility at the University of Washington, the Pacific Northwest being one of their stronger bases. They demonstrated at the University of Wisconsin at Madison against Dow Corporation recruiters, Dow being the maker of both Agent Orange and napalm. They poured red paint on draft files in draft offices around the country and on anyone trying to intervene; they made gasoline bombs and burned out recruiting stations. They half-heartedly worked out so that when one of them was grabbed the rest could come and fight to free them.

Pressed flat by time to the bottom of the pile, I was surprised to find two pages of newsprint from the student paper, dated April 13th, 1969, with two inch headlines, THOUSANDS ATTEND ANTI-WAR RALLY. The text explained that most classes were cancelled, some spontaneously, to let students hear Mark Rudd of Weatherman speak at the Hawthorne Student Union, denouncing the war, the government and, by extension, our society. Someone from the University of Massachusetts chapter of SDS warmed up the crowd, and following Mark was a list of others championing women's lib, black liberation, sexual liberation; it seems now, in my curmudgeonly years, like everyone with an axe to grind was just jumping on the stage. Then I was shocked to see, on Page two, below the fold, a photograph of me at the microphone with caption: Lecturer Peter Dumont speaks at rally. My hair was shoulder-length, and though the photo cut off my legs I know I was wearing bell-bottoms. I had a scraggly beard—only in my forties would my beard grow in completely, and by then I didn't want one. But me speaking at the same mike as Mark Rudd: I somehow forgot that day completely. I must have been something.

I wasn't the only loudmouth on campus. An associate professor of anthropology, Karen Black, also spoke that day and I remember her joining a few picket lines in those years. I admired her for her convictions but was not surprised a few years later when she was persuaded to leave. And for the first time in years I was reminded of David Crockett, a lecturer in political science, who tried to persuade me to join him in a picket line at Draper Laboratories, a military research facility in nearby Cambridge. I didn't remember where any of them went, though if I asked around someone would know. I'd just let that time lie dormant, like the mercury at the bottom of Lake Erie, hopefully buried and no longer dangerous.

I survived them all at Hawthorne. Such is the revenge of time.

I finally found the clipping I was thinking of, Carl and Tom, in handcuffs, arrested after some demonstration—there had been so many—and both had long hair, both wore bell-bottomed jeans, and both looked so altruistic. Carl was medium height, stockily built, a linebacker. Tom was, or is, or was, a little taller, lean, with a Roman nose and deep brown eyes. As a woman she was intimidating. There were other clippings, one from the Boston Globe noting that two former Hawthorne students, Carl Krajewski and Thomas Rose, were suspects in the bombing of the Buffalo recruiting office, for which the Weathermen had claimed responsibility. And as a final reminder to the American public of 'the struggle', these two wanted to blow up a statue of the enemy.

At least the statue couldn't fight back.

What dreams I had. My subconscious isn't usually so permeable as to take the day's events and immediately recapitulate them in a dream, but the gates were wide open that night. I was in the chopper. I was flying it, and the lights of Washington resembled an amusement park, including a Ferris wheel. My guns wouldn't fire, though. I remember pulling the trigger—there isn't actually a trigger in an Apache gunship—and hitting the RESET button—there definitely isn't a RESET button in an Apache gunship, but there is on my computer—and hearing someone say that if I could fly the chopper in a somersault that might unjam the guns. But when I did the somersault—not actually possible in an

Apache gunship—I ended the night. Daylight came up and I was immediately aware that it was a stupid place to be, up there in a military weapon flying over Washington in daylight, so I landed it fast and while running away I woke up.

My dream stayed with me too, which is rare. It was vivid, and for a brief moment at waking I was awash in relief, glad to be out of that anxious dream, glad to be awake and back in my non-anxious life. Then I remembered yesterday and the anxieties came down on me like a blanket dropped from the ceiling.

I got up and listened at the doorway and heard nothing. I opened my door, stepped into the hallway, still hearing nothing. I opened the second bedroom door, which was slightly ajar. The bed hadn't been made but it was empty. No duffel bag. No strange apparel on the floor. In the kitchen there were some dirty dishes, more than I usually create in an evening, so I hadn't dreamt Carl and Rose, but their van was gone and so were they.

Relief really washed over me then. I thought I had displayed a lack of enthusiasm for their plan, and maybe they smartened up and left before I woke up. I smiled as I made myself some breakfast. Until I sat down to eat, and saw that Rose had left behind, on the kitchen table, the article she'd clipped from the Globe about Westmoreland's statue. My appetite disappeared.

By ten there was still no sign of them. "Well, I can't live today waiting for them to maybe return," I decided in a bold voice. I had papers to correct, and the weather was gray and rainy, so I turned on channel 38 and they were broadcasting the third Freddie Krueger movie. It set the perfect mood for me to grade tests on Reconstruction.

Leon Turbo wasn't his legal name, but that's the name he gave me. Leon knocked on my door in mid-day. He wore bib overalls and had long, grayish-brown hair under a baseball cap, and he was paunchy, looking like either a farmer or a tow-truck operator. He didn't use my doorbell, he knocked. I opened my front door, leaving the storm door latched. "Hello? Is this Professor Dumont's house?"

"Yes," I answered in my most professorial tone, "can I help you?"

"Carl asked me to stop by and introduce myself," Leon said.

That wasn't an answer I knew how to respond to. "He what?"

"I was in the Weather Underground. Back in the sixties?" he hinted.

"I know when the Weather Underground existed," I answered, somewhat curtly. "How do you know Carl?"

Leon glanced left, then right, then said, "I was in school a little while with him. Him and Tom. I didn't take your American history class, though. I had to take a Bio Lab." Leon looked like he'd had damn little use for that Bio Lab. I smiled agreeably; those life science courses eat up a lot of the kids' time. "Would it be alright if I came inside?" he asked.

For a moment, I struggled with my sense of hospitality, and won easily. "I'm sorry, Leon, but I don't think so. Do you live around here?"

"No," Leon said, "I live in Maine. Outside of Kittery. Tom called me last night and asked me to come here."

I didn't remember a phone call; perhaps before I regained consciousness? So they were rounding up cronies? How many other backwoods college dropouts would be appearing on my doorstep? My earlier anxieties roared with fresh worry. "Leon, I'm sorry to be so inhospitable, but I'm not letting anyone in that Carl invited. He doesn't live here." Leon looked a little perturbed but resigned. "There's a pizza parlor across Route 9, it isn't bad, if you're hungry. Maybe you could call from there later and I'll tell you if they have returned?"

Leon capitulated gracefully and I watched him walk off. He didn't seem to have a car. Had he hitchhiked from Kittery? I felt badly then, but I was giving serious thought to changing my locks, quickly. I sat back down and was into the next test when the doorbell rang. "I think I know who this is," I said to myself. Yep, Leon again. "What's the problem?" I asked, irritated. "Couldn't you find it?"

He shrugged. "They wouldn't let me smoke." He pulled a stout handmade from his coat pocket, the tip twisted tightly and singed. "It's good shit. I grow my own."

I sighed. Where to begin? The anti-smoking ordinances or the lamentable fact that cannabis sativa itself remains outlawed? "Should have pulled out a gun first," I suggested. "Those laws aren't so tightly enforced." He looked at me with the same, dull, expectant look. "You don't get out much, do you Leon?"

"I don't like people much," he admitted. I stepped back from my doorway and waved him in. He nodded his thanks, paused to wipe his gumboots on my stoop, and then headed straight for the kitchen. There he pulled out a kitchen chair, rummaged around and couldn't find an ashtray. "Just use a dish," I advised him from the living room. Did I want this stranger smoking pot in my kitchen? For the first time I wished Rose or Carl were here. "So, where do you know Carl and Rose from?"

"Who's Rose?" he asked. Oh, I realized, he hasn't seen Tom lately. "Are you wanted for anything?" I asked, to be conversational. "I'm not looking to turn anyone in," I thought to add as he turned to give me a look through the kitchen entry, "just that…most of the Weathermen were in trouble with the law."

"I had an outstanding warrant in Boston, for resisting arrest in 1969," he said, "and I turned myself in in 1975." I nodded politely. "Charges dismissed. I don't even have speeding tickets on my license." I smiled. "Carl and Tom and I were arrested together in Springfield at the Armory, a demonstration in October, 1968. Carl saved my ass when the Guard started with the tear gas. He got me a wet rag and led me to a first-aid tent. Actually, he pulled half a dozen kids out of the tear gas. Including Tom. It was kind of scary. We saw their rifles and, everyone was an American, but we never knew when they'd give the order to use live rounds. My dad came down to make my bail and I talked him into covering for Tom and Carl."

"That was generous of him," I said.

"Yea," said Leon, "my old man was okay. He thought the whole Vietnam thing was a complete screw-up."

"Were you in Vietnam?" I asked, unsure now, for Leon looked like he'd been a tradesman all his days, not a protestor.

"Yep." He was silent for a moment. Then he said, "did a tour in '64," making it sound like a nursery rhyme, "came back. Thought I'd start using my GI benefits. Wondering how I got mixed up with the two college kids?" he asked, one eyebrow raised.

"You joined Vietnam Veterans Against the War?" I asked. He nodded, smiling, pleased that I knew of them. "You ever throw a medal at the White House?" I asked. His smile faded. No medals, nothing to throw. "I…so you and Carl and Tom got arrested together?" He nodded, smile gone. "You share any other adventures?"

He prepared to speak, thought about what he was going to say, then said, in a lower voice, "I helped them rob a Armory," his pronunciation clunked in my ear. "In New Hampshire, few weeks before they did the armored car job," he continued, a little boastful, a little threatening. I now knew a little more than I wanted to, and Leon was no longer an amusing country fool. "Any idea when they're due?" he asked.

"Soon, I hope."

Leon lit up and a nostalgic smell wafted through my house. I did my best to concentrate on my tests, but they're a strain in the best of times. I re-read the same dull, grammatically incorrect paragraph twice, and my ears picked up the sound of tires in my driveway. I sighed in relief this time. "I think they're back," I announced. Leon was holding a lungfull of smoke as he nodded.

Like they owned the place, they came through the front door. "Leon!" Carl called him in happy surprise, and he and Leon exchanged bear hugs. "Good to see you, man!" "Yea, good to see you, too!" They separated, and then Leon saw Rose.

"Who's she?" he asked Carl.

"I'm…I was Tom," Rose half-smiled shyly, "now I'm Rose." She apparently hadn't had a lot of contact with the old crowd. "Hi, Leon," she said, in the meekest tone I'd heard her use. "I'm a woman now," she explained anticlimactically.

Leon, though at least a little worldly from fighting in Vietnam, was clearly uncomfortable. "Carl?" he said, looking at Rose, "is this some kind of fucking joke?"

"I go by 'Rose' now," Rose persevered. Carl was staying out of it for now. "It's good to see you, Leon. How's your father?" Oh yes, I remembered, the father that posted their bail, just before they took off. He must remember them fondly.

"Dad's dead," Leon said, "leukemia. About a year ago." Carl mumbled his apologies, as did Rose, but Leon only responded to Carl. He was studying Rose's face and clearly recognized Tom's features. Then his eyes ran down Rose's body and he shook his head in disbelief. Rose blushed. In a voice of undisguised disgust he asked, "Tom, what the fuck were you thinking?"

"So," I stepped in, "now that everyone has met everyone, what's going on? Meaning no disrespect, Leon, but why is Leon here?" I asked Rose.

Again the two Weathermen exchanged looks, this time of something akin to embarrassment. "Well, we tried to make contact with whoever we still had any link," Carl explained. He had carried a brown bag in and now he picked it up off the floor and set it on the kitchen table. "We had a few numbers, and they were all, what, about thirty-some years old. Leon's was the only one that still worked. Still in Kittery, huh?"

"Still in Kittery," Leon said, and he was trying not to look at Rose. "So what the hell's up, man?" he asked Carl. "Why'd I hitchhike from Maine? To see that?" he indicated Rose.

Rose darkened with anger, but held her tongue. Carl looked distressed. "It's just an operation, man," he said, "Tom's brain is still in there. Now he's got tits is all." I noticed Rose glanced at Carl, perhaps uncomfortable with his description.

Leon wasn't convinced. "You two ever…" he raised his eyebrow quizzically.

"No!" Rose said, her patience worn thin. "We didn't do this so we could fuck. I chose to do it because I was miserable as a man."

"You never got laid, did you?" Leon sniggered at Rose. "This is doing it the hard way."

"Leon, hear me say this," Rose said in a voice that could have cut Leon's tongue out if he'd been so foolish as to expose it, "I find this society almost tolerable as a woman. I don't know how I lasted my first twenty years. It's dick-heads like you that made me ashamed to be a man."

At least Leon shut up.

"Leon," Carl tried to change the subject, "first, I want to say thanks for coming down here." I noticed he didn't thank me for letting a complete stranger into my house. "Rose and I wanted to make a statement before we get too old to be crazy. We thought we'd see how many of the true believers were around. You know of anyone else?"

Leon shook his head immediately. "Everyone I knew either sold out or cashed in. There's nobody underground. I even used my real social security number when I started working a regular job last year."

"What do you do?" I asked, wondering where the old Weather Underground fit into today's economy.

"I work in a sporting goods store, in an outlet mall up there," Leon said dismissively, not proud of his lot in life, "but I get medical benefits. That's why I took it."

"You feel like doing one more crazy thing before we're all in wheelchairs?" Carl asked, with a mischievous smile. Leon looked intrigued. "Show him the clipping?" he asked Rose. Leon took the clipping from Rose, reluctant to acknowledge her.

"They're putting up a statue to Westmoreland," he read; Leon was a fast reader. "Down in the Pentagon?" He nodded understanding. "Don't tell me, you want to throw a bucket of pig's blood on the statue?"

It had been a favorite Weather Underground tactic, but the blood was usually red paint. "No, man," Carl corrected him, "we're going to blow it up."

Leon's eyebrows rose. "Seriously? Blow it up? With what?"

Carl dug out the AVIATION WEEKLY. It was getting pretty battered.

"We're going to need money, and we don't have enough," Carl announced when we'd all set down to eat, Carl and Leon and Rose and I. I'd cooked up a bowl of spaghetti; I still hadn't gone for groceries. I flinched at the announcement; the Weathermen historically raised funds by borrowing from wealthy leftists—most of whom were dead now—drug dealing, and credit card scams. A few had odd jobs.

"How much money?" I realized that it was me speaking. I knew by this time that I was very, very curious about their plans. I wasn't sure yet how far I could go with them. I hoped to learn enough about their plans to write about them before having to decide whether to put on a ski mask, hold a submachine-gun and call myself Tanya.

"Well, it's three weeks until the statue is unveiled," Rose said. "We have a plan but we need to find a place to stay in Washington." Leon nodded.

"I have some savings," I finally volunteered. Nobody else spoke. "And we can probably get good weekly rates if we stay outside the capital. D.C. is very expensive." They stared at me.

"Dumont," Rose said, in her kindest tone, "this is the Weather Underground," she reminded me. "We're plotting a criminal act."

"And to finance it you're going to sell cocaine, or knock off a bank or armored car, or steal some credit cards? That's what got you in trouble in the first place." They looked at each other deadpan but no one denied it. "So, does that mean you'd refuse a donation? You used to be more than happy to borrow from rich liberals."

Rose looked at Carl. "He has an interesting point," she said. "I recall we even tapped our parents, initially, for bus fare to Washington for demonstrations." She looked pale, remembering her parents. Were they still alive, I wondered? Did she know?

"And bail bond," Carl added.

"And how," Leon found his tongue. Carl looked uncomfortable; that was an old, unpaid bill.

"Still," Rose pressed on, her memory unfurling, "that was SDS. Non-violent protests and all that. When we joined the Weather Underground we decided that if we were at war with a capitalist society, we were ethically obligated to steal to meet our needs, because—" she bulldozed past my raised eyebrows—"working meant we were submitting to capitalist society instead of rebelling against it."

I wasn't happy with that. "That felt good in 1969. But have you spent the last thirty years stealing to feed, clothe and shelter yourselves? You've worked as a beautician," I nodded to Rose, "and you," I looked at Carl, "you're in the Air Force Reserve. You must have given yourself a dispensation of some sort, no? Live and let live with capitalism? Get jobs, get paid, pay rent?"

That struck a nerve, and it struck them silent for a long time. I was surprised, and not just at them but at myself. For a moment there, I sounded like I cared about the revolutionary tradition Tom and Rose had embraced.

"Peter," Carl began, "you have a point." He was looking at his hands as he used his fork to push a string of spaghetti on his plate. "It was impossible to maintain our anger at the level we had when we were twenty. We did make compromises. And that's not something I'm proud of," he looked up, looking relieved at having found the words to answer me, "and this legacy, this last act of defiance, is what I'm hoping will redeem me. Redeem us," he nodded to Rose. "As for accepting a donation," he grinned, "that's funny. What's next? A bake sale?"

"Why not?" I pressed my point. "Because once you've done it, it's easier to steal than to work?" Carl's grin faded. I realized then that whatever I said from that point on I would have to live with, and that felt okay.

"I'm offering you the money to do this, without resorting to theft and you'd rather pull a ski mask over your face and rob a gas station. That's just another form of childish, trivial anger at the system. That's how the James brothers went from broken Confederates to bank robbers."

"Who?" Carl asked.

"The James gang," Leon said. He brightened at my analogy. "You know much about the Civil War?"

"I teach American history," I reminded him. "The point is that you want to steal for the sake of stealing. You've been underground for thirty years. Nobody knows where you are. In Rose's case, who you are. Now you want your legacy. Your greatest advantage is your anonymity. You'll squander that if you pull a bank heist, and you won't even be close to your legacy." I was listening to myself, wondering where these words were coming from. Looking back, I think that moment I knew what it must have been like in those Evangelical tent meetings of an earlier time, where the saved got saved all over again in a chorus of overheated religious ecstasy. "I've got enough in savings to handle…" I did some quick calculating, multiplied it by four, "all of us in a decent motel, legally. Doesn't it make more sense to avoid trouble until the main event? It will cramp our planning to have to avoid police while we're planning."

The Weathermen were confused. Carl and Rose both looked about to speak but were bereft of words. It was Leon who spoke. "I have an idea. If we could steal the money to finance our operation," he said to Carl and Rose, "but do so in a way practically untraceable, and that won't force us to dodge cops for the next month," he offered me, "would that be a good thing?" None of us knew what to say to that. Leon warmed to his topic. "I've been doing this for the past five years," he began, his eyes moving steadily around the room to keep us all attentive, "and I've never been caught because I'm careful and I'm not a pig. I haven't been living a luxurious life, but I'm also not wanted." He had all our attention. "Ready to hear more?"

I nodded just a little, maybe moving my head a centimeter. Rose's eyes were lit up and Carl nodded eagerly. "Talk, Leon."

He smiled. "I've been skimming bank accounts, electronically." We were lost, and looked it. "Banking is all done electronically, numbers for accounts, numbers for dollars, all of it's just data swimming in phone lines from one computer to another. Most accounts include dollars and cents. Twenty-four cents, fifty-nine, the small change." We nodded. "I bought a used computer a few years ago, old Leading Edge. I got software off the Internet and I bought some passwords through a contact. It cost me a thousand bucks, but it's been a damn good investment. Every couple of months I go online at night and run this software in two or three banks. I only take small amounts, nine cents or less from any account. But it can sweep through thousands of accounts in a few seconds. Then it transfers all it has to an account I set up just beforehand. I log off, go in and withdraw most of it."

We had a lot of questions.

"Nobody ever questioned your withdrawals?" I asked.

"I don't get piggy. The guys that get caught with this usually increase the deduct option to dollars and try to get one big score," Leon explained, "and they get caught. Nobody balances down to the penny. Or, if they do, they don't usually have the balls to go complain at the bank. And if they did the bank would probably figure they'd made a mistake and give it to them." That sounded simple and true.

"How much do you usually get?" asked Rose.

"Depends on the bank. Five thou or so from a small to medium sized savings bank, that's if I want to be very careful and only hit random accounts," Leon explained, "they also tend to be the easiest. If you want bigger paydays you need to hit bigger banks." He looked smarter now than just a middle-aged hitchhiker from Maine. "Of course, they have better security. I've historically stuck to small banks. It kept me fed and out of jail."

"Whose money is it, really?" I asked.

"Some of the accounts are business, corporate accounts. Most are private citizens," Leon admitted. "But no citizen gets hit for more than nine cents."

That did stall my primary objection. It was like snitching the change that had fallen behind the back seat.

"So why, with this clever banking technique, did you take a job at an outlet store in Kittery?" Carl asked.

"My old lady wanted a medical plan. You know how much they cost?" Leon asked, looking wounded. "The store pays for most of it. And it gets me out of the house, which was the other thing she wanted."

It was hearing Leon's plan that made this whole affair start to sound, if not easy, then viable. We could actually finance it by skimming thousands of dollars from the spare change of society in seconds, eliminating the horrific bank robberies and shoot-outs that stained the memories of the Underground. That feeling of being 'born again' hadn't washed away, and my career crisis was feeling less menacing with each passing moment. Maybe this all could work. I couldn't fully imagine the risks, but I knew planning to attack the Pentagon represented treason, and if caught, I would lose my teaching job and pull a long stretch in prison. That was chilling.

Then history shone through. This plan would very likely execute like their other plans, i.e. poorly. Like, the helicopter would run out of gas thirty miles short of its target, or the missiles wouldn't work. There was a good chance I could be part of this operation and the first anyone would actually know of it would be when I published my account of it. I was ignoring a lot of other plans they had executed—armed robberies, bombings—that were executed and turned violent, and in retrospect I know I was rationalizing because I truly wanted to join them. So I convinced myself that being part of a plot created and executed by two old Weathermen was as exciting and harmless as going backwards in bumper cars.

Still, I insisted we try the money skimming outside my house, on a strange phone line. Motel 6 had a cheap room, and few innkeepers today look twice at the number or gender of folks going into a room with one double bed. I paid cash for the room. I also bankrolled the purchase of a dirt-cheap computer capable of handling Leon's needs, but for that I had to use my credit card. I had a sturdy desktop model of my own, but we had decided that the mission required a laptop.

Our first logistical challenge: the phone was wired into the nightstand behind the bed. The nearest floor space big enough to accommodate the computer and Leon was six feet away, and the phone line with the laptop was five feet long. "There's an electronics store in the mall down the road," Leon directed Rose, "get me at least a twenty-foot phone line."

"Does it need to have any special jacks?" Rose asked deferentially, struggling to be, temporarily, a good soldier while Leon was running the show.

"No, it should be fine as it is," Leon answered, a little kinder this time. Rose left and Carl and Leon and I finished loading the computer's software, creating the phone connection. Then Leon dialed his number in Kittery. "Line's busy," he discovered, "Emily, I bet you've been talking with Abby since the minute I left."

We waited. "So, what was it like being underground with a freak?" Leon asked Carl.

Carl struggled to be civil. "Leon, when did you become such an asshole? Rose is Rose. Accept it. She doesn't want to fuck you. Do you want to fuck her?"

Leon blushed. Maybe he did. Rose had strong features and the doctor had shaped her bust expertly. "Where you guys been living?" Leon asked to change the subject.

"Places," Carl answered, also grateful for the new topic. "We thought we'd be in Europe for six months, but Ruby Tuesday wasn't home when we called." He looked angry then. Leon and I glanced at each other, equally lost. "Our signal that it was safe," Carl said. "When we did come back, we moved a fair amount. Early on we suspected cops or the FBI were following us, though in retrospect I think we were just paranoid. The Weather Underground helped us with phony Social Security numbers. We worked to pay our rent. We lived almost everywhere but Texas. Rose said she'd rather cut off both of her twenty thousand-dollar boobs than live in Texas. Florida was nice, until about 1983. Traffic got terrible. Then Chicago, and then Seattle, and we stayed there awhile. There were some Weathermen out there, and they helped us out with jobs and stuff. But they decided to go straight and it was better for all concerned for Rose and I to scram. That was in 1987. We came back to the East Coast, and we've just moved around here since then."

"Nobody ever suspected you?" I asked.

"Of what?" Carl asked. "The robbery was a long time ago, and we never stayed in Ohio. We haven't committed any crimes since. There was an article in TIME back in 1982, after the May 19th clowns shot up Nyack, when the FBI admitted they hadn't been actively hunting for Weathermen. And after the shoot-out, when they busted everyone they could find, they thought they caught everyone. I don't avoid driving by police cars anymore. I don't even have any speeding tickets."

"And Rose?" I asked.

"That's a different story. Don't let her drive," Carl warned, shaking his head. "She's got lots of speeding tickets. I think the sex change affected her driving skills."

Leon stepped outside to smoke a cigarette, leaving Carl and I alone for the first time in decades. I said nothing for a minute, and Carl looked around the room at the modest furnishings. A truck roared by on the nearby Mass Pike. "Carl?" I asked, "can I ask a personal question?" He shrugged. "I apologize in advance for such an intrusive question, but in all those years living with Rose, didn't you guys ever experience," I looked away from him, casting about for the most diplomatic version I could find, finally say, "sexual tension?"

Carl already looked tired of this question. How many people could have asked him over the years? "Professor," he began, so I knew he wouldn't get physical, "Rose is the sister I never had. And, like she said, we aren't all that attracted to each other." 'All that attracted' tinged in my ear. "To tell you the truth, I don't know if Tom or Rose has actually had much sex. Tom was not a virgin, courtesy of Debbie Ginsberg, who certainly fucked him, but it was probably a pity-fuck, since she was always hanging around David, our cell leader. It was part of our early beliefs," he said, as though we were anthropologists, "to have random sex in order to break down our monogamy, which was one of the bourgeois conventions we were supposed to be purging. So Tom got laid, but just once or twice. Rose?" He thought for a moment. "She had a guy in Seattle, Richard Longacre, they met working at a food pantry, and they were hot and heavy for almost a year. In fact, I found myself planning on going it alone, which didn't happen. I'm sure there was some sex there. But between her and me, strictly Platonic, brother-sister."

A key in the door was our warning. Rose entered, tossed her jacket on the bed and fished a plastic-wrapped package from a paper bag. Leon followed her, trailing the smell of tobacco. "This long enough?" she offered it to Leon. It was a fifty-foot cord.

"Jeez," Leon chuckled, "were there any longer ones?" Rose smirked. Before they got friendly, he turned gruff again and plugged the phone line into the computer, then, because I was the slimmest, I got the job of groping for the wall jack behind the bed, finding it with my fingers and working it into the jack until I felt the 'click'. Leon was typing at the keyboard, and a moment later we heard the whistling noise of the modem.

Screen after screen flashed by as Leon used his Internet account to pull down the necessary software and load it on the computer's hard drive. Then he disconnected from the Internet and dialed into the first bank, Dime Savings Trust. "The main branch is in Providence, Rhode Island. They real-l-l-l-ly should have beefed up the protection for their credit unions," Leon said as the modem whistled its way into another computer. He waited a few more moments as the computer on the desk introduced itself to the one in the basement of the Providence bank. “Okay,” Leon said softly, as though we were in the basement of the Providence bank, “let’s start off small. Four cents per donor, please,” he asked, keying and then hitting the <Enter> key. “Dialing for Dollars.”

Electronic theft was a little like riding down the first, steep slope of the roller coaster. My throat constricted as the monitor flipped from one account to another. Almost every account was a private citizen, and I could see glimpses of names and addresses. When the program ran and no alarm went off, no BUSTED message came up, when the bank’s computer let us take the change and go, I got the rush I was afraid I’d get. Then a column of numbers flipped by and a small window in the lower right hand corner updated the total transferred. In seconds it went from pennies to dollars, and then to tens of dollars, and gradually to hundreds. When we hit a thousand, Leon hit <Enter> again and did some furious typing.

“I just hit this bank two weeks ago,” he said. “More than a thousand dollars might trigger something. Someday they’re going to find a cheap enough program to catch me at this.” He ended the call, began another. “This one’s for serious money. Fleet Bank.” The computer played fetch again. “I’ll go for five thousand, and we’ll get it in less time. Bigger the database the faster and the easier.” I wondered if Leon wasn’t also aiming for corporate accounts that time as well, for I saw addresses flash by and none that were private citizens. And he had five thousand in the box in less than a minute. “Okay, kids,” Leon keyed the machine again, “let’s make life really simple.” He dialed into Citizens Bank.

“Hey, that’s my bank,” I said. Then I reached into my pocket. “I’ll make my donation in person,” I said, and tossed a dime on the bed.

We all laughed. “Thank you, Professor Dumont,” Leon said with mock politeness, “but your bank is just going to be the pay-off point. I’m creating an account for myself, and I’m transferring the funds from both banks to that account. Tomorrow we’ll go in and take the money out. And that’ll give us six thou in seed money." And then he finished keying the computer, and I got to exchange the phone plugs again. With Leon carrying the computer, we exited the motel room, Rose and Carl lagging to wipe fingerprints off doorknobs and phones and police the room.

Jesus Christ, I realized, as I sat behind the wheel of my Corolla, Leon smoking a cigarette outside. I've just been party to a felony. I've just watched a man electronically steal six thousand dollars. The ease and speed of the theft was what kept me from hyperventilating. I had wanted to play with the big boys, but just then the game got scary and I was having second thoughts. I felt I could almost claim coercion for most of the day's events. When I provided the funds to buy the computer and rent the room I either toed the line or crossed it; the difference would rest with a good or bad lawyer.

Without alarm, without difficulty, Leon left the next day and returned with six thousand dollars. I did hyperventilate then, because cold cash is more frightening than numbers on a screen. "Maybe I've over estimated my capacity for this," I said as I sat and leaned forward, my head between my knees, until my breathing calmed. Rose got me a glass of water, which helped. My lungs heaving and my pulse fluttering, I felt weak and foolish. "I'm alright," I said, convincing no one, "I'm alright."

Leon put the money away and seemed unconcerned. Carl frowned when I admitted my anxiety. "Dumont, so far you haven't done anything, really," he tried to comfort me. "If they catch us, they'll be more than happy with Rose and me. Leon might get a slap on the wrist. I don't think they'll bother you."

All my anxieties had roared up and were consuming me. "Would it be rude to ask you guys to please leave?" I asked, suffocating in my fear. "And forget you saw me. I just don't think I'm up to this. I'm sorry." I kept saying I was sorry, like a mantra that would make them disappear. I then put my head between my knees longer than I needed to, to avoid looking at them. They were looking at each other, I guess, but not speaking.

"We've got six thousand dollars," Leon pointed out. "And if the Professor will let me keep the computer I can raise more easy."

"Keep it," I mumbled, still ducking them, mumbling 'sorry, sorry'.

Rose sounded like there were a few thousand words she'd like to say, but Carl wasn't letting her. "But he—we only asked...why can't I?" I raised my head a little and watched Leon carry the computer back out to the van, and watched Rose and Tom carry their duffel bag out. They didn't say a word to me, they just collected all their stuff, put it in the van, and a minute later I heard the van start and back out of my driveway.

And as the anxiety faded I felt embarrassed, and ashamed of my panic attack. The bubble of exhilaration I'd ridden last night popped, and all my excited plans of resurrecting the Weathermen and my career popped with it.

Initially I was never so happy to be grading essay tests. It spared me from thinking. Never before had I given such generous grades, and this from the campus' greatest grade inflator. After finishing, I congratulated myself, having finished in half the usual time. Of course, giving out grades like I just had would make every grading session only as stressful as making toast. I even carved Art's multi-volume paper down to about seven good paragraphs and gave him a 'B'.

But I was bored. And that was odd. I loved my privacy and guarded it carefully, avoiding any serious commitments, as Linda could testify. I had projects I worked on, primarily my book—my conversation with Winfield rang fresh in my ear.

My new book was about the Weathermen, and my thesis was to de-romanticize them. A big stumbling block to my thesis was that, thus far, I'd found almost no examples of the Weathermen being romanticized. I'd seen no kindly documentaries or movies casting them in favorable light. No novelist had made them lovable. The whole era was missing from television. Rose was right, the Weathermen *were* faring poorly at the hands of history.

The Vietnam veterans had, not surprisingly, belatedly won some grudging respect from society. President Carter gave draft dodgers an amnesty, though few took advantage ten years after their flight. But the anti-war protestors were still *persona non grata*. True, society forgave most of them, but there was only one place in our society for SDS, the Weathermen, and the Black Panthers—history classes.

So I had an outline for my unwriteable book. In Part One, I was to review the Weathermen as they were (not) depicted in the press, in popular culture, movies or TV or videos or wherever. In Part Two I used my extensive collection of newspaper clippings and videos of old news footage to remind the reader of what truly hard-bitten and deadly serious and lifelong committed revolutionaries the Weathermen were. But they weren't, for the most part, hard-bitten or lifelong revolutionaries. They were called 'Mustang Bolsheviks', after the sports cars their parents gave them; they drove to Washington for the weekend to demonstrate instead of doing Homecoming. Most of them became straight citizens. So if my book was written as conceived, it would be a novel, not a history.

That morning I finally accepted that fundamental flaw in my book, because of Rose and Tom. Unlike all their contemporaries, they were the most romantic Weathermen of all. They hadn't surfaced in thirty freaking years. Instead of planning retirement funds, they were planning a futile assault on the Pentagon. It doesn't get more romantic than that. So I was in a state of creative confusion. It was eleven-thirty in the morning, an hour and a half since they'd left—since I'd thrown them out—and I deeply regretted it. There went my damn book. It was at precisely that point that I willingly joined with Rose and Carl.

And where were they?

Ten minutes, more or less. It was ten minutes after that that my phone rang. "Dumont?" Carl called. "I'm sorry to trouble you further, but we really need your help."

"Where are you?" I asked frantically, tucking the wireless phone under my chin as I looked for my car keys.

"Framingham Police Station."

My stomach quaked. "They caught you—"

"No!" Carl cut me off. "We got stopped for running a stop sign."

"In Massachusetts?"

"And Leon gave the cop some shit so the cop searched him and Leon was carrying."

I'm glad Carl never saw me smiling. "Leon's interpersonal skills aren't good, are they?"

"No," Carl admitted. "Rose was pretty rude too. Then Leon started talking about Rose's operation, and I don't think the cops like her at all." Carl stopped talking for a moment and I heard Rose in the background, sounding defensive. "Could you please come down? We need to get...we need to get Rose out, anyway. This fucking Nazi desk sergeant says Rose was born with balls so he—she—goes in the tank with the boys."

"I'll be there in ten minutes."

It's amazing to me the effect on others that my job title can have. 'College Professor'. The effect can be negative as well as positive, but when it works it seems to rest on the assumption that college professors are the smartest people in the world, perhaps a half-step down from the legendary 'rocket scientists'. I find, incidentally, that when this works positively it's usually with folks who've never been to college. One step inside a hall of higher learning and all the illusions evaporate.

This is all my way of explaining how I got Rose, Carl, and even Leon released on personal recognizance. Desk Sergeant Mulcahey, a young man with close-cut dark hair and a thick native accent, lectured Leon in my presence as he must do to many a child in his parent's presence. "I'm gonna cut you some slack because you were in the service. Now, the next time you think you talk smart to an officer, you think about how close you came to a night with the brothers in the holding tank. You understand?" Except that 'smart' became 'smaht', 'officer' became 'officuh'.

Leon, smart enough to sullenly nod, led our entourage out of the building and across the street to the parking lot and my trusty Corolla.

"Fucking-Nazi-bastard-asshole—" I thought it was coming from Leon. It was coming from Carl, and from Rose.

"What kind of little shit hole town is this where they give you the chair for having a joint?" It was a rhetorical question—Leon's.

"Rose?" I asked hesitantly, "how are you?" Rose was wearing jeans and a blouse. Her clothing looked intact. Her hair was a little disheveled but she was combing it back even as I thought to look. The stern, resolute look she usually wore was no angrier, no darker than usual. Perhaps Carl had exaggerated the threat to her.

"I'm fine," she said. "No bruises, no cuts." But the real damage would be a grope, a menacing glare from a person with a badge, nothing that darkened skin. But she wasn't nearly as pissed as were the men folk. I let them walk ahead of me, since they were still cursing a blue streak in public.

"Where's your van?" I asked, "I assume they impounded it?"

Carl stopped dead in the parking lot. "Right. They gave us a ticket on the stop sign." He fished in his pants pockets and came out with a crumpled form. Unfolding it, he looked it over. "It's going to cost us a hundred-twenty. Fifty for the ticket, seventy for the impound. Do you know where on Worcester Road it is?"

I did know, having once had my car towed from the college, and the guys still had plenty of cash, so we all squeezed in to my Corolla—built for four, it's true, but only comfortable for three—and within the hour the car was also out of jail. Their duffel bags and other gear were still in the van, and Carl fussed about things not being where they'd been left and someone must have gone through the van searching for something, but he couldn't find anything important missing. "Listen, guys," I finally said, when Carl's paranoia was waning and we'd driven the van out of the lot. "I had a chance to do some thinking, and…"

Rose's eyebrows rose and for the first time in some decades I saw her genuinely smile, "Du-mont found his prin-ciples, Du-mont found his prin-ciples," she sang in a child-like nursery rhyme. "I don't know guys," she said then, smiling coyly, "do we want him in on this?"

We returned to my home. We had to figure out precisely how to do the job. Then we had to keep it secret. I still figured Carl would run out of gas halfway to the Pentagon, but now I was committed to being there too.

D.C.

Leon couldn't handle Rose, especially if she was at all assertive, which made the ride to Washington, D.C., in the van a version of Hell I'll never forget. He wouldn't address her by name. After a furious argument over lunch was mediated with a fast-food drive-through that made no one happy there was further ugliness. "You ate my French fries?" he glared at her. She responded by speaking to him in the third person. "Leon didn't order French fries, he ordered a burger but forgot to order fries." Rose also insisted on driving into Washington "—I know how to drive in this town—" and within seconds of getting onto local roads I was certain we'd end up smeared on a guardrail.

"Watch out!" Leon ordered as Rose tailgated a mini-van. The mini-van's tail lights lit up and Rose stomped the brake and we were all launched forward, straining against seat belts, as the van stopped centimeters short of collision. Rose cursed everyone in general and wheeled around the mini-van, almost side-swiping a car that was already in the spot she wanted. "Rose," I said, "how about if Carl or I drive?" Ignoring me, she decided the light hadn't been red long enough to count for a stop and we barreled through to a chorus of honking horns. I found myself in the fetal position. "We there yet?" I asked.

We spent the first night in a Holiday Inn in Bethesda, Maryland, not in the capitol, as DC was hosting a VFW Convention that took almost every room within fifty miles of the Capitol. Even that room was available just for the night. The next morning, with two hours' rest amongst us, and not all at one time, we doggedly worked through the phone book and cruised motel strips and, in the evening, we found one room for all of us in a Best Western in DC. Chapter One of my new book: 'the revolution was postponed while we found a place to sleep'. But the sleeping quarters were still cramped, to say nothing of bathroom access. Four adults, two beds, one potty.

"Are we sure there weren't any more rooms?" Leon moaned as we stepped into the tiny room. "Cancellations, maybe?" I had an overnight bag, Leon had a paper bag, and with Rose and Carl's bulging duffel bag, our modest luggage seemed to fill the room.

"Can that software get into the reservations database here?" I asked.

He sadly shook his head. "I wish. I don't like the idea of being in a room with It," Leon looked at Rose. Rose returned his look with one of boredom.

"Leon survived one night with me, because I was feeling kindly," Rose hissed. "Did I tell you I've begun killing in my sleep?" she asked me. It was late, about ten in the evening, and a series of coin-tosses landed Leon and Rose in the two beds.

"Did you hear that snoring last night?" I asked Carl rhetorically. He shrugged; Carl was one of those fortunate souls who could sleep in the front seat of a high-speed chase. "Maybe the van would be quieter?"

"Colder, too," Carl commented. "I remember sleeping in a van with, was it five of us, Rose?" Carl asked. "We were on our way to that student strike in Ann Arbor. The bathroom was a bush off the interstate."

"You were, what, about twenty years old then?" I asked groggily. "Older folks don't tuck into tiny sleeping spots as easily. And our sanitary requirements are higher, too." But there was nothing to do but try to find the softest piece of floor and pray Leon would not snore. I might as well have prayed for a socialist revolution.

"First thing I need to do is locate a base with Apache helicopters," Carl announced, and there was no arguing with that. Carl and Leon donned their old fatigues to insure the salutes of over half the population. We were all mired in groggy crankiness. "Do you have any idea how fascist you clowns look?" Rose sniped at them as they were leaving. "Carl, you've got clean jeans. What's the point of this dress-up game?"

"We're going to be gathering intelligence in a town full of military dudes," Carl explained, sounding appropriately like the only well-rested one in the room, "and in our fatigues no one will give us a second look." Even Rose couldn't argue with that, so she shut up and our soldiers left.

At my suggestion, Rose and I got out of the room for fresh air. "Let's check out the pool," I suggested, but the pool was closed so we ended up in the bar at ten-thirty in the morning. It was already crowded. And, after ten minutes of Rose's ceaseless stream of sarcastic comments about men with beer bellies crammed into their old uniforms, I decided to go out, too. It was April in Washington, flowers were blooming, and it was pleasant outside. It had been almost twenty years since I'd seen the capitol, and, it being the City of Monuments, it's a pilgrimage every citizen should make at least once every twenty years.

Of course, my first stop was The Wall.

It's not as barren a monument as was originally intended. In part that's because so many people leave personal mementos that humanize the granite. In part it's also because other forces of war insisted on more traditional monuments—statues—nearby. One shows three guys in jungle fatigues. Another, a few yards away, is dedicated to the women of Vietnam, the nurses. While both statues are decently executed they are an anticlimax to the Wall.

Like most others, I found myself in front of a panel, in a spot where I had some elbow room, and my eyes picked out names. Some kid graduated Hawthorne and, degree fresh in his hand, went off to Vietnam as a second lieutenant. He came home in a box seven months later. My first year teaching at Hawthorne they named the library after him. So I stood there at the Wall trying to remember the name of our college library; it was 'initial-Smythe-something-WASPY'. I couldn't find him.

"Do you know him?" A young boy who'd strayed from his father stood by me. He looked—sorry, this is for the romantics—sort of angelic.

Him? Who? I looked at the granite. Oh, 'John Paul Bobo', another lieutenant. No, I didn't.

"Terry," the father, a little younger than I, arrived to take his boy's hand, "don't disturb this gentleman."

And then I realized little Terry and his father thought I was there to mourn a lost comrade. So, I'd managed to pass as a Mourning Veteran. It was yet another successful pose by the Man Who Never Marched, Never Protested, Never Draft-dodged, and Did Not Fight. I didn't say anything, didn't try to ease their momentary embarrassment by saying, "no, no, I'm just here to appreciate the monument." Or I could have said, "I didn't have to go. I had a college deferment. I'm just here to honor those who went."

Oh well, Terry and Dad were long gone by the time I figured out what I should have said. I decided to check out the Smithsonian's Air and Space Museum, as a chilly breeze had come up.

Someone else took my spot in front of the Wall.

Wednesday evening, we had our first logistics session; in retrospect we should have gone to a movie instead. "It's not going to be easy," Carl said with a morose, sullen look as he sank into one of the lumpy seats. It was his first admission of any degree of difficulty in this grand plan. He popped open a beer and took a long swallow. In his Army fatigues he looked like the antithesis of what he was, perhaps a clearer picture of what he'd always intended to be. "I spent most of the day around three bases. One Air National Guard, one Air Force, one Marine Air Corps."

"Isn't there just one Air Force?" I asked. What did I know?

Even Rose shook her head at my naivete. "Every branch of the service has an air arm," she said, and though Carl and Leon winced at her nomenclature, they agreed.

"So there must be twenty thousand airfields you can pick from?" I asked, knowing that probably wasn't right, or Carl would be looking happier than he was.

"I've got clearance to get on the bases," Carl said, "so I can get into the PX, and I can bum a ride on a cargo plane, but the armor is always in a separate part of the field and security is tighter than at Westover."

[That was the first real clue I had as to where Carl and Rose had spent their underground years. Near enough that Carl did his weekend warrior hitch at Chicopee.]

"None of this sounds surprising," Rose said, "do you have a plan to get past the security?"

Carl nodded, took another drink of beer. "I thought of something. I saw that they're using the new electronic keys down here to get into the hangars. There's a guard, but he's just there for emergencies. If you have an activated badge, you get in. So I hung around the cafeteria and met a couple of the maintenance guys. One of them lives in a house out in the country. I thought we could get in and out of his house without a lot of attention."

"So you're going to break into his house, steal his card and get access to the choppers," I summarized.

"Correct," Carl agreed. Then he noticed my shopping bag. "What'd you buy?"

"Some cellular phones, and a really cool video camera." I pulled out the surprisingly small appliance, a lovely Japanese camera that provided instant playback as well as recording. "It's supposed to be the best on the market for filming at night. I thought tonight I'd test it."

Then I distributed the phones, with the extra batteries. Then I explained what took me hours to learn, that the phone's memory would keep each of us in one-touch contact with each of the others. "That should make communications much easier," Rose said approvingly. She was being much nicer to me in Washington, probably because Leon was being such a prick.

My role, as Rose and Carl and I had discussed it, would be to film the attack on the statue. Once filmed, I would copy the tape and send the copies to every major news organization we could contact, domestic and international. "We might also be able to upload the tape to the web, though I think we need a few thousand more in clever electronics," I added.

"We'll let CNN worry about it," Rose said.

"Well," Leon chimed in, "I was checking out replacement vehicles. We can use the van to go get the access badge, but at that point we've committed a crime, and the police may be after us, which means we need at least one new vehicle and as many different license plates as we can get. I figure a mini-van or one of these sport-utility vehicles would be the least conspicuous and have room for all our gear." We all nodded agreement. "I could steal one, but we don't really need that kind of trouble." We nodded again. "And I don't really want to spend all our money on a used car, 'cause you never know what kind of problems you're getting."

"Is this your round about way of saying you want to buy a new sport-utility vehicle as our escape vehicle?" Carl asked, a Mona Lisa-like half smile on his face. "Spare us the bullshit."

Leon smiled. "I just need to borrow the phone line tonight for a little while."

"Oh God," I groaned, "how much per account you going for tonight?"

He shook his head to negate my concerns. "Pennies. And I have to set up a savings and checking account, and if I remember how, try to create a certificate of deposit. I'm going to use them as bank references." We waited. "And, yes, I'll probably put a few thousand in each of them," he conceded. "So, when is this operation a go?"

'Go' meant execute the plan. Bomb the statue. My throat tightened. All of this had been the prelude to the actual event. "When is 'Go'?" I asked.

Carl looked at Rose. "When is 'Go'? Well, we have to wait until the statue is set up," he said. "When's that?"

Rose was hooking the computer into the phone line. "Let's get on the web and see if they've updated Army Times." She typed a few keys, I heard the modem whistle.

I closed my eyes and rested them. The day's activities had been a pleasant departure from my customary duties. I taught no students, I didn't even see the campus. I spent the morning at the Wall, then admired the Air and Space museum, then caught a bus and did my shopping. And then the night's sleep on the floor started catching up to me.

"Well, I've got no news," Rose said, studying the laptop's display. "This section was supposed to be updated by now and it hasn't been. Typical." I moved around to see the screen. There was a story about General Westmoreland's military career, and a link labeled 'UNVEILING SCHEDULE'. Rose had tried it and the link had come up empty. "The last time I saw this the statue was going to be installed Friday." Today was Tuesday. "Let's keep going. Leon, buy us a car. Carl, plan to get that access card and be sure you can get to a chopper."

"And me?" I asked.

She looked out the window. It was dark. "Go practice."

I spent maybe twenty minutes playing with the camera, but then tucked it into the vinyl carrying case. People haven't been the same around video cameras since the Rodney King incident, and I felt conspicuous. I aimed it up the street, and the people walking towards me froze, then gave me unpleasant looks as they doubled their pace to get past me. Must be what it's like in North Korea. But after a few test shots I saw how glaring a streetlight looked on video, how sensitive the camera was in picking up the flashing red brake lights of cars at an intersection, and agreed with Consumers Report that the camera did well with night-shots. Then, reminded by a Domino's Pizza delivery man of Hawthorne campus, I thought to use my telephone calling card to check my machine for messages.

First message was Linda. "Mom's out of ICU, her doctor says she's stable, but Mom say's she's dying. I have to stick around here at least through tomorrow, and I'll probably end up here the rest of the week." There was a pause on her end, then, "God, I miss you." My heart caught in my throat. I don't think I ever used the word 'love' in describing my relationship with Linda, though I think it was just from my severe discomfort using the word. "God, I miss you," I heard her say again, and then she got control of her emotions. "I'll call you Thursday." My own heart tugged, and I wished I hadn't been speaking to my own machine because I wanted to say, "and I miss you. And I wish you were here," and I felt my eyes misting up; something was happening between us.

Second message was Art. "Professor Dumont? I finished the draft of my paper on the Weathermen? I've got a thesis about failed revolutionaries and I'm on page thirty-three. And you had said no more than fifteen pages, so I wondered if you could meet with me and help me cut it down." Art did this to me each of three semesters. He wasn't Lenny Bruce, and he wasn't brief. Thirty-three pages of his writing could be boiled down to a page and a half. Suddenly it felt so good to be in Washington.

Third message was a hang-up. Telemarketers, probably. Fourth message was in a foreign language, probably a wrong number. South Framingham is heavily Brazilian, and I get wrong numbers in Portuguese. That was the end of the messages. I hung up the payphone, stepped out of the booth, and felt the nip in the night air. I really didn't want to go back to that crowded room, with Leon scowling at Rose, Rose taunting Leon, and Carl getting exasperated at both of them. So I went back to the bar.

It was noisy there, a long narrow bar with lots of stools, a few tables, and almost every seat filled with a gray veteran in his fifties or sixties, or a woman of similar years, and there were two TVs at opposite ends of the bar. At one end was a baseball game, and at the other end was some sitcom. I ordered a beer at the bar and took it to the baseball game end of the bar. It was Boston playing Kansas City. Nobody seemed to be consistently cheering either team. "That guy is the most over-paid lunkhead in the major leagues," complained one rotund, aged fellow with a farmer's tan. He paid the same compliment to every batter that stepped up and flew out or struck out that inning.

"You got to admit it," said one other fellow, stick-thin by comparison and a perfect fit in his old uniform, "that this is the greatest game in the world. Gree-e-e-e-e-atest game in the whole God-damn world." He looked too cheerful to be sober.

"No need to start cursing," complained the woman next to him, perhaps his wife. "Everytime you have two beers you say the same thing, and you start cursing." Perhaps they came from the Bible Belt, I wondered. They had soft, southern accents. Probably good Baptists, go to church most Sundays, and live the kind of quiet lives that make a veteran's convention in Washington the high point of the year. I found myself liking them.

"Yeah!" "Whoo-hooh!" "Run you son-of-a-bitch!" The batter had a stand-up double and was bringing in a run, and Boston was ahead. The room was festive for a minute, until the next batter struck out and the inning was over. More beer was ordered, nobody ordering liquor. I liked these folks. They were laughing and smiling at a baseball game; hell, they were probably doing here what they did every Saturday night in Hooterville. No night spots, no walks around the Rotunda, no special Washington parties. They would behave the same way next year when the convention was in Orlando. I had nothing in common with them, but after the company I'd kept for the past couple of days, I liked these aging veterans more than the aging revolutionaries up in room 202. If, however, I wanted a chance at a decent pillow I had to get back up there, soon. I finished my beer, left a modest tip on the bar, and reluctantly went back to the room.

The lights were out. I flipped them on, and discovered everyone was in bed, or, in my case, a blanket and pillow were on the floor awaiting me. "It's only nine-thirty," I said, "what's going on?"

Rose spoke, face into her pillow on the floor. "Leon started getting verbally abusive and before I ripped his dick off and stuck it in his mouth, we decided it was time for bed. Sorry you've got the floor, but tomorrow it's your turn for the bed."

"I thought tonight was," I groused, "I've been on the floor for two nights. It's Leon's turn for the floor."

Carl said, "Leon wouldn't agree to light's out unless he got the bed. Could you just hang with it again tonight?"

Leon had turned his back on us all and was asleep or pretending.

"Well, the convention winds up tomorrow," I announced, "so another room should open up. I think Leon should rob another bank tomorrow and we can each have our own suite. Is everyone agreed?" There were mumbles and grunts. "Fine. Floor is mine. Anyone need to go to the bathroom?" More mumbles and grunts.

I found a soft spot and tried to look forward to the four-hour sleep I might get.

The two days following can be compressed somewhat. Leon raised almost ten thousand dollars by penny looting several area banks, and came back on Thursday in a very sleek black Mercedes SUV. "Leather seats," he pointed out, "CD player. Power everything. Tinted windows. Interior temperature control. Kicks on the air or the heater, whatever it needs." I sat in the back seat. It felt better than the couch in my living room.

"A Mercedes?" Rose asked in dismay. "Don't you think buying a Chevy or Ford would have helped us blend?" But it was a nice vehicle, and even Rose enjoyed sitting in it.

"I still have seven thousand in the checking account," Leon boasted. I did a little math. He claimed to have skimmed ten thousand, and there I sat in a forty-five thousand-dollar vehicle. Even with favorable loan rates I knew Leon was rounding off dramatically. A sick feeling developed in the pit of my stomach. I was in the company of thieves. More precisely, thief. Leon was closer to the May 19th Coalition now than the Weathermen, becoming one of the James gang.

Carl located the home of one Jerry Bergen, a Sergeant who had access to the hangar sheltering the attack helicopters. Bergen was forty-five, and he had a wife and a couple of cats and no dogs. "Last two nights he went home, stayed home, went to bed early. Not a party animal. I think he's a creature of habit." That based on one day's surveillance.

So the plan was set. Carl and Leon would follow Mr. Bergen home tomorrow evening, Carl in the old van, Leon in the Mercedes. Leon would park the Mercedes a short distance away from Jerry's home. Leon and Carl would invade Jerry's home shortly after he arrived and get his access card. "He might cooperate, but it's smarter to presume not," Carl said. They would cut the phone lines and duct tape Jerry and his wife to the basement water heater or staircase or whatever. The van they would leave with Jerry.

"Shouldn't we just take Jerry's car?" I asked.

"Too easy to trace," Rose and Carl and Leon answered in unison. Okay, I thought, so I'm new at this, no need to rub my nose in it.

So Carl and Leon had thirty minutes to get to the base.

Leon would drop Carl off at the base. Carl would single-handedly get into the base and get the chopper. I glanced at Carl to see if he was serious; he was; I identified that as Weak Link #2, with breaking and entering and getting the access card and code from Mr. Bergen as Weak Link #1. Leon would return to the Best Western and pick up Rose and I, and he would drop Rose off at a shopping mall in Falls Church. Carl would land, pick up Rose, total time on the ground less than a minute, and they would head off to glory. Weak Link #3.

I would have plenty of time to make my own way to the Pentagon. I would use the cellular phone to keep track of everyone, and when the action began I would capture it all on video.

Leon would eventually show up at my position, in the northwest parking lot. He would arrive just five minutes before Carl and Rose's ETA, and as soon as the statue was blasted we would head north. Weak Link #...oh, I thought, why bother.

There was a good long minute of quiet as the plan simmered. "Question," I broke the silence. "How do you two get out?"

Rose looked positively beatific as she said, "Dumont, we initiated this plan expecting to be captured. Or...killed. It's fair to say that the police and military will be all over us when we're done. Escape for us was never an option." My eyebrows went up. Leon looked passingly impressed. "The only thing more important to us than blowing up that statue is for you two to distribute the tape with the lesson to America on why we did it." She sighed. "And speaking of lessons, we should start writing our statement." I'd claimed that this group was suicidal; now I had first-hand proof.

The statement: Rose and Carl were going to compose a statement on why they were doing this. Remembering the Port Huron Statement, remembering the Weatherman Statement some years later, I wanted to suggest they keep it minimally theoretical so folks could understand it, but dictating to someone their own suicide note is in poor taste. They adjourned to the other side of the room, using the round coffee table with the lamp, and started writing in a lined notebook. And arguing. Mostly arguing, as the night went on. Leon tried putting on the TV but both of them barked at him. "Can't think with that thing blaring!"

"Let's go for a beer," Leon said to me. Sounded good. This time I got to ride in the front seat.

We started driving, but the traffic was miserable so we ended up parking back at the Best Western and returning to the bar I'd visited. The VFW conference was winding down and the bar had a more varied clientele. Leon ordered a pitcher of beer and we took a table in the corner. "This is more like it," he smiled, and I realized it was probably the first time I'd seen him smile. His smile was a half-sneer, so I wouldn't miss seeing it again. "Another hour with that freak and I'd probably kill it." Seeing that I didn't join in Rose-bashing, he poured one for himself, one for me, then drank off a third of his mug. "This isn't turning out like I thought it would," he admitted.

"What did you expect?"

"It was fun back then," he smiled again. "We were fighting for a cause, and the streets were friendlier to us. Seemed like every college campus had a chapter of SDS, and they could always put you up for the night, and sometimes you got laid to boot." Leon's eyes looked wistful for the days of yore. "We all had long hair, and the music was good, and the dope was plentiful and free." Leon was beginning to remind me of the old veterans I'd observed two nights ago—everything but the long hair and the dope and the music. And the sex. "But the war is long gone. After Desert Storm people even like the military." He took another swallow. "I came down in '69 with the Veterans Against the Vietnam War. John Kerry was one of our leaders. There was this demonstration planned where all the guys with Purple Hearts, Silver Stars, any kind of battlefield decoration, were going to line up at the Pentagon and throw their medals back." He was silent a moment. "I didn't have a Purple Heart. All I had was a Good Conduct medal and my badge qualifying me on my rifle, shit any kid can get for fifty cents in an Army-Navy store." He looked down at his hands. "But I threw my Good Conduct medal, right alongside those Purple Hearts and Stars."

"And did it help to do that?" I was a very poor interviewer.

He looked sad. "I went back the next day when everybody was heading out, and I tried to find my Good Conduct medal. But someone had collected them all and I was shit out of luck." He sighed heavily. "And it's been like that ever since. I hung out with Tom and Carl. Carl was into the military stuff, and he was like having a little brother. He told me about how his father didn't talk to him, because of him being in the Weathermen. Never bought Carl's argument that he was in the service, just not the government's. Tom was more intellectual, but he respected my military time and we were a cool bunch. Now it's all changed," he sighed again, clearly not for the better.

I didn't know what to say. I didn't quite like Leon. I was impressed with his experience, but his behavior was otherwise juvenile and his excessive bank robbing made me suspicious of his motives. Now he had shared a personal story with me, and I felt locked into a relationship I wouldn't have created on my own.

After his hitch, Leon came back to Massachusetts and used his GI benefits to start school at Hawthorne College. Dropping out in his sophomore year, he tried living in a commune in the Berkshires but none of the free spirits wanted to get even a minimum wage job to keep the lights on in the commune. "It was a complete pig-sty. They felt they should either panhandle, whine to Mom and Dad for money, or even commit petty crime. Getting a job, even selling vegetables at a roadside stand, was a sell-out. That wasn't my version of New America."

It sounded to me like Leon had never come close to embracing Weatherman's call for socialist revolution. I guess he got into it for the promise of action, and probably for the sex. "After Carl and Tom pulled the robbery, we split up. I knew they were heading out of the country, and I didn't want to. A guy I knew from Nam, Everett Jacobs, lived in Kittery. I went home in December for Christmas and ran into him. He was living in a camp of his, back in the woods. Not the kind of crazy survivalist stuff you see now, just him living by himself. He had a good cabin, and his GI benefits were paying his bills, and he was trying to figure out what to do with himself. I hung with him for a while. We saw Tricky Dick go down in flames, and Jerry Ford pardon him. Then Carter comes in and we were hopeful. I stopped voting when Reagan got in."

"So what did you guys end up doing?"

Leon looked shy. "Well, there's always guys wanting to go on hunting trips up in Maine, and Everett and me started guiding for money. We didn't know much about tracking moose or anything. We just knew how to go in and find our way out. It kept us in beer money. Then I met my wife, Emily, and we built our own cabin on a piece of land a little closer to town. And then the PC came along, and I've been making a living off it, one way or another."

"Were you ever in my classes?" I asked, hesitantly.

"I sat in one once. Tom strongly recommended it," Leon answered, strong emphasis on 'Tom'. "You were pretty dull." He was smiling, looking to see if I could take it.

Even dropouts are entitled to their uneducated opinions, but I was feeling unusually feisty. "I was probably having a bad day. Or you were." I paid more attention to my beer and we were dividing the rest of the pitcher when Rose came into the bar, looking like a truant officer bagging two tardies.

"Here you are," she announced, glaring at us. Leon looked quite willing to knock her on her ass. "We have news," she said, not happily, standing next to me.

"What's the news, Rose?" I asked, sounding a little sloshed.

She drew us out of the bar, into a corner near the elevator where we were briefly alone. "The statue won't be dedicated tomorrow. It's probably going to be postponed at least six weeks." She was pissed. "Six frigging weeks. It was in Army Times, just posted on their web site. Fuck, fuck, fuck, fuck!"

"Postponed?" Leon reiterated. Shaking his head, I saw him work his lips around 'fuck, fuck, fuck' but he kept the volume to himself.

"Postponed," I repeated. "What do we do now?"

"C'mon back up when you're done with your beer," Rose said. "Carl and I are cooking up alternatives. Goddamn Army."

Maybe Leon and I should have returned immediately, but he ordered another pitcher, and I guess I liked Leon more than I thought because I stayed to help him drink it. We must have wanted to get drunk. We barely spoke, just watched TV and took long swallows until we each had to pee, then the pitcher was gone. "Let's go up and see what the freak has found," Leon announced. I remember thinking, at some point I have to defend Rose, but I wasn't up to it then.

Rose was animated when we entered the room. Carl was studying the computer screen and she was pacing back and forth, groaning as the screens slowly loaded. "C'mon, c'mon!" she demanded.

"There," Carl pointed at something on the screen. "Look at that."

Rose stopped and looked. "God, what kind of line we working off here?" she complained. Then, for the first time, she noticed us. Smiling now, she beckoned us over. "We've caught a great break."

Leon let me lead the way, and I realized he was having trouble staying upright. Some hunting guide, I thought with derision, gets plastered on two pitchers. Then I realized the chair I was heading for really was moving, somehow. "What?" I asked. Rose pointed at the screen, but the display was too small for me to read. "What's it say?" I asked.

"Westmoreland, Retired General Westmoreland, will be giving a speech in ten days, to the directors of the Boston Historical Society. He will be giving this speech at the Park Plaza. In Boston." Rose beamed. "In plain sight. We don't have to settle for a statue, guys, we can get the real pig."

Then the floor really started moving and I sat down hard.

Leon argued without much conviction that, having gotten ourselves here, perhaps we could go through with the attack and find another target. "No," Carl insisted, "it's got to be Westmoreland. I'm not trying to make a statement against the military itself. It's got to be about Vietnam."

"We could bomb the Vietnam Memorial?" Leon suggested, though even he clearly didn't like the idea.

"Bomb the victims?" Rose retorted, and that time Leon took it.

"No, it has to be Westmoreland," Carl said. "The only other person still alive who had as much involvement with the build-up besides Westmoreland was Robert McNamara, and he's too much of a pussy to bother with."

It was an eight-hour drive from Washington back to Framingham, with rest stops. We started at eight in the evening and drove through the night, not my preference but sudden pangs of guilt were drawing me back to Hawthorne and the classes I was missing. I had called in with a 'family emergency' that would take a week, the first such emergency of my many years. I wanted back, because after five days with the Weathermen I was desperate for familiar sights; my own bed was especially seductive.

Carl and Rose drove in their old van, and Leon and I rode in his new Mercedes truck. I think Leon wanted Carl to ride with him, but Rose had a typical fit over Carl riding with her. It forced Leon and I to get to know each other a little better. "So why do you have so much trouble with Rose as a woman?" I asked in my best nonchalant manner as we rolled into the Maryland countryside.

"It's un-fucking-natural," Leon answered. "You don't change your gender. It's mutilation." I was quiet. "I don't care about race, or religion," he proclaimed like one who will always care about race and religion, "but if a person can't stick to their gender they are sick. I also don't like transvestites, or fags."

I have found that vocabulary often establishes a person's true feelings faster than any ideas they try to convey. 'Fag' says more to me than any statement on homosexuality. I have heard 'fags are okay by me so long as they stick to their own' and know that the first contact, however accidental, that the speaker has with a gay man will be hostile and, if opportunity arises, violent. Leon went on about his liberal approach to sexual diversity for a while, and was quite the bore. Maybe Carl was right, I wondered, maybe Leon is actually sexually attracted to Rose and contempt was his only way of dealing with that boner. He finally got tired of his own opinion and was quiet for a few minutes.

"What about Vietnam made you decide it was wrong?" I tried a safer—relatively—line of discussion.

Leon sighed. I'd touched a nerve. "I did a tour in 1964. I was a grunt and I was at Ben Suc." He took his eyes off the road for a moment to look me in the eye. "You're a history professor. You know what I'm talking about?"

"Ia Drang. The Iron Triangle?" I answered, and he nodded. It was the first major military operation the US Army tried in Vietnam. Like a sacred mantra I recited what that village made infamous. " 'In order to save the village it was necessary to destroy the village'." He nodded. [I later learned that Leon hadn't been at Ben Suc. He'd spent his year pushing papers in 'Supply' at Tan Son Nhut airbase. He was another version of 'Missing the Show'. Just as I had Never Marched and Never Fought, if one had to be in Vietnam, and later endure the societal abuse accorded to those who went, one might as well have been in the field mowing down the enemy, rather than assigned the boring, depressing task of typing and filing and trying to stay close to the air conditioner in the tropical heat. Leon and I had more in common than we knew.]

But it was a good icebreaker. Leon talked, but now he was interesting. Some things were unchanged since the sixties. The government was still a lying, deceitful, self-preserving organism, and changing presidents and legislators every four or so years didn't make a damn bit of difference. "The military does its job, obeys its orders," Leon said, underscoring his loyalty to his khakis, "but the government is seriously fucked up." When he began to speak of the Zionist Conspiracy I felt the hair on my neck rise. "It's all part of Z-O-G. You know what I mean?"

"Popular expression among the militias," I answered, "Zionist-Occupational-Government, or Washington, DC, as some of us know it." I broke a sweat. "So, have you read the Turner Diaries?"

"Damn good book," Leon answered, and then I knew for sure I was trapped at eighty miles per hour in a Mercedes truck with a Weatherman-turned-Militia-man. I should have seen it coming a mile away. "And if you're wondering, am I in a militia, the answer is, technically, no." I watched a U-Haul truck up the road a few hundred feet, a little afraid to look at Leon. "I have some friends who are sort of organizing in our region. There's a lot of sympathetic folks. But after Oklahoma City everyone's a little afraid." He let it hang there.

Immediately upon our return to Framingham at five in the morning, having grabbed about an hour of uneasy doze, I showered, shaved, inhaled a cup of coffee and a Pop-Tart, and then dashed off to get the class material to teach my 8:30 American History survey course. I don't even remember teaching that class; the sad part is the students probably don't either. After that I retreated to my office to compress the two sessions of each class I had missed into the rest of the class meetings. After that I collected two more messages from Linda, back at work, and deliberately returned her call at the bookstore. "Peter?" she sounded surprised. "I heard you took a sudden trip to Washington?" 'Sudden trip' wasn't a concept people associate with me.

Carl and Rose and Leon were still at my house, and I was still frozen in fear that their new target was the living, breathing general they'd sought to disgrace. "Yea," I answered, trying to sound casual, "I went to Washington." Linda and I had been close enough for too long for me to create an old friend she had never heard of. "I can't really explain just now," I said. "I will be able to, soon. It's nothing for you to be worried about," I tried to reassure her; that phrase never worked, but I kept trying. I heard a cash register clang from her end of the phone.

"How about lunch?" she asked expectantly. We agreed to meet in the Greek pizza parlor across Route 9 from the college. I hung up the phone and sighed with relief. Then I remembered who was at my home.

I was first to the pizza shop and had a table staked out when she came in through the screen door. We hugged, hers more heart-felt than usual, a quick peck, and then we both ordered a big pizza to share. "So how's your mother?"

Linda frowned. "She's probably got another year left in her, but I'm not sure I do. If I could just get Richard to help out." Brother Richard was an assistant lecturer in the Creative Writing Program at Iowa State, lowest possible rung on the academic pole, with at least twelve other overeducated and underpaid bards over his head. "He says he's 'just swamped'. I think he's full of swamp gas."

Linda had lost sleep. Her deep brown eyes seemed larger than normal by the dark shadows under them, and she yawned repeatedly—of course, I was also working on about seven hours of sleep over three nights, but I look almost the same either way. She usually reminded me of a brunette Stevie Nicks, and just now it was Stevie Nicks in her Klonopin years. "Mom really wore me out. And the bed is the same bed I grew up in." Yawn. "But I had a chance to think about us, which is something I'm often too busy to do here. All the time I was in bed not sleeping, I was thinking about you." Her tired eyes were smiling and she seemed so very happy to see me.

We didn't do public displays of emotion, so what she had just said, coupled with that phone message, was a clear call that she was getting more serious than we had been. She's going to want to move in, I thought, or she wants to be engaged; perhaps both. "I thought of you, too," I said, not even squirming over the exaggeration. I had thought of her while I was in Washington, but I had had a lot on my mind.

"I'm sorry," she said, "I know I'm dumping this on you. But it has been bothering me, and then Mom pushed all my buttons. We've been dating for years, Peter," she continued, "and my mother asked if we were engaged, or planning to be engaged, or planning at all, and I," she was studying her school ring, which she wore on her left ring finger, where an engagement ring would be, "didn't know what to say."

"I...don't know..." I caught myself before I said something wrong.

She blushed. "I know, I know," she apologized, "I'm caving to Mom here. But I do want to know..." she shyly looked up at me, completely reviving the Stevie Nicks look, "what is your commitment? Where do you think we'll be in a year or two?" This time she looked at me, and she had that childish grin that put out pheromones like Niagara Falls.

So, Mom had lit a fire under Daughter to 'get a commitment', though it sounded like Linda had been simmering on her own. "What sort of commitment are you looking for?" I asked in what I mightily tried to make a gentle, vaguely loving but ultimately neutral tone. Not Clinical Neutral, not 'I'm afraid that tooth's going to have to come out' neutral, but 'Rhett Butler looking with brotherly affection at Scarlett's sister'-neutral. I still hadn't caught up on my own sleep, so whether it would have been an honest suggestion or not, saying 'let's sleep on it' seemed a bad idea if I didn't want to wear pizza. "I want us to be together in a year," I finally answered, but my voice sounded like I was struggling with a multiple-choice test. Her sweet smile sagged. "Tell me what you want," I begged.

"I thought we might want to try moving in together," she answered, but she was disappointed. "But seeing your response," she shrugged, "never mind."

Bells ringing, alarms sounding. I hadn't dated at all for the first five years here, and I vividly remember my loneliness. Our first meeting had been in the bookstore, an unpromising start. Then one rainy evening we were parked together in the parking lot when...was it my car that wouldn't start? I know she was the one who had jumper cables. Story of our relationship. I had been very happy with her. In love? I didn't know.

How would I feel if she left me and dated someone else? Like a cold winter wind gusting over a frozen steppe in north Siberia, I felt the edge of despair touch me. And with that brief foray into my emotions—all my emotional explorations are brief—I knew I must be in some sort of love with Linda. "Then let's do it," I said, taking her hand, and I sounded certain enough to bring back her smile.

Then Rose, Leon and Carl appeared in my memory. "*When* did you want to?" I asked, as though I was scheduling soccer practice instead of an act of love.

She smiled mischievously; she had a spontaneous streak I'd failed to stamp out, "tonight?"

Oops, I remember thinking, logistical problem. Did it show on my face? No, she was still smiling. How to accommodate three unwanted visitors and my love? Not possible. "I do have a little problem," I admitted. "I've got three guests."

Linda's eyebrows arched. "You have guests?" she asked, amazed again.

It was a fair response; a companion jolt to 'sudden trip'. "Who? Are they old friends? I want to meet them," she said, her smile dazzling. "They can tell me old stories about you."

Nothing you'd want to admit in front of a judge, honey, I thought.

"Pizza's up," the counterman called. When she'd put away two slices and paused for air, she asked, "so what made you run off to Washington in the middle of the term? Testing the power of tenure?"

That reminded me of the talk I'd had with Winfield. "Interesting word you mentioned," I said. I gave her the short version of my chat with Winfield. "And the reason I went to Washington was that I was contacted by some old...acquaintances from my radical days." Saying that I had 'radical days' was stretching the truth like plastic wrap under a thousand pounds of pressure, but Linda ignored it. "They wanted a sort of reunion. I thought I could get something from it, maybe an article. Something. So I jumped on it." Linda was very accepting, positively enthusiastic. She nodded and said she'd like to see what I wrote on it—if I ever did. Then it was time for her to get back to the bookstore and time for me to finish any damage control from my trip.

By two in the afternoon I had caught up with the two graduate students I had skipped out on. I had some papers to correct, as well as Art's magnum poopus to pare down to readable length. When I returned to my home I felt comfortably esconced in my old life again, and less tolerant of the rolling stones in my living room.

Rose and Carl were on my phone. Leon was sitting in the Mercedes in the driveway, playing the radio. I glanced in the kitchen. They had fed themselves and the dishes were in the sink. The refrigerator looked bare. "Is anyone planning on going to a supermarket?" I asked. "And will the culprits who dumped their dishes in the sink be washing them soon?" Nobody responded. In some respects nothing had changed; the Weathermen were still complete slobs. I went into my office and pointedly closed the door until the latch clicked.

Back In Boston

The next morning I emerged from by bedroom to find my house even messier than the night before. Leon was stretched out, asleep, on the couch, one bare foot dangling unappetizingly in space, the comforter I'd bought in Ireland stretched taut over his unwashed corpus. Carl was watching a morning news show on TV and Rose was at my dining room table, finishing a breakfast of eggs and toast.

"Morning," she acknowledged me with a bare glance. She was reading my copy of 'The Economist', and I looked over her shoulder for a moment. She was underlining passages she found especially irksome and writing obscene responses in the column. "Ever try the crossword puzzle?" I asked. She ignored me.

Dirty plates from a meal I had missed were on the dining room table, the kitchen table, the kitchen counter and the dining room floor. Cooking pots were stacked in the sink, above the faucet. I started inventorying my cupboards. There were no clean coffee cups or dishes. All my silverware, even the decorative pieces, like the butter serving knife, were mingled with the plates and collecting in the sink, with hardened crusts forming on them. Leon's other clothes were strewn around the couch and someone had microwaved popcorn at some point and, so it appeared, tried to sow it into the carpet.

"Alright," I announced, my chronic morning crankiness peaking, "everyone listen to this." Rose looked up, Carl turned down the TV. "You have two choices. Two," I held up two fingers. Leon was still asleep. I marched over and kicked his exposed foot and he woke. "Two choices, Leon. Choice Number One is to clean up this mess immediately. Choice Number Two is to leave immediately. There are no other choices."

Linda pulled into my driveway at about three in the afternoon, just three minutes after the Weathermen finally took off to the Park Plaza Hotel. I was still airing out the pot smoke and the dishwasher was on its second load. Linda's ancient VW Rabbit was filled with clothes, some plants, and some photos. "This will get me through the night," she grinned facetiously, and then she kissed me. It was a warm, sexy, wet kiss and it turned my day around. My heart, and my lower regions, began pumping. Linda had definitely moved our relationship up a notch. Her kissing was coming from a much hotter source than before.

We brought her stuff in, and I put her suitcases on the guest bed. "Hello?" she stood in the doorway, arms full, smiling, "what's wrong with this picture?" I looked back and forth, and blushed, and collected her suitcases and took them into my bedroom. "And now," she announced, "you have to clear out a drawer or two for my things." I nodded. "For your reward I'll make us a nice surprise for dinner," she offered, and gradually we emptied her car.

"What kind of surprise?" I asked with some trepidation, after making room for feminine items in the bathroom. She shooed me out before unpacking her little suitcase. "What kind of surprise?" I asked again, through the door, in part playful, in part anxious.

I followed her to the kitchen. "Beats me," she smiled, and opened cupboards. "What have you got here?"

"Well, I haven't been shopping this week," I began defending myself. "Toothpicks, grape jelly, some tuna fish, that mayo is probably gone. I don't know why I have so many cans of beans because I don't like them, and that's organic macaroni and cheese," I identified for her.

"Organic macaroni and cheese," she said in delight, taking out the box, and I knew it was like finding caviar by the beef jerky in the corner convenience store. I'd bought four boxes of it and my Weather Underground guests had consumed three of them. We ate and Linda mentioned, "stopping at Stop-n-Shop to get some food in. I like to make dinner. And two can eat cheaper than one," she said, nuzzling up to me. She was radiant. I was pleasantly surprised to find I liked it too, but I was distracted. Even as my lover and now housemate was warming her space my mind was about twenty miles east-bound in a suite that cost, per night, half of my mortgage payment. And hundreds of thousands of Americans had paid for that suite with their unwitting four-cent contributions.

It was five days before Westmoreland was to speak at the Park Plaza. Carl and Rose were in a lavish suite with two king-sized beds and a living room, with Leon in a suite on another floor, on the other side of the building, which was still not far enough away from Rose for him.

I went in that evening for a meeting. "Okay," Carl said, that first evening with us all together, by way of reviewing the new plan, "I'll be picking up the chopper at Hanscom Field. Rose'll be in the van. I'll arrange with her where to pick her up." Leon and I glanced at each other—they were cutting us out of these details—"and when I'm about to pick up Rose she'll call you," Carl indicated me. "And you will be where?" he waited for my response, schoolmaster-in-training.

I didn't like his tone, but I kept my attitude in check. "I roll film as soon as a helicopter appears above the Public Gardens," I answered. "How will you know your target?" I asked him.

"It'll be the only limo flying a four star general's flag," Leon reminded me. We all nodded.

"Sounds like a plan," Rose wrapped up.

Actually it was so spare, so simplistic, that it compared poorly with previous poorly planned Weather operations. Carl would go to

Hanscom and steal an armored combat helicopter, encountering no significant resistance. And then he would fly it over Rt. 128, and Lexington, and then Belmont, and Cambridge, none of these metropoli being rural, under-protected small towns without police forces. Then he would land at some place only he and Rose knew of, where they would not be spotted, and she would join him in their quixotic assault. Meanwhile, Leon and I would be loitering on the Common waiting for retired General Westmoreland's four-star rented limo to leave the Park Plaza Hotel, drive down Charles Street, and come under attack. "Just one question," I thought to ask, "Leon, you're going to have our Mercedes get-away vehicle waiting?"

Leon nodded.

"Where?"

"How about by the 'Partisans' statue?" Leon suggested. I nodded; it was a good symbol. [It's a statue of four defeated soldiers being led away, bound, on horseback.]

"And you two?" I addressed the dynamic duo. "Still planning on being guests of the gray-bar motel? Or are you going to land the chopper and run for the escape pod?"

"If we can escape, we will," Carl answered soberly, which was less dramatic and much saner than they'd sounded in Washington. "If we can get to you, fine. Maybe we'll fly out," he shrugged. As plans go, it was a joke. As the Weathermen went, it wasn't bad.

And for me, it was perfect. If they hadn't done any planning, I finally had. I'd get a book out of this, and it was a virtual certainty that neither Carl nor Rose would get within ten miles of Westmoreland. I doubted Carl would reach the median of Route 128. So I'd get my book and no one would get hurt. When Westy's limo double-parked in front of Bullfinch's, Leon and I would be hauling ass…where? "Where will we go?" I asked, "after."

"A safe house," Leon answered, and I'm sure he didn't know of one closer than Kittery. No, I thought, I'll run for the Boylston T stop, ride to Riverside. I will want to go home to Linda and tell her all about it while it's still fresh in my head. And when the police came knocking, I'd go willingly. If they didn't come soon enough I'd call them. That was my own escape plan.

En route to the bathroom I saw two packages, the size and shape of a loaf of Wonder Bread, packed securely in heavy brown paper and heavy duty tape; there was also a black plastic device trailing a cluster of wiring. "What's this?" I asked, holding the plastic device. "Where'd you get this stuff?" I asked, trying to heft a loaf; it was heavy.

"Dumont, have you ever heard of the Internet?" Rose asked in an exasperated tone from around the corner; then she came around and saw I was holding the plastic with wiring and she reacted like her little boy had just grabbed the sharp end of a knife. "Put that down!"

"What's it for?" I asked, sounding wounded, ignored, and suspicious. I wasn't really feeling wounded or ignored, but I was powerfully suspicious.

"I can't explain it right now," she said, and I picked up a mystery loaf.

"If I knew what bomb components looked like, I'd say these looked like…is this explosive?" I asked of the package that I hefted like old cheese.

Carl had come to see, and he turned pale. "Yes, it is. Put it down, now. Carefully."

"Oh." I set it down very lovingly, very gently. I'd been kidding; they weren't. "You guys have a backup plan? Are you going to kill him here? Maybe…we're," I indicated Leon," the backup plan?"

Leon, who'd come to see the fun, turned his head left, at me, then right, at them.

"Rose and I are considering bombing the banquet," Carl confessed, "after Westmoreland leaves, so will his security detachment."

"Leaving a hundred old officers and capitalists in one room," Rose added. Her eyes lit up. "It's too tempting a target," she said urgently. "We've looked it over. It's easy to get the bomb in there, and we've made this kind of bomb before."

That was a sobering moment for me. They'd made that kind of bomb before. They should have been incarcerated. And suddenly I was in way over my head. "When were you going to tell us?" I asked, sounding hurt.

"You would have been told when it was necessary," Rose answered in an irritated voice, "you were a little more observant than I thought. Let's get on with it."

Oh God. They'd gotten greedy. The beauty of the first plan was its threadbare complexity. This other plan was simple, so it could work. I could have complained more urgently but there wasn't enough time or trust in the room. "Bombing is so messy," I improvised, "and you'll kill innocent people. This is Boston. The waiters are probably undergraduates, just reading DAS KAPITAL. What's wrong with just attacking the limo?"

"It's an opportunity," Rose said, "and by the end of the evening we'll be wanted again anyway. This will be a night people will really remember. For a long time." She was savoring that thought, as was Carl. Even Leon looked a bit starry-eyed.

"I have a suggestion," I said, hesitantly, "something I was going to mention earlier, before all this," I indicated the bomb. It had come to me while driving in, that I might be able to turn the point of this knife. "Instead of shooting Westmoreland, which is technically murder, remember how you guys used to make very eloquent statements by dumping red ink or pig's blood onto draft files?" I checked each of them to be sure they were listening. "It made the point, it embarrassed the draft boards, and nobody was killed. It was great PR. It was a great way of making a statement. How about we pay homage to the old Weather Underground tradition and dump red paint on the limo?"

Boy, was that a metaphysical wrench into the gears. All three of them stared at me like I'd farted. "Red paint?" Rose asked, as if reminded of an old irritating song.

"This is not 1968," Carl said, "no one will remember what it's for."

"I don't know about that," Rose said, "symbols are never outdated. CNN will have a retrospective airing thirty minutes after we do it," she deadpanned. Their debate accelerated, and went back and forth. Leon looked at me as if to say, 'why didn't I think of this?' and then I knew something. I knew that Carl and Rose were prepared to die, and I knew Leon wasn't, and I think he was grateful. I got up and opened a beer and started reading a Boston Globe I found on the floor.

Carl and Rose adjourned to the bathroom and shut the door for a Senior Staff Argument. Leon changed the channel on the TV to an adult movie. I moved my seat, in part to see the adult movie a little better, and to overhear the bathroom conference. "You do the flying, I handle the shooting," I heard Rose say. "Dumont is just scared."

"But he has a point," Carl argued. Now *he* liked my idea, as a tribute to the pranks of the past, and now *Rose* was against it. Get two Weathermen in a room and you'd have three political parties. I heard something like 'fuck it' and then I got away from the door as it opened. "Leon, turn off the Porn Channel, please," Carl said. Leon was motionless. "It's rude to Rose," Carl reminded him, which only made Leon dig his heels in.

"Let the asshole pretend he has a penis," Rose dismissed him. "We have to discuss this," she spoke to all of us as though we were in a parliamentary setting. "Dumont has suggested that we deliver a non-lethal message to Westmoreland by dumping red paint on his limo. I still feel we should have Westmoreland pay the same price he forced thousands of conscripted young men to pay."

Never mind that Rose and Carl had been thirty years underground, that they had probably conjured and debated a dozen plans for their legacy. The Weather Underground was notorious for over-debating their plans. They analyzed, they criticized, and they debated, symbols attacking symbols. They also attacked each other in organized sessions, hours upon hours of targeted character assassination, trying to root out bourgeois influence. It must have been like trying to piss on a forest fire. "Dumont," Rose turned to me at one point, her eyebrows knit with suspicion, "are you just scared of killing? Is this about symbolism or about your cowardice?"

I thought for a moment about the answers that I could give her. Then I said, "both. I was pretty comfortable blasting a statue. A little property damage, nothing to get sent to Cedar Junction over. But blowing up the limo and killing people is murder. Whatever happened thirty years ago, this is still murder. And I have never had any stomach for murder. So why not invoke some symbolism without murdering? It'll have more positive effect than killing will."

"And what effect is that?" Carl asked, more curious than antagonistic.

"Surprising the shit out of the entire world that the Weather Underground still exists," I answered. "The first story the news will carry will be this bizarre attack on Westmoreland. Someone dumped paint on him. You'll get more press from that than crude assassination. Dumping red paint? Nobody under forty will know what it's about. The networks will take five seconds to remember the Weather Underground, ten minutes to dig up archival footage, which they'll run and they will explain to the totally clueless what you've done, and bingo. You two want a legacy? That is your legacy. That your ideals sustained you for thirty years. That you still cared after all this time. That you carried the revolution to another generation." They looked at me, then at each other, eyes narrowed suspiciously at first, then evolving into curiosity.

I pressed my point. "If you dump red paint on the limo, and I can get good pictures of Westmoreland in red, that image will be seen around the world in under five hours—" like I had any idea of how fast news disseminated—"and people will, at worst, be irritated with you for spoiling the old man's uniform. At best, they'll remember the sixties, will remember Vietnam and the protests, and will honor you for reminding them." I let that image warm them, then said, "if you shoot up his limo, then the images will be of an old man murdered by terrorists, and most folks will want to see you following Timothy McVeigh on Death Row, and they'll happily pull the switch themselves. Their kindliest thoughts will be that you guys used to stand for something, but now you're just murderous punks." I let that thought simmer. And, thinking of Carl's grandiose Operation Brainless, I added, "and if you shoot and don't kill, you'll be remembered like Squeaky Fromme. You want to end up as a footnote next to Squeaky Fromme?"

I think that made them think hard. Nobody wants to be remembered like Squeaky Fromme. To start your adult life as a follower of Charles Manson displays bad enough judgement without concluding it as an inept attempted-assassin of President Ford, who has a national profile substantially lower than the current White House pet. Rose was having cold shivers thinking of herself in some history book with a photo of Squeaky on the same page.

She took Carl back into the bathroom for a minute, then they came out. "Okay, Dumont, you have a point," Carl said, sounding tired. "We'll go for symbolism. Feel better?" he asked, like a parent to a child getting over the flu.

"Yes." I felt very tired, but very relieved. "Leon?"

For the first time since BABES IN TOYLAND had begun, Leon took his eyes off the TV. "What?" he asked, irritated.

"We're going to dump red paint on Westmoreland, not kill him."

Eyes still on the screen, he smiled, whether at them or at the news I couldn't tell. "Woosies."

Driving home, I was so pleased with myself over the change in plans that I almost forgot about the second plot, to bomb the room after Westmoreland left. That plan was still 'go'. How were they going to get the bomb in? There were ways. When Westmoreland left the room, so would all the security. It would be just another banquet. Getting a bomb inside was no harder than getting in with the dessert cart. What mattered was that people were still in real danger.

And when I reached my home and stopped my car in the driveway, I realized that I was in danger, too, danger of prison for conspiracy in a bombing Carl and Rose could easily execute. Conspiracy. That phrase put a chill up my spine and in my groin.

I needed help.

I turned off the car and she surprised me, coming from the house in her bathrobe. "Where the hell have you been?" Linda asked in her anguished voice. It was nine-thirty, I'd said I'd be home by seven, but I wasn't used to being held responsible. Linda was painfully punctual—life was going to get hard.

It was time to share my experiences. We went inside. And, as I asked her to sit down, in so doing warning her that it wasn't a simple story, I saw something new on my wall that made me smile: I saw her family photo and was reminded of Linda's 'baby' brother, Lieutenant James Falcone of the Massachusetts State Police.

Linda thought I was pulling her leg, but I convinced her I wasn't. "We have to tell someone," she said, the first wave of panic washing over her.

"How about your brother?" I asked. "I'd rather not start telling this story in a police station. Can he come over?"

"It's a little late tonight," she pointed out, "but maybe I'll call him anyway." And at least I was out of the doghouse for that evening.

James Falcone, "please, call me Jim," was a solidly built fellow of thirty, Linda's youngest brother in a family with six siblings. He had a geometrically flattop haircut and didn't look to be carrying any more than the necessary six percent body fat.

Jim had instantly agreed to come over, in part to check me out. I'd been dating Linda for years, and Jim was her nearest relative, but I had avoided meeting him. There was no avoiding him anymore. When he came in he was just big enough to fill the doorframe, and that intimidated me. "Hi, Peter," he said, smiling politely. That I could have been Jim's uncle—Linda and I were eight years apart and she and Jim were another seven years—didn't help our tension. We didn't have anything in common, except Linda. We each had a beer and Linda started telling each of us about the other. That lasted about five minutes. Then Linda and Jim shared some inside jokes for a couple of minutes. I got more beer for everyone; it couldn't hurt.

"Jimmy," she grinned at his boyhood name, "has been in the State Police now for three years, right?" she checked with him. "Yeah. Peter's been teaching at Hawthorne for thirty years." Jim was impressed. Linda looked a little awkward. "Jimmy, this was a good opportunity for you two to meet 'cause Peter's got a problem." I watched Jim's brow furrow slightly, though his smile remained. "You should tell him now," she said to me.

So I told him. I told him about being kidnapped from my class, about the electronic bank skimming, and the abortive trip to Washington. That all took about forty-five minutes—Jim was a good listener and he didn't interrupt—and I paused when I'd brought the adventure to the present. "They're staying in the Park Plaza Hotel now. I think they're expanding the plan from stealing a helicopter to include planting a bomb in the hall after Westmoreland leaves." I realized how tense I was then, holding the glass bottle tight. "I figured that the more complicated the plan got the quicker they'd get caught. That's why I stayed quiet, up until now."

"And collected material for your book?" Jim asked, and he looked just a little amazed. "You're an educated man," he began the sentence, so I knew it wouldn't end kindly, "so I'm kind of amazed at your judgement."

I nodded. "I know I've been a jerk. Anyway, last night I learned they were changing plans. So I knew I had to do something."

Jim got up and borrowed my cordless phone and took it into the kitchen for some privacy. Linda sat next to me protectively, out of instinct or to specifically keep Jim from clubbing me with my own phone, I wasn't sure. He was on the phone for a while, and when he hung up he redialed and made another call. Five minutes turned to fifteen, then half an hour. Linda said, "I think it's a good move you made." She got up and went into the kitchen to make coffee, which is her tried and true way of easing herself through stressful experiences. She makes at least half a pot but won't drink more than half a cup. This time she returned quickly. "He'll be in in a few minutes." A few minutes later the phone rang, which surprised us, as we thought Jim was on it.

Linda and I were stretched out on the couch and wondering if turning on the TV for the news would be rude, when Jim finally came in. He dropped into the chair opposite me and he sounded tired. "Okay, I called my captain, and gave him the general story. He told me to immediately contact the Barracks, and I had to wait a few minutes on hold, because I had to explain it all to the Anti-Terror squad."

'Anti-Terror Squad'. I turned pale. Linda did too.

"Westmoreland's visit is scheduled for Friday, right?" Jim asked. I nodded. It was midnight Monday. "And your comrades are in the Park Plaza Hotel, Suites 515 and 705?"

"I, uh, didn't tell you that. I didn't even remember what—"

Jim smiled. "Two people matching the descriptions of Carl Krajewski and Rose Thomas purchased some sophisticated and illegal bomb components from a fellow in Revere who also happens to be a reliable informant of the State Police."

I felt embarrassed, then relieved. Not only did that lend proof to my story, but I was relieved that the forces of law and order had been hovering in the wings all along.

"You sure about this plan to steal an armored chopper and shoot up the limo?" Jim asked, with that air of disbelief almost everyone had.

"I might have talked them out of shooting up the limo," I answered with a little pride, "I convinced them dumping red paint on the limo would send the same message without unnecessary death."

Jim was looking at me like a precocious child he'd been stuck with for hours. "The chopper," Jim focused, "they still plan to steal the chopper?"

I nodded. "Okay," Jim said, getting up, "enough for one night. Peter, this has been a more bizarre introduction than I'd expected, but I'm pleased to have met you," he said, offering his hand. "I'm going to talk with you tomorrow. Are you supposed to meet with them tomorrow?"

"They call me when they want me to come in," I said. "I'm sure I'll hear within the next two days."

"What if you asked for a meeting?" Jim asked.

"Huh?"

Jim's brain took over. "I want you to contact them. Do what you must to convince them they have to do a dry run of stealing the chopper. We want to catch Krajewski, but the best way to do it would be to catch him at Hanscom, trying to get to the chopper. Can you convince them to try a rehearsal?"

Preparation was always a poor second to polemics to them, but I nodded and said I'd give it a good try. "It would make life simpler, for everyone," Jim said pointedly, and then we bid him goodnight.

Art was waiting at my office the next morning when I arrived at 9:15 a.m., after calling and leaving a message for Carl and Rose. "Professor Dumont?" he asked, like Stanley finding Livingstone. Then I remembered I hadn't returned any of his messages from when I was in Washington a week ago. I tried to look guilty.

"Hi, Arthur," I greeted him, "I got your messages, but I've just this morning been able to get back to people. You were on my list," I added, and that always, everywhere, sounds unconvincing. "Your paper?"

He unveiled from his backpack what had to be fifty pages. It had multiplied. "I thought we'd cut it…way down," I said, unlocking my door. He followed me in.

"Yeah," he said, "but there's so much to cover with the Weathermen."

The irony was not lost on me, but giggling would have been devastating to Art's fragile ego. I didn't giggle, but just because I'm not a giggler. "What's your thesis?" I asked, knowing Art would need at least five minutes to get it out.

Ten minutes later, having hung up my coat and opened my briefcase and gingerly sorted out the papers and mail and stacked them on my desk, having adding "uh-huh" once or twice to keep Art talking, and having glanced at the 'Call For You' messages that the department secretary had left in my mailbox, Art was winding up. "The Weathermen were suicidal," he'd gotten out first, "but at the same time were very pragmatic because they were political and politicians are always pragmatic." That was my summation of Art's thesis; I've just saved you nine minutes of your life that I've lost forever from mine.

"The Weathermen were pragmatic?" I posed to him. He froze. My tone was inquisitory, and Art had been in my courses before and knew I started tearing something apart by first posing it as a question. "How pragmatic were the Days of Rage? Their plan in 1984 to free two Puerto Rican separatists from a federal prison with helicopters and Stinger missiles?" I should have stopped there but I didn't. "All their plans to recruit high school students to bring violence to the streets, to believe they could use violent revolution to change this society, the best armed in history. Are these practical people?"

He was silent, and then he looked at his paper and began sifting through the pages. "I've got a part here," he said, scanning his writing, "this part I wrote," he said, "that talks about that." He thumbed through his epic paper a couple more minutes and then I rescued us both.

"I think if you try to look at every incident with every Weatherman, you will find periodic episodes of pragmatism," I pontificated, trying to use the letter 'p' three words in a row, "but when you get a little distance, which is the lesson of history, you will find they were primarily dreamers who periodically got practical." Art was back in 'worship' mode, and was trying to scribble notes on the margins of his paper. I babbled for another minute or two. "And you really need to keep it to fifteen pages, okay?" I asked. He nodded, joked about how it was easier to type fifteen than fifty, and then I smiled and waved him off to pester some other tenured soul.

I had a lot of papers to correct, and some phone calls to return. Winfield had sent me an email reminding me of 'our conversation', reminding me of the journal editor's name and address and phone number and noting 'he likes email'. My choices were to correct papers, email the journal editor about the article I was to prepare, or prepare for my eleven o'clock lecture on…I checked the syllabus: the Great Depression. Instead, I went for coffee and a muffin, and when I returned to my office, the phone's message light was flashing. "Dumont," I heard Rose's voice in her commanding mode, "what's the problem?" I had deliberately rambled a bit in my early morning message to her, hoping a sign of instability would get her attention. "We'll be in and out. Call back."

I shut my door and dialed. On the fifth ring it was picked up. "Hello," Carl answered cautiously.

"Hi, it's me." Carl called out to Rose and another phone picked up, to make it a three-way conversation. "I started thinking very carefully about our plan last night, about—"

"Dumont," Rose interrupted, "phones can be tapped. Just call it 'the plan'."

"Okay," I agreed. "I think Carl should do a dry-run."

"Dry-run?" he said.

"If you really think you can get…access to the…aircraft—"

"Dumont!" Rose screeched.

"I think you should test that part," I finished. "I think you need to be sure that that part's possible. Everything else is pretty certain, isn't it?"

Rose put her hand over her speaker; I could hear the crunching sound of the plastic being squeezed. I could also hear her voice distantly through Carl's speaker, which he'd not muffled. Dumont's up to something, I heard her say. "Like what?" Carl asked. I don't know, she said. "Dumont," Carl asked, "what's the sudden concern?"

"I just hadn't paid much attention to that part of the plan until last night," I said. "I don't want to be sitting on my ass on Common—"

“Dumont!” Rose was back online.

“—freezing my ass off for nothing,” I finished.

Carl and Rose both muffled their phones a minute, then Rose came back. “C’mon in tonight. We’ll talk about it.” She sounded irritated. I said good-bye and then dug out Jim’s number to give him the news.

The Great Depression is best taught with a black and white slide show, some Woody Guthrie tunes, and outtakes from ‘The Grapes of Wrath’; at least that’s how I taught it. I dug out some horrific statistics from the USDA several years back that put numbers to the misery. How many millions of acres of farmland disappeared in the Dustbowl, how many Okies there were, the story of the dust storm of April 13th, 1934, that actually crossed the continent days later to darken high noon in Washington, D.C., and how high unemployment was at its peak in 1933. I got a little jaded at the annual repetition, but the class always ended in stunned silence, which is usually a good sign. It is comforting to me to remember that some days I did teach.

The day crept by. I met Linda for lunch, which she’d packed for both of us and which we ate in my office. “I called Jim,” I told her. “I’m meeting them again tonight, in Boston.”

She nodded; she hadn’t slept well. “Has this sort of thing ever happened to you before? Students coming back as dangerous criminals? I mean, I assume not,” she added uneasily.

“No, nothing like this has ever happened to me,” I assured her. “In fact, it’s making me look at my teaching materials in a whole new light. What lecture am I delivering that could incite students to violence? Who knows?” I shrugged. “You hope to inspire your students, but you really don’t have much control over it.”

“You don’t have any hostile lectures on gays or lesbians, do you?” she asked in a worried way. I shook my head. “I didn’t think so,” she said, “since I order the books for the campus, I have an idea what people are teaching. The gay and lesbian stuff is mostly for the Psychology department.”

I had make-up meetings with graduate students until six, and then I had to drive straight to the Park Plaza for the meeting. I found Carl and Rose finishing off subs in their suite. "No room service?" I asked.

"We've been doing room service for days," Rose said, "and today we were out, and I smelled a veggie with cheese and fell in love." I grinned; Rose hadn't let levity into her voice since returning from Washington.

"Where's the Maine boy?"

"He said he was catching a 4:30 flesh-tone on the hotel's pay-per-view, so I expect him anytime now," Carl answered. It was half past six.

"Porno films last two hours now?" Rose asked.

Carl shrugged as he jammed his steak and cheese into his mouth for a juicy bite. I hadn't actually had time to eat. My stomach growled. "Can we get started?" I asked, dropping into a deeply upholstered chair. The tension of waiting on this meeting all day had left me very tired.

"Okay," Carl began, setting his sub down. "What's your concern about getting a helicopter? I said I could do it, and I can." I guess I'd challenged him.

I started with the old 'Weathermen don't plan well' speech, but I beat around the bush trying to avoid further offending Carl, and then Leon showed up, and he insisted I start over. I also couldn't help glancing at the remainders of Carl's sub. "Your point," Carl interrupted a minute later, "is that the degree of difficulty logically requires rehearsal." I nodded. "On the other hand," he said, "surprise is important, too. If I pull a practice run, I risk blowing the surprise."

"No," I responded, "not if you're as slick as you say you are. If nobody catches you, you've still got surprise working for you."

That seemed to be just the right touch of logic. Rose nodded slightly. Carl looked thoughtful, looked at the TV for a minute, then started discussing the steps involved. "I have to get through the gate, which my ID will do," he said. "The armored material is through another gate."

"How do you know?" I asked. "Have you been in Hanscom?"

He shot me an irritated look. "No," he admitted. "But it's standard. I have to get through the second gate, but I've got a couple of ideas on how that'll work." Rose's brow furrowed. "Security isn't that tight these days unless you look like an Arab."

"But Westmoreland's coming," Rose chimed in, "so Security will be tighter." I almost sighed in relief. If Rose hadn't come in on my side I wouldn't have had a chance. Leon never said a word, just kept watching COPS on the TV.

Carl looked at both of us, then blew air out between his lips as if to whistle. "You two don't have a lot of confidence in me, is that it?"

"No, no, that's not it," Rose responded, and I let them go at it. I looked at the TV and watched some blurry footage shot through a police video camera, showing someone in a gray American car driving through traffic and against traffic and then colliding head-on with a truck. "Ooh!" Leon grunted with a smile. Carl's sub remained untouched. I wondered if he'd notice if I took a bite.

"Alright, alright, I'll test the fucking plan!" Carl suddenly erupted. "You two are so fucking concerned that I can't do this, so I'll fucking prove it!" Rose and I both drew back slightly.

"When?" I couldn't believe I asked that, but I was really hungry by then and the sub going to waste was making me cranky.

Carl looked wounded. "Tomorrow good enough for you?" he asked angrily. "I mean, I'd go now but you probably want to go home to your nice little life fucking up the youth of today, right?"

I answered softly, "tomorrow will be fine."

Then Carl stood, headed toward the bathroom, but paused to ask in a maddened tone, "oh, what form of proof do you require that I was able to get through? Should I buzz Hawthorne? Which side of the campus is your office on?"

Rose had risen and was standing in front of him, trying to play mother and sister at the same time. "Just tell us when you get back that it was a piece of cake and Dumont worries too much, okay?" She was torn between agreeing with me and her sense of betrayal of Carl.

Carl mumbled something with 'fucking' in it, went into the bathroom and slammed the door shut.

"Can I go home now?" I asked.

"Please do," Rose answered, deadpan. "And take It with you," she referred to Leon. I decided leaving the sub was the wisest choice. Leon had said nothing; now he just got up and followed me out. We went to the elevators and waited in silence.

He was going up, I was going down. When an 'Up' arrow lit, Leon said, "you were right to get him to test his plan." Then he got in and threw me a half-smile as the doors closed.

I walked to my parking space, shivering a little in the cool dark. Inside my car, after navigating the city streets to the quiet Pike, I let out a sigh to the rear-view, watching the road roll away behind me. "You could have *tried* to write your paper."

As the exits rolled past and I reached Rt 128, I thought of Linda waiting for me at home, and felt very tired. In the rear-view I could see my red, sunken sockets. I hadn't been sleeping much since coming back from D.C. Having Linda next to me in bed once every wee or two had certain delightful benefits, which I'd come to look forward to. Having a bedmate every night was different. Some nights were just for sleeping. And I never shared a bed with anyone, and having the bedroom to myself was a longtime habit. Linda liked to read in bed, and she typically turned in around eleven. I stay up a bit later but when I go to bed I turn out the lights and expect darkness. "Could you turn that out, please?" I'd asked her each night, and she always did, but sometimes her answer was, "soon as I finish this page," and the damn page took forever. There were other adjustments to be made, in many small ways. I'd survive, I knew, I'd adapt. But I was damn tired too.

I spoke with Jim Falcone that evening from my home, and Linda and I stretched out on the couch, watched mindless TV and ate popcorn. She had showered and was wearing a fluffy bathrobe and we cuddled. "This is the kind of night I've been waiting for," she said, curling up and positively purring. "What else is on TV?"

"I don't know." Neither of us was paying attention to the television anymore. Our relationship had moved to a new plateau, and there were new tests involved. Do you like the living room this way? Can you please pick up your underwear from the bathroom floor before I come in? I think we're eating too much fat and salt, so I want us to try eating vegetarian for a week, okay?

We had had sex before but not since she'd moved in; our sex life was a roughly once every week or so event. Last night had been too stressful even for sleep, much less carnal pleasure. Tonight she was clearly aiming to make up for lost time, and I was at once pleased, very tired, and a little anxious. I was fifty-three at that time, and Linda was forty-five, and I didn't think eight years meant much and I still don't, but call it Fragile Male Ego. How many times did she expect to do it, now that we were both 'home'?

I needn't have worried. She was also short of rest and fell asleep at nine-thirty and I couldn't even rouse her to move to the bed.

According to Carl, he was almost home free when the guard discovered him, asked him for identification, then marched him to a holding cell. According to the Hanscom Base Military Police, 'Joseph Ventry, ID 497721332, was apprehended in an off-limits area of the base. He did not have authorization and was detained. He later escaped custody by means unknown.' And, according to Jim Falcone, "the Hanscom Base cops have their heads so far up their asses they have to fart to smile."

Carl was discovered trying to run a piece of aluminum foil through the magnetic lock restricting access to the hangar housing the Apaches. The guard who found him was confused, not apprehensive. Carl tried a line about forgetting his ID, but the guard didn't recognize him, so Carl dropped the excuse and just kept repeating his name, rank and service number. The guard took him to the Security Office, and put Carl into a room used to hold 'detainees'. The guard called for his sergeant, having never actually arrested anyone before. Before the sergeant arrived, Carl asked the guard for a bathroom visit and climbed out the window.

My first call was Jim, and I got his version of the story. "So Carl isn't under arrest?" I asked, just to be sure.

"No, he is not under arrest," Jim said. "He is wanted for questioning, and he is not in custody." He swore, primarily to himself. "A very juicy bust, and I still can't believe they blew it. We've put out a description, and we've got plainclothes' watching his room at the Park Plaza, but he hasn't shown up. The woman hasn't moved from the room today. The other clown has been in and out. Are you expected to check in with them?"

There had been, as usual, no plans. "I guess Carl was going to call this evening, telling me he had succeeded," I said. "I guess I can call the room this afternoon and ask if he's back yet." Jim gave me his beeper number and told me to call him no more than ten seconds after I heard from Carl.

So Carl had tried to get to his chopper, and gotten caught, but then escaped. So the plan to steal the chopper was probably history, but Carl was still free. Shit. I had a faculty meeting to attend that afternoon and feeling like shit was the perfect preparation.

The Department of History had twenty faculty, just nine of us full-time, just eight of us tenured. Attendance at the faculty meetings was not limited to full-timers, but we were the only ones the school paid to be around all day so we tended to dominate the meetings. Assistant Professor Sylvia Medeiros was our only female full timer, thus far non-tenured. She was hired a year ago to cover Women's History and make our white boy's club look a little more eclectic. If we'd been put in old suits and lined up we could have passed for the Rotary Club, 1918.

Erich Thurber was our youngest tenured professor at thirty-eight, and he shared his time with the Computer Department and did History of Technology. Erich was the guy to call when your PC coughed up the Blue Screen of Death. He was a pure geek, and no fun at a party—as though any of us were. Almost all of us were members of AARP; some were 'short-timers', counting the months until retirement and monitoring the financial pages to see how our pensions were fleshing out.

Then there were the part-timers, out-numbering us and presumably doing a sort of journeyman's work until a permanent full-time slot opened up. Some had been part-time for a decade. Some, like Lincoln Philbert, in his early forties, was also part-time at Metrowest Community College, and sold real estate. Michael Xavier Collins was our only black faculty member. The sole benefit of such an Irish name was that he could legitimately ask us to address him as Michael X. Michael had begun teaching two years ago, and there was considerable pressure to find him a full-time slot. Collins was very bright, politically sensitive, and a good teacher. And he dressed like an Oxford don, making the rest of us look like old sheep dogs. I was sure Winfield was going to bust a gut to keep Collins on board, and rightly so. He should have fired one of us to fit Collins in, but that's tenure for you.

Those were the usual attendees. Winfield, of course, presided; we sat in lounge chairs in the faculty room and politely heard as a group what we'd already heard from him individually. "The fact is that at least five of us will be unemployed by the end of the term," Winfield said, and he looked sad.

Philbert raised his hand. "Are part-timers also subject to this?"

Winfield nodded. "Except that it means two of you to equal one full-timer."

Michael X asked, "I realize how stupid this may sound now, but are there any plans to increase the faculty? I don't wish to sound boorish, but as you may know I've been teaching at Boston College, too, and I've been approached. If something comes up there, I'd feel compelled to take it."

"Wouldn't you anyway?" I asked. "I mean, I would." Turning to Winfield, "no offense, Winfield."

Winfield smiled. "Michael, I'm still hoping to broaden the range of this department, but this is probably not the year for it." Philbert tried to not look too snubbed, but the fact was that he taught a dull Classical History course straight from ten-year old notes—a method I was intimate with—and if all of us full-timers dropped dead that day he'd be lucky to get one of our jobs.

"I want to suggest something today that's radical, but that might work for us in surviving this bloodletting," Winfield took over. "I've told each of you to make a special effort to add fresh publications to your bibliographies. There's a new journal starting up, and I don't think we can co-opt it, but it's a quarterly and if we've at least got papers being reviewed, I'll have fresh ammunition. Now," Winfield shifted in his seat, and looked pained; he'd had hemorrhoids removed a month ago. "Has anyone here ever been part of a peer-review board for papers?" Had any of us read scholarly papers submitted for publication? Read and digested and then asked questions? After a moment, only Michael X raised his hand, slightly. He glanced around, and rested his hand.

"I've been reading a friend's manuscript on women's sexual freedom," Sylvia offered, hesitantly. Her hair, of that intensely curly texture that looks like a brush if it's over four inches long, was carrying a static charge that day and it reminded me of a long-ago science project.

"Okay," Winfield forged on, looking pained at this reminder of the quality of the crew he led, "I'd like to establish a reader's group. I think it'll motivate us."

I blushed; we all did. None of us wanted to have to read, much less critique, each other, because we were all sure we stank. Our silence filled the room. Winfield sighed, "I thought that would be your response. I wouldn't suggest this if I didn't believe it would be useful." He went on, explaining his 'mission statement' for our to-be-overhauled department.

My mind wandered. Somewhere, Carl was hiding out, probably hatching an alternate plan that might involve nuclear weapons and hijacking the space shuttle. Rose was on the Internet, perhaps trying to buy used satellites from the Russians to aim at Retired General Westmoreland. Leon? Leon was the most interesting, somehow. Heeding an old friend's call to spit at capitalism, he was enjoying himself in a four star hotel. And as I wondered which porn film Leon might be ogling I realized I'd missed an important discussion. Winfield's plan was now a circle-jerk, and Sylvia was saying, "where each of us passed our paper to the person to the right and read the paper of the person on our left." I looked to my left. Lincoln Philbert. Sylvia was on my right. She was smiling nicely, so I tried to do the same. Lincoln was looking at the floor as though down there was his lottery ticket without a single good number.

"Okay," Winfield smiled, pleased his plan had survived in any form, "can we set a deadline for each of us to have something for our reader by the end of next week? Outlines, some text, something?" We mumbled. A few minutes later we were done, and if I thought my students cleared a lecture hall faster than a fire drill, they couldn't beat the faculty escaping that meeting.

Changing Names to Protect the Innocent

I almost flinched opening my office door, knowing what I'd see; yes, my telephone's message light was flashing. I dialed and listened. First message: "Dumont, this is Rose," and she sounded quite panicked. "Carl's been busted! I'm sure we're under surveillance! If you get this message before noon—" it was now five o'clock. "—call me. After that I may be gone, and I don't know where I'll end up." Probably at my front door again, I grumbled. Second message, at 3 p.m.: "Dumont, this is Rose," and she was calmer, and angry. "Leon is still at the Park Plaza because I couldn't convince the dick-wad we were under surveillance. I'm at the Hilton, in the Back Bay, under the name Linda Prescott." I scribbled those details on my pad.

Third message: "Hi, hon." That sent a chill up my spine, but I liked it. "It's me. Linda. What should we have for dinner? I was thinking of stir-fry but I don't remember, do you own a wok? I've got one at my old place, so maybe I'll just stop by there and pick it up, plus some other stuff…" she started talking about some irritation at work. "Okay, this is turning into a book instead of a message. I'll see you at home. Bye, hon." Fourth message: "Dumont, this is Carl. I'm hoping Rose called you. I'm back at the Park Plaza and she's gone. Please call me at," and he gave me his cellular number, which I already had.

I called Leon first, through the hotel switchboard. The telephone clicked and hummed a little. "Yea, what?" he answered, and I heard a movie soundtrack in the background.

"Leon? It's Peter. Have you heard from Carl or Rose?"

He adjusted the phone, and the soundtrack faded. "What?"

"I said, have you heard from Carl or Rose?"

"Uh," he thought, "no," like a boy queried by adults.

"Did you know Carl was arrested at Hanscom?"

"Oh, yeah, Rose did tell me that."

"And she's left the hotel. I guess you weren't worried?"

"They're fuck-ups. I could care less what she does," he said, sounding like forty-something going on nine.

"So you're just going to stay there and live off room service for the present?"

"Got a better plan?" he asked, and I really wanted to reach through the phone and smack him. "So where's Carl?" he asked.

Sighing audibly into the phone, I answered, "Carl is in or near the Park Plaza somewhere. There will probably be a change in plans. It might be helpful if you moved to the Hilton."

"Did Cousin It remember the explosives they had in the room?" he asked. "Did she remember to take them?"

Oh shit. "Good question. What do we do?"

"I don't know. Call me when you hear from Carl." Then he added, "Dumont, let me give you some advice," in a voice intended to be both kindly and snide, "Carl and Tom weren't too organized on their best day. The armored car job, the demonstrations, couple of the draft-board bombings, none of it ever followed plans. In the end we just improvised." I said nothing. "Oh," he groaned, "it's an old Traci Lords flick and I am hanging up!" And he did.

I called Carl on his cellular and there was some background noise. "Where are you?"

"I'm in a coffee shop around the corner, on Tremont," he said. "Where's Leon?"

"Still in the Park Plaza. And Rose is now...Linda Prescott at the Hilton." I heard him mumble as he scribbled the alias down. "Did you remember about the, uh, stuff—"

"Yes," Carl interrupted. "The gear is still there but fuck it. It's not important now. I mean, the feds are on to me now." I closed my eyes in prayerful thanks. At least that plan had been ruined.

"Are there police down there?"

"Oh yeah," he said, "there's a couple of folks here I'd bet are undercover cops. And a few in uniform. I'll be in touch. And Peter," he added, concern clear in his voice, "try not to use the phone so much. It'll get you in deeper than you deserve."

After he hung up the phone hummed a moment. It was, I sensed, already too late for that. I calculated that the police would probably have all three of them in custody well before Retired General Westmoreland set foot on Massachusetts's soil. Sitting, sinking into my chair, I relaxed for the first time in weeks. I remember feeling so warm and safe out in Framingham.

So Winfield wanted us to start writing, to each other for starters. It was a horrific idea for a group that struggled to stay civil in faculty meetings. But, given the derailing the Weathermen had suffered, I had no reason to further avoid the task. So I dug out some notes I had written a year ago, a series of questions that I somehow thought would bolster my thesis on 'De-romanticizing the Weathermen'. 'How many Weathermen died for the cause?' I'd written. 'Aside from the townhouse explosion, had *any* Weathermen died for the cause?' 'How many draft-dodgers went to Canada—compared to how many joined Weatherman?' More went to Canada, I guessed, but I had no idea. 'How many live abroad as expatriates?" I read through it three times. "Where did I come up with these questions?" I asked myself. "It's like the category 'Weathermen' on an episode of 'Jeopardy'." I couldn't even read my handwriting in some spots and couldn't remember now what I'd been thinking. It was all junk anyway. Crumpling the page into a ball, I sank a three-pointer. I turned on my word processor and typed in my heading, then deleted the 'De' prefix. I knew at least two Weathermen to whom I could apply the term 'romantic'.

A half-hour later I was still staring at my computer screen, blocked, for the hundredth time in ten years. My peripheral vision reminded me of my students' essays, and I picked up one out of my sense of duty and with a powerful sense of loathing. But loathing disappeared. The first, by Judith Rosen, gave me a jolt. 'The Days of Rage saw hundreds of Weathermen with amateurish weapons throw themselves selflessly at the most powerful symbol of oppression in the country in 1969, the Chicago cops who had clubbed protestors in 1968.' I flinched at Judith's bold stroke, a behavior our profession would drum out of her if she pursued graduate study. But I kept reading, and saw that Judith had done a masterful job. In fact, and I read it twice to savor it, she had in fifteen pages outlined the book I'd been struggling over.

I remember reading that paper and having the sensation of being 'lapped', of being the slowest car in the race, so slow that the leader overtook me and started a new lap. It was a little like dying must be. The next generation had just blown past me on the racetrack. And what happens to the car that's so damn slow it can't even keep in the same race? If it has any dignity it throws a rod, or blows a tire, or crashes into the retaining wall.

By my own definition—by *any* definition—what I did next was wrong, but I like to think that I was very busy and just using time efficiently, and that I had thought of this concept first, she'd just executed it better. I was in the middle of this covert operation and my job was in trouble. I looked over my own outline for the few shreds of original thought contained therein, but I hadn't thought of anything Judith hadn't covered. So I rewrote Judith's paper in my own, academically correct, dry style. Then I tucked it into an email message and sent it to Sheila. 'As per Captain Winfield's' orders, here's a draft of something I'm working on. Please be gentle. :<)'

It was pure plagiarism. For a teacher to steal the work of a student is like chugging Jonestown Kool-Aid, presuming the teacher is stupid enough to get caught. I did pause at the moment of clicking on 'SEND', aware that I was technically committing a terrible act, but decided that, the jurisdiction being Hawthorne College, the scale of this crime was really a petty misdemeanor.

In retrospect I can explain it more honestly: the excitement of the Weathermen plot had made me very aware of how bored and sick I was of teaching at Hawthorne, of teaching, period. The burst of excitement had left my palate too bored with my job to tolerate staying. I wanted to quit, but I didn't have the guts. So, 'suicide by plagiarism'. Like many crimes it was a crime of the moment, a crime of passion, not a planned and carefully executed crime. I might as well have been a Weatherman.

I called Jimmy, and started telling him where Rose and Leon were, which he already knew. "Where's Carl?" he asked.

"Around there somewhere," I answered. "When will they be arrested?"

"Rose and Leon we'll pick up this evening," he explained, "we're hoping to get a fix on Carl, and if we find him we'll grab all three immediately, but if we can't locate him by this evening we'll grab what we can. I'll talk to you later."

According to Rose, here's how they got the idea of trading the helicopter for a seaplane. They hooked up at the Hilton. Somehow they got past the plainclothes and regular officers watching them, and they promptly bailed out of Boston and rented a room in a Best Western in Gloucester. I don't know how they did it, but they'd become adept at hiding. Carl fashioned himself a disguise, which included brown colored contacts for his blue eyes, a decent wig, and a phony moustache. In times past, following the collapse of a plan, they would have gathered in a group therapy setting and 'analyzed' the plan and each other's parts in it in a highly critical vein. It could go on for hours, even days, people accusing each other of any of the Socialist Sins—being materialistic, monogamous, obsessed with sex, racism, or the all-purpose 'flawed Socialist thinking'. But Rose and Carl were older, calmer, and beyond couching every bodily function in Marxist-Leninist terms.

They re-planned in the safety of the Mercedes, where Carl conceded, "I can't get close to the Apaches here. I could get to them at Westover, but I can't fly across all of Massachusetts. They'll force me down in no time."

"So what do we do?" Rose asked, angry and desperate. "We've come this far! I did not surface just to disappear for another thirty years!"

"Do you still want to attack from the air?" Leon asked. They did. "Well, up in the hunting camps in northern Maine, seaplane is the only quick way to get in and out. I was working in a camp that had two seaplanes. You think you can fly a seaplane?" he asked Carl.

Carl, of course, shrugged and then nodded. "I can fly an Apache, which is a lot harder," he argued. (Actually the two craft have different aerodynamics, and skill at one does not equate to skill at the other, but as has been previously pointed out, these people are not strong on logistics. Or details. Or timing.) New plan: they would get to Leon's hunting camp in Maine, fly a stolen seaplane along the coastline in daylight and, with luck, they would land in Boston Harbor about six in the evening of Westmoreland's speech, and not drown. Rose would meet them, in a boat; presumably, Leon would give her his seat in the plane—

"What?" Rose interrupted, "I'm not sitting here while you and Carl go off into Moose country. I'm coming too!"

Leon started insisting that he and Carl could make better time, but Carl interceded as he saw Mount Rose getting ready for a blast. "It would be safer if we split up, but Rose and I have planned this from the beginning, and she should come," he said.

Leon didn't argue further.

The phone rang at my house, and I was expecting it to be anyone telling me the Weathermen had been arrested. It was Rose and she told me they were heading up north. I covered my surprise pretty well. "So what's the new plan?" I asked.

She gave me a sketchy idea, which was all there was anyway. "You need to be down by the end of Rowe's Wharf at six p.m Friday. We're going to land and taxi as close to there as we can, and then Leon is going to row to shore in a lifeboat, and you need to pick him up and get to the Common."

"I thought Leon was the get-away driver," I said, "is he planning to get us out of town in a dinghy?"

I heard a rustling noise on the phone. Although I knew my phone was tapped, it was actually the cell phone switching relay towers, and I heard Rose and Tom and Leon talking, and I waited and waited, and tried to call her back to the phone. I sat down, turned the TV on low, and waited for a half-hour, realizing they'd forgotten about me. I was too pissed and curious to hang up. After I began calling "Rose, Rose, are you there?" I heard conversation. Rose had 'muted' me and, perhaps accidentally, hooked me back in to the talk in the Mercedes.

"What can we shoot at the limo?" Rose asked.

"That we can fire from a seaplane," Leon said. "I don't think missiles will work. I doubt you can rig a seaplane to fire missiles," he said to Carl.

"I guess we can use automatic weapons," Carl said, his voice childish with disappointment. Once one had feasted on the vision of firing missiles into a limo, popping away with an M-16 must have been a big disappointment. There was a moment of silence.

"ROSE!" I screamed.

"Oh, fuck," I heard, then, "Dumont? What are you doing on the phone?"

"Remember, forty minutes ago, I asked about a getaway?"

"Fuck," I heard her curse. "Let us think about it," she said a moment later, "when we drop off Leon he'll tell you." She cut the call on her end.

Fine, I decided, thoroughly pissed-off, I'll just show up at the end of Rowe's Wharf with Jimmy the Cop and two-dozen of Boston's finest.

"That was Rose?" Linda asked. I nodded. She was cleaning up the kitchen, which, after she had cooked, should have been my chore. "I know you're working with Jim, so everything will go okay, but I'm worried about you," she said, giving me a loving, worried look. She was leaning over the kitchen sink, where she was washing my dinner dish. What I should have done was go into the kitchen, put my arms around her, and hug her. She would probably have set the dishes aside, turned around, and kissed me, and things could have accelerated from there. But I had a mildly sick sensation in the pit of my stomach, no connection to the stir-fried vegetables. It was that feeling I was now calling 'dead race car', and it made me feel old and feeble, and not sexy. "Don't worry, Linda," I answered from the table, looking at my scribbled notes from Rose's call, "I'm not going to get in trouble."

Jimmy was very excited at the new information. He hung up, then called back half an hour later. "Thanks for the lead. Yeah, one of our surveillance units is with them now," he said, "and they reached Kittery about fifteen minutes ago. They're coming back in a seaplane?" he asked for the second time. "A seaplane? Did he say from where?"

"Somewhere in Maine," I said.

"I have to get the Maine boys in on this anyway. It's their jurisdiction. Did Leon mention any contacts up there?"

"Just his family, but they're around Kittery." Jimmy said goodnight.

"Fine." I finally got up and was going to go into the kitchen and hug Linda, but she had finished the dishes and was in the bathroom with the door closed.

The next morning, at 9:30, I had to cover a lot of ground with my classes. I'd missed some meetings and I anticipated missing another one or two. I spent the morning grading more essays. Judith got an 'A', and most of the rest got 'B', including a 'B-' mercy grade for Art. Grading the essays took care of class preparation—I'd hand out the essays and we'd 'talk about them' for an hour. Maybe less. Then I'd assign them some reading that would leapfrog from the Days of Rage through the New York townhouse bomb that killed Diana Oughton, finishing with Nixon's Plumbers. The ones that liked to skip class preferred lengthy reading assignments, and I had noticed that attendance was down about a third. That was typical, for me.

The graduate students, unfortunately, were more demanding. I thought up a discussion question: "on several occasions members of the Weather Underground visited Cuba, usually for training in political and military philosophy and techniques, or weapons training. Was Castro getting us back for the Bay of Pigs Invasion and the ensuing blockade?" There was plenty of room for the brain-dead to say 'yes' and for the hardened leftists to say 'yes' and still make the brain-dead sound wrong. Since any scrap of hard information on the Bay of Pigs will be CLASSIFIED until at least 2061, it's a safe place for unsupported opinions. And if you ever want to see some people squirm like worms on red-hot hooks, ask a room of graduate students to answer a question based solely on their opinions. They are all professors-in-training in their own minds and they see what mincing cowards instructors are. Was I torturing my students? Yes, a little.

After my morning sessions were finished I atypically stopped at my office and saw my message light blinking. Shutting my door I called up my messages. First message: "Dumont, this is Rose." Then her cell phone died. There was a second call and again it was Rose, "...going-to-lose-the-signal-so-I'll-talk-fast. We're in trouble. This place is a bunch of fucking fascists and Leon's a god-damned fascist prick!" I knew that, I wanted to say. I heard a knock on my door but I didn't move. Her cell phone died again. Then Rose's voice, one last time. "Please be at your phone at four o'clock. It's imperative I talk to you directly." The call ended.

The hours crept past. What was worse was my afternoon schedule, with two students I had barely spoken to that semester. Dredd Levasseur was a visiting Haitian student taking a highly customized round-robin sort of study, whereby he met with professors in practically every department, from History to Biology to Physical Education, and read what we directed. His English wasn't great, but it was much better than our Creole, so we'd give him a reception and a 'Pass' at the conclusion of his American semester. Dredd was actually a breath of fresh air on Hawthorne's campus. He wore dreadlocks, he had wildly colorful clothing, always smelled of cologne, and any girl at all adventurous tried to date him. He also won over the guys by whipping three of them solidly in an informal soccer exhibition.

Dredd and I had met a month ago. I dug out my notes and was reminded that we had discussed Haiti's American colonial influence on the current political situation, which, prior to us invading, I'd say was nil. But that was generally Dredd's streak of curiosity, so I'd assigned him some articles from…good God, did I really assign him a Reader's Digest article? I powered up my PC and did a quick web search on 'Haiti' and 'politics' and found some recent postings that had more meat. "Hello, Professor Dumon?" he greeted me at my office door, pronouncing my name as it was by my French forebears. We actually had a good chat. He expected little and I delivered it. Plus his delightful cologne left my office smelling better than it had prior.

My next meeting was with Judith Rosen. She requested the appointment after class Monday, and one would have thought that I was the student, not her, and that my grade was F, not A. She showed up a minute early, dressed in blue jeans with the knees stylishly ripped out—I was surprised that she would indulge in such conformity—and a t-shirt from Umass Amherst. Was it a new one, I remembered thinking? "Hi…Judith," I greeted her, wanting to say 'Judy' but I had felt absolutely no encouragement to informality.

"Professor Dumont," she answered, a gentle, polite smile on her face. "Thanks for meeting with me." I shrugged and grinned. "I'm interested in applying for a special program and I need some letters of reference." Oh God, I gasped to myself, she's out of here?

I was standing, and then I thought to sit and invite her to as well. "Tell me about it," I asked, smiling.

"It's a semester abroad," she said, "at Oxford College, in England."

"That's where it's always been," I joked, relieved. "And what do they want from you?"

"Well, my grades, of course," she joked, blushing. I knew she had no reason to blush. She was a top student. "I'm hoping to study history there, so I need to send a paper, and the paper I just did for you, on the Weathermen, I really enjoyed doing." My palpitations kicked in again, double-strength. "They want twenty-pages, and your page limit is fifteen, so I'd like to do the same topic, but explore it a little more. Does that make sense?" she asked in that vulnerable voice students have.

I was thinking fast, very fast. I had sent Judith's paper to Sheila Medeiros yesterday. I had, in fact, puffed it with some academic verbosity, up to eighteen pages. If I were a real gentleman I should have offered my paper to Judith and even things up, but it couldn't be that way. "You wrote about the Days of Rage, correct?" I asked, pretending I had too many students to track each one.

She nodded. "Yea, about them being romantic idealists for attacking the Chicago cops when they were so outnumbered?"

I nodded. "Good paper." She blushed again, for both of us. I thought quickly about what to give her. "What you might want to do," I began, scanning my shelves, then a file of papers, "is look through...this one."

I retrieved DEAD IN THEIR TRACKS, a forty-seven-page stem-winder of an article of so-called psychohistory, a specialty in which psychologists try to psychoanalyze people posthumously. Martin Luther was one popular target; the paper I had, by some quack from Sequoia College of The Redwoods or some-such institution in

California, analyzed Diana Oughton and two minor Weathermen who had died and were, therefore, available. The therapist believed Diana showed depressive behavior, and one of the other Weathermen had committed suicide, so the therapist called their behavior 'romantic idealism', which mixed badly with Marxism. I had read it almost all the way through and suspected it was crap, even though it was one of the few scholarly twigs I'd found in support of my unwritten book's unproven thesis, but I hadn't gotten around to thinking it through and knew Judith would. I briefly explained the paper's topic to her. "Try this, and then try rewriting the paper?"

I should have been shot. I remember thinking, I haven't been able to prove this thesis of romanticism myself, so how can I guide a student in proving it? Perhaps she could guide me? Hey, just so long as one of us did it.

And as she smiled again and bade me good-bye and left my office, I glanced at my desk clock and saw that it was 3:49.

Their road trip from Kittery, due north, paralleling the New Hampshire border, left the four-lane Maine Turnpike in favor of the local highways. It was just dawn, and they stopped for coffee and muffins, then took to the road again. Rose fell asleep, somehow, though the local highways were rolling, uneven, and badly potholed. "I remember driving through one little village after another," she told me later. "Maine goes on forever." After five hours of this, with another stop in the town of Gilead, where they ate sandwiches while watching the white water rush past exposed rocks in the fall-dry Androscoggin, they resumed their ride. "At one point, Leon turned off the paved highway onto a dirt road," Rose said. "There was no sign, it looked like someone's private driveway. Except that we drove up a hill, bumping, grinding along in second gear a lot, down the other side of the hill, through a swamp. He had to use four-wheel to get us out of a mucky section. And up the next hill, except he kept calling them 'mount this or mount that'." Rose and Carl both dozed and Leon kept soldiering through the Maine woods until the afternoon sun came in just over the tops of the evergreens.

Rose smiled in spite of herself as she remembered, "then, after driving for hours down this dirt road—and there were other dirt roads that intersected it every hundred million miles or so—we come out of this very, very dense pine woods, and there's a log gate across this miserable little road. Like there was a chance in a million that someone might stumble upon it. Like they had to screen unwanted visitors." What took some of the humor out of it was the armed guard at the checkpoint.

Henry Arsenault, thirty-one, a rotund, teddy-bearish five-seven in his uniform of Army fatigue jacket and cap, Levis and LL Bean gumboots, also had an M-16 resting lazily over his right shoulder. "Get the fuck out of the truck," he ordered in a bored tone, as though they were just one of a parade of unwanted visitors. "Michelin? Is that you? You dumb prick!" [That was when I learned Leon's real name.]

Leon got out first, and tried to make this meeting the reunion of old friends. "Hey, Arsenault, how the hell—"

Arsenault wasn't happy to see Leon. "You got a lot of nerve coming back here, unless you got that money you owe me," Arsenault warned him, now holding his rifle on Leon, aiming for his mop of gray hair.

Rose and Carl stayed in the car. "Arsenault, I told you before, I didn't take your money," Leon argued. "You just play poker like a blind man."

CRA-A-A-CK! Rose and Carl hit the floor. Leon was still standing, but he was silent. Smoke curled from the tip of the rifle, and Arsenault no longer looked so ludicrous. Leon was holding his hands up, and Arsenault had stepped towards him. "You owe me six hundred and forty-seven dollars," he said, in that distinct Down east drawl where 'forty' sounded like 'fawty', "any disagreement on that point?"

Leon shook his head.

"So, who you got in that Mercedes?" Arsenault asked, and saw Carl and Rose. "Tell them to get out." Rose and Carl got out, shut the doors, and stepped slowly up to stand just behind Leon. "Who the fuck are you?"

"They're friends of mine from a long time ago," Leon said.

"That's nice," Arsenault half-smiled. Pointing his rifle at Carl, he asked again, "who the fuck are you?"

As Rose told me the story later, she and Carl were afraid to speak. "Strangers in paramilitary gear with M-16s in the north woods in this day and age probably are not left-wing radicals," she explained. "So the last word we were going to say was Weathermen. Although Arsenault was probably too young to remember the Weathermen."

This being a scene with men and guns, Carl did the talking for Rose. "Leon was telling us he knew of a good hunting camp up here."

"You guys hunters?" Arsenault asked, saying 'huntahs'. "What do you hunt?"

'A retired general' was the right answer. "Oh, deer...some...moose," Carl conjured, and knew when Arsenault began chuckling that his answer was probably bad.

"Dear and moose?" Arsenault asked, sounding a little like Boris and Natasha speaking of 'moose and squirrel?' He indicated Rose. "Do you hunt too? Or do you just stay behind and clean it and cook it?"

Rose was now expected to speak. "I watch TV until they say it's done," she answered in undisguised disdain. Arsenault seemed to like her response.

"Well, the hunting camp is closed," he announced, and Leon darkened. "And you have a problem, Michelin, because you are in the middle of the fucking wilderness and I'm going to take the Mercedes truck as a down payment on the money you owe me." The words chilled the Weathermen, and Leon looked frustrated. "Any argument with that?" Arsenault polled them.

"If the camp is closed," Carl said, "how do we get back to Boston?"

"From Bah-ston?" Arsenault asked, not realizing that he couldn't mimic the accent if he was a user. "Well, you got a hell of a long walk, don't you?"

The air was crisp, the sun warm where it penetrated the foliage. Rose pictured hunters finding her bones in a few months, picked clean by whatever picked bones in the woods. "Quit being such an asshole," Leon said. Arsenault's nostrils flared with the scent of a fight. "Take us up to the camp. The truck is yours, for now. We aren't walking all the way back to town."

Arsenault was quiet for a long, frightening moment. Then he pushed Leon aside, headed for the vehicle, saw that Leon had left the keys in the ignition and hopped behind the wheel. Starting it up, gunning it violently, he whooped like a thirty-year-old child delighted at his surprise under the Christmas tree. After he figured out how to put it in gear—with a shriek—he drove straight into the log barricade. With a crunching noise, he broke through and disappeared down the dirt road.

Leon sighed as he saw his Mercedes disappear into the woods. "It's about a mile further up the road," he told them, "I guess we walk."

"Needless to say," Rose continued, "when we reached the camp, we were expected."

The hunting camp was a clearing on a lake that linked to another lake, in a string of small lakes. The camp was set in pinewoods, the tall trees hissing when the light breeze gusted. Two rusting Quonset-huts, fronted by big, steel garage doors, were tucked into the woods, and there were a half-dozen big propane tanks in a row between the huts. Tire tracks had rutted the ground in front of the huts. A log cabin with wood smoke lazily curling out its chimney was the building closest to the lake, and a pathway led from the cabin's front door to the shoreline, to a dock that jutted out into the lake. Stacked against the back of the cabin was a cord of split firewood, and a man was setting up a section of wood to split with a maul, and the crack and whine of the wood splitting echoed a moment later. Three aluminum rowboats with outboards were tied off to the dock. Further out in the water, two seaplanes floated on their pontoons. And a flagpole in the middle of the site flew and American flag flying upside-down.

Three men were warming their hands over a fire they'd built in an oil drum. There were about a dozen trucks parked haphazardly, all of them mud-spattered four-wheelers. Some of the trucks were painted in camouflage and had white stenciled numbers on their bumpers, either government property or painted to look like it. The Mercedes, already dirtier than when they'd left it, and a piece of its chrome grill broken by hitting the log gate, was parked by the log cabin, and when the Weathermen stumbled into the clearing, one of the three men whistled sharply and more people came out of the cabin. In a few seconds there were at least a dozen people, four women, the rest men, most of them either in their twenties or their fifties. Arsenault was the middle child.

"Is that my sorry-ass husband?" asked one of the women. Judith was barely five feet tall, and big in bust and bottom. She was dressed in denim with a dirty buttoned-up fleece-lined jacket. "Leon?"

"Hey," Leon called back, not too happily.

There was some discussion among the militia members. "Morry Shaw isn't here," Leon explained in a soft voice, "they can't shit without him here to supervise." And unfortunately, they couldn't begin to sort out the strangers without their leader. The Weathermen were herded into one of the shacks, wherein two cots with rumpled blankets and a pile of dirty clothes indicated someone lived. "You stay in here until the Major gets back. He'll sort your hash," Leon's wife said with a snarl aimed straight at her husband.

"There was a pot-bellied stove and firewood, so we were warm," Rose recalled. "There were stacks of their fascist right-wing propaganda, so we read a couple of those and decided that wood was too precious, so we burned their pamphlets instead. They brought us some awful sandwiches made from some dried-up cold cuts, and I had to share a water bottle with Leon." She stuck her tongue out at the memory. "We were only in there for about four hours, but it seemed like much longer."

In mid-afternoon they saw a truck with plates drive into the camp and honk its horn twice, and the camp came to life. "Hey, it's the major," they heard a man call out, "did you remember the beer?"

An hour later, Judy came to get them. Herding them back into the clearing, they stood like slaves at auction.

From the cabin came a man the others looked at, their leader. He said nothing as he swaggered across the clearing. He was sixty at least, dressed in fatigues, his figure modeled on Jack Lalanne, with a carefully trimmed snow-white beard, a service sidearm tucked in a web belt, and his mouth marked by the half-burnt cigar he clenched in his stained teeth. "Welcome to Camp Freedom," he greeted them brusquely; they were not, in fact, welcome. "I'm Major Shaw, Commander." He had flinty blue eyes up close, and he stopped inches in front of Leon, like a drill sergeant about to chew out a recruit. "Leon, I'm a little surprised at you coming back, and bringing two strangers," Shaw barked. "Explain yourself."

"I'm a member," Leon said, a little flippant, more than a little defensive, "I took the oath."

"Repeat it," Walsh ordered.

Leon licked his lips and recited, "to follow the rules of the Church and drill with the defenders of Camp Freedom, and prepare to rise when the time came to overthrow the Zionist Occupation Government. I haven't broken the oath."

"Except our rule against gambling on the Lord's Day," Shaw said.

"You didn't kick out Arsenault," Leon argued, "just me."

"Fleecing him seemed punishment enough," Shaw said, with a hint of a smile, and the men around the fire chuckled. Arsenault wasn't laughing, but he toyed with the keys to the Mercedes.

"No hard feelings," he laughed in a harsh way. "I like the truck. We're even."

Leon wasn't at all happy with the deal, but said nothing. "So that's the end of that, right?" he dared to smile.

Shaw wasn't smiling. "No, you still must submit to the judgement of the Sergeant-at-Arms for gambling on the Lord's Day." He turned and called to the house, "who's Sergeant-at-Arms today?"

"It's Judy!" laughed the oldest woman.

"There's justice," said one of the men at the fire.

Leon's wife strolled across the clearing. She had a pleasant face framed by brown hair, cut in a pageboy that made her a somewhat plump pixie. "You also left without telling me where you were going, or for how long. Which isn't against the rules of the militia, but which I'm going make you pay for," she said, scowling and revealing half the teeth she was entitled to.

Rose and Carl had been standing silently. Major Shaw took over the situation again. "Leon has failed to introduce you," he said, "could you do the honors?"

Carl spoke for them.

"Are you husband and wife?" Shaw asked, wedding bands conspicuously absent.

Rose sighed. "No, we are not. Neither do we have sex. Is that okay?" she asked in her trademark attitude voice.

Shaw also smiled. "Platonic relationships are out of style, but not forbidden. We have a women's barracks, separate from men's. Miss Thomas, Mister Krajewski, how do you know Leon Michelin?"

Oh, the truth would hurt. "We were old college friends," Carl said. "We wanted to go hunting and Leon said he knew of a good hunting camp," he said, hoping Arsenault had already spread the story.

"So Henry told us, though he didn't seem to believe you," said Shaw. "Well, I'm afraid the hunting camp went bust." He scowled. "We gave up trying to function in the United States. It's a toady for the United Nations, working to strip true citizens of their freedoms while taxing them into servitude. We are now Camp Freedom, an independent political entity. What's your political affiliation?"

Rose told me later she kept sane by imagining ways of slowly killing Leon. "We're no friends of the government," she said, "and I notice you probably aren't either. Is that flag flying the distress signal?"

Shaw locked onto Rose as though seeing her for the first time. "It is," he answered. "We're a self-sustaining unit of freedom fighters. The surrounding five hundred acres have been declared independent of the State of Maine. We cooperate with the county sheriff, but we disavow Federal jurisdiction. We pay no taxes and we expect nothing from the government."

"Ah," said Carl, "that would explain the absence of license plates on any of the trucks. Just out of curiosity, how long has Camp Freedom been established?"

Shaw frowned. "That's none of your damn business. Are either of you federal agents? If you are, admitting it now will save us all a lot of grief."

Rose laughed, involuntarily. "Hell, no, we aren't federal agents. They might be following us, though."

Boy, was that the wrong thing to say.

Ever pour water on an anthill? Or watch sped-up film of people walking through a mall? The members of the camp suddenly began running frantically in what appeared to be aimless animation, yelling to each other, running into each other, as though someone had tossed a firecracker at the propane tanks. "Sentries!" Shaw barked, "to your stations! Women and children inside! All troops, prepare for imminent assault!" Carl and Rose and Leon stood frozen as the men of Camp Freedom ran to wherever they'd left their rifles or side-arms. Two ran into a corrugated metal hut and came out lugging what appeared to be Stingers, surface-to-air anti-aircraft missiles made famous in the Afghan War when Afghanis used them to down Soviet helicopters. The ones with the Stingers jumped into the two camouflaged trucks. One tore off down the road the Weathermen had just trudged down, the other off in the other direction. And Major Shaw seemed, belatedly, to remember in the midst of it all to escort the Weathermen, at the point of his pistol, into the log cabin and the tender mercies of the Sergeant-at-Arms.

"These people may have brought federal infiltrators down on us," Shaw told Judith and the two other women. "We'll be establishing and monitoring the perimeter. I expect you to judge and punish accordingly." Judith had an Uzi, and Shaw watched as she expertly inserted a clip and loaded the chamber. Then he left and they heard more men yelling and engines running, and a few gunshots of insuppressible exhilaration.

"Sit." Judith ordered Leon onto a stool. She pointedly double-checked the magazine on her gun, pulling it out and shoving it in until the metallic 'click', then sighted just over his head, her finger on the trigger, then letting the weapon drop until it aimed at his chest. "My mother told me you were a sack of shit. I should've listened. Right now I'm just thankful we got no kids, so when I kill you I don't make some child fatherless." Carl raised an eyebrow and he and Rose backed up a half step, and felt the wall behind them. Leon was pale. "So, Mister-I'll-be-gone-for-a-day-or-so, just to see a college buddy, how many bimbos you been humping behind my back?"

"Hon, the closest to a woman I've been is It," and he pointed his thumb at Rose. "And she started life with a pecker, so you know I've been faithful."

Judith scowled at the lie she sensed, but when Rose didn't protest the slander, she looked at Rose. "Is what my sorry-excuse-for-a-husband said true?" Rose was poker-faced as she nodded. Leon's gamble worked; his wife was now focusing her anger on Rose. "Step over here," she ordered, and slowly walked around Rose, checking her shape and only after she'd done the tour did she register an emotion. "Dear Lord, our God in heaven, you have mutilated the Temple of God," she said in a hushed, dramatic, mildly horrified tone to Rose. Rose looked bored. "How about you?" she looked at Carl. "You start out life as a man?"

"Yea," Carl said, laconically. Anxious to change the topic, he asked, "you're the Sergeant-at-Arms?"

Judith nodded, propping her Uzi on her hip to emphasize the barrel to Carl. "Sergeant-at-Arms," she said, emphasizing 'arms'.

"Is there a trial process here?" Carl asked.

"Trial process?" she asked sarcastically, "you mean, is this some faggot-loving, liberal-ruined federal court where freaks and criminals can run amuck?" Her disgust seemed from the heart. "No, this is a militia, we support, protect, and defend the Constitution of the United States, and we worship our Lord Jesus Christ. You want a jury of your peers?" She sneered at Rose. "Them kind of peers we are fresh out of!" She laughed, as did Abby.

"We came up here hoping to rent one of your seaplanes," Rose said, in her most deferential tone, "and if you have since become a militia, that's cool. We didn't know. He led us here," she indicated Leon. "We haven't done anything to you, not knowingly."

Judith looked perplexed. Rose disgusted her, and she didn't seem at all happy to see her husband back. And, with the men gone into the woods to 'guard the perimeter', she and the Major's wife, Abby, and Abby's useless daughter-in-law were left to guard and judge these freaks, and probably to have a hot meal ready when the boys returned in an hour or so, tired of shooting at rocks and listening to pine cones falling in the woods. "You," she indicated Rose, "know how to peel potatoes?"

Rose nodded; Judith pointed the barrel at the sink, and Rose followed. Abby handed her a peeler and Rose picked up a misshapen Maine spud and started hacking away. "You," Judith looked at Carl, "might as well help her." Carl nodded and joined Rose. "As for you," she looked at her husband, "you are a member of this militia. Major Shaw asked you, but I didn't hear your answer. Why did you bring two strangers into our camp?"

Leon looked bored and tired with the scene. "Two weeks ago the Detached Maine Militia," he exaggerated the name's importance, "was a group that met on Sunday evenings in the family room, with camping trips up here in good weather," he reminded her. "I brought up two customers for the seaplane, business for the hunting camp. How the hell was I supposed to know in that time Shaw would declare war on the United States?"

"You could've called home once, you son of a bitch." Judith looked very angry then, and she prodded Leon out the door. They could hear her outside, "just once call home! I could've been hurt! In the hospital! Dead in a ditch! You think I'm your goddamn doormat?" They watch Judith march her husband down the pathway several feet, then behind some birch trees around a corner of birch trees. Out of sight she then ordered Leon to kneel, and then there were five quick shots from the Uzi.

"Peel, Rose, peel," Carl whispered urgently to Rose, and they tore into the potatoes.

[Jimmy wrote a report later on all of what happened to him in Maine. The following is the only part that didn't bore me to tears. See, cops have to account for each interview, and if they fire their weapons, for each bullet. If they actually hit or arrest someone, that's another dead tree, and all of that means police reports are a tie with legal boilerplate for dull reading.]

"Detective James Falcone," Jimmy introduced himself to the two Maine State troopers he'd met at the Gilead Post Office. "Massachusetts State Police. Very pleased to meet you." He was in Gilead, a crossroads in Maine just about ten miles from New Hampshire to the west, Canada to the north.

"Detective Fal-cone?" Maine State Trooper Gordy LaSalle, himself approaching his eleventh year with the force and deeply ingrained with the minimal necessary level of cooperation with the Massachusetts brethren, "Gordy LaSalle, pleased to meet you. Why don't we have a cup of coffee while we're talking?"

Jimmy followed them into the coffee shop next door to the Post Office. The two buildings, along with a general shop—*Cold Beer* **LOTTERY** *Cigarettes*—that sagged away from the street, and a gas station with a relatively jaunty SHELL sign, were the business district.

Winter seemed to be on its way, a cold wind blowing as the cops hustled into the overheated donut shop. It was outfitted with huge windowpanes. Newspapers were scattered along the ledge, left folded to inside stories, and some dead flies rested against the window's edge. Behind a scratched, well-used Formica counter was a seven-burner stainless steel coffee maker that looked up to the job of keeping the locals well caffeinated. The teen-ager serving donuts was leaning against the cash register, reading a well-used novel. She was mildly plump, with dark hair pulled back in a ponytail, and she smiled at the cops.

Once seated at one of three tables, LaSalle picked up the conversation, "so what sort of problem you got? I mean," he glanced at his younger partner, Trooper Joe Gallant, who was smiling at the teenaged girl behind the counter, "we were monitoring your radio communications, but why don't you fill in the blanks?"

"Of course," Jimmy agreed. Gallant got up first and asked the girl for an order. A minute later he brought three tall Styrofoam cups of steaming coffee and some donuts. The girl was giggling at something Gallant said, Jimmy wasn't listening, but they seemed to know each other.

Jim explained to them what I had told him about the Weathermen, omitted much of what had transpired, then explained their desperate plan to attack Westmoreland with a seaplane, and then he said, "and there's a fellow from Kittery involved, calls himself Leon Turbo? Former Vietnam vet. Worked up here at a camp for a while, now he works at the Kittery Trading Post?"

"Haw!" Gallant laughed and snorted coffee, and took a minute wiping his face with a paper napkin. "That would probably be Leon Michelin. Fuck-up supreme."

Jimmy looked attentive. "Can you be more specific?"

LaSalle took over. "So, Leon Michelin was a Weatherman? Huh. Michelin is one of them burnt out Vietnam vets. He and his wife, Judith, she's a good girl, she deserves better, and a few others worked a hunting camp up in the woods. Michelin has been in and out on petty theft. Usually involved stealing beer, and gas and getting arrested for drunk-n-disorderly. Had a job down in Kittery for a couple of months. He probably walked out on that. And now you're telling me he's involved in this…whatever you call it?" LaSalle pushed up the brim of his hat. "That's a surprise. That's working the other side of the street."

"He's in the company of two other Weathermen, Carl Krajewski, and Rose Thomas," Jimmy paused, "formerly known as Thomas Rose."

There went the now customary exchange—"he did what? Cut it off on purpose?"—and then they got back to Leon. Jimmy asked, "what did you mean by 'working the other side of the street'?"

LaSalle groaned and Gallant took over. "There's a wild bunch up in this camp Leon hangs out in. The owner, he's a Vietnan Vet named Maurice Walsh, he's had financial problems. From what I hear, he didn't make the last three payments on a loan he took out, putting the property down as collateral. And when the bank sent him a note threatening foreclosure, he put up barricades, dug out his fatigues, and him and some of his hunting pals, including Leon, started walking around with hunting rifles and forty-fives, calling themselves Camp Freedom."

"Oh," Jimmy said. "I see. So the Weatherman is now a Militia-man." All three cops took sips of coffee and chewed pieces out of their donuts. "How many in that camp, you think?"

"We're guessing about a dozen, with Leon's wife and Abby Walsh, and her daughter-in-law," said Gallant.

"How long have they been up there?" Jimmy asked.

"About a week or two," said LaSalle. "We wouldn't have even known they were up to anything if Walsh hadn't blasted off his big mouth, written a letter to the editor of the paper here, declaring his camp independent from the state. Said that the current government, state and federal, were illegal, called them the Zionist Occupational Government, all that crap."

"So he's read The Turner Diaries," Jimmy noted. "And if the government is illegal he doesn't owe it taxes. How's he dealing with his loan?"

"Bank got a check drawn on a non-existent account, from a non-existent bank," LaSalle said. Jimmy nodded; the Freemen of Montana and others out west had taught their brethren the art of kited checks. "He also said he tossed his driver's license and registration into the lake. Like I said, we wouldn't have known if he'd declared himself Head of the Mugwumps but for that letter. Far as I know, none of them've stirred from the camp, and the bank still hasn't run the clock out on him, so I'm just hoping they get tired of it soon. Otherwise I guess he'll come to town in his unlicensed truck. Then I'll run him in for not having license plates and then we'll go up and clean the place up. Until then, he's not hurting anybody, and he's not guilty of anything except lunacy, which thankfully ain't a crime."

"Do they have seaplanes up there?" Jimmy asked. LaSalle and Gallant compared looks, then nodded. "Well, I have a feeling my Weathermen are up there, and they are planning to murder General Westmoreland using a seaplane. In this case, lunacy may be a crime." The Maine troopers frowned.

"Looks like we got to go in, don't it?" LaSalle asked rhetorically, and he ate the rest of his donut in one bite.

Cold wind started blowing when the defenders of Camp Freedom scrambled to defend their camp. They took up positions in the woods overlooking the logging road that was the only access. Having grown up hunting in the woods, the militiamen were well prepared to sit and wait whilst hiding behind fallen logs or inside dense foliage.

The wait was about an hour and a half. Three had novels, two had CD players, one hummed to himself as he struggled to write a country song he planned to send to Garth Brooks, and the camp owner and head of the militia and eldest at fifty-eight, Maurice Walsh, soon fell asleep. It is probably no slander to note that Walsh's hunting camp never won any state competitions for slaying the largest, fleetest, or strongest of any breed. It also explains why the three officers of the law who approached the hunting camp from the south encountered no initial resistance when they reached the log gate Leon's once-perfect Mercedes had smashed.

Since the officers did want a confrontation, they got out of the cars and LaSalle hollered, "Walsh! Maury Walsh! This is Gordy LaSalle! I want to talk to you!"

Some birds tittered and flew from tree-top to tree-top. "Walsh!" LaSalle tried again.

C-R-R-R-A-A-A-CK! A bullet zinged by, ricocheted off a slab of granite and into space. The officers ducked behind the car doors for cover. "Guess we've made contact," Jimmy said.

LaSalle was red-faced, and had drawn his service weapon by instinct. "Where'd that come from?" he asked angrily. "Who the hell just shot at me?" he demanded of the woods.

A not-too distant sound of leaves and sticks crunching under footsteps drew the officers' attention to the driver's side of the road. "Walsh?" LaSalle called, "I want you to come out and drop your weapon, now, before someone gets hurt. You'll get five years, minimum, for that shot. Trying to kill a police officer is frowned on in Augusta."

From the opposite side, from the passenger side, up a wooded slope, they heard a man's voice call back, "that was a warning shot. Next one will be fatal. You're trespassers. This is Camp Freedom and you have no jurisdiction here. If you want access, you have to write to request permission. Now turn your car around and leave."

Jimmy broke a sweat under his heavy coat. "Fuck. You guys got anything like shotguns in the trunk?"

Gallant answered, "yea, but don't bother. If these bastards are serious, we won't get out of here with shotguns. Hey Walsh!" he tried, "we know you got money problems. That's no reason to get crazy. It can all be worked out."

P-I-I-N-G-G-O-W-W. "Bullets make funny noises up here," Jimmy said as another bullet hit the same slab of granite and ricocheted. "Do you really think that's a warning shot, or is it that all he can hit is that piece of granite?" Taking off his service hat, Jimmy used a stick to raise it and wave it. BOOM! A shotgun blast ruined his service hat. "I guess we either back our asses out of here or back our asses out of here," said LaSalle.

The Busiest Day of My Life

I was standing by my office phone at four in the afternoon but it didn't ring. It didn't ring for forty-five minutes, and when it rang it was Linda. "Hi, hon. Hear anything?" she asked, her own voice casual, bookstore chatter in the background.

"Uh, no," I said, standing because I was too tense to sit, "and it's way past deadline."

She said 'thank you' to someone, then, "I wanted to call earlier but I didn't want to tie up the line," she said. "How're you?" I mumbled 'okay'. She's a thoughtful girl, common sense to boot. I was finding that each day I cared more for her, and that I didn't mind sharing my space with her. I hadn't gotten any lectures on leaving toilet seats up, or squeezing the toothpaste tube, not even on underwear on the bathroom floor. Truth be told, I'm pretty tidy anyway but I'd left some bloomers out as a test, and she just walked past them, on them, and made a crude joke about them. Then she hung three bras to dry on the shower curtain rod. Maybe it was retaliation; I actually found them kind of nice to ogle, much easier than pretending to 'accidentally' stroll through the lingerie section of a department store. I was growing accustomed to her face in the bathroom, the kitchen, and especially the bedroom.

Anyway, she asked, "is Jimmy up there now?" 'Up in Maine,' she meant. I knew he was, but I didn't know how things were working out with Jimmy and the Weathermen. I wanted to screen Linda from any possible bad news about her brother. "Yea, I think so, but there aren't a lot of cell phone relay towers up there. That's probably why we haven't heard from anyone."

We got on with our day. I was finishing up my prep for the next day's class, on the Greenwich Village townhouse explosion which triggered the rush underground for the Weathermen, when my terminal 'bipped'. I had email. It was from Sheila Medeiros. My blood ran cold. Opening it, I read: 'Peter, got your chapter. Very interesting stuff.' Stuff? It was cracks like that that had kept my writing blocked for a decade. 'I need to talk to you about a student of ours, Emily Rosen. Mail me. Thanks, Sheila'

Sheila's message triggered such an anxiety attack that I was certain I was having a heart attack. I had all the signs: sharp pain in my chest, pain in my left arm, difficulty breathing. And, being almost fifty-five, the age at which my father died—in a car accident—made the alleged coronary very real. Do I dial a nine and then nine-one-one? I wondered. Or should I try to limp over to the campus infirmary. No, they'll just call the ambulance, I decided, might as well cut out the middleman. Linda, I thought, I was falling in love with you. What an inconvenient time to die. And those damn Weathermen up in Maine, about to commit the political crime of the year, and I've got an exclusive. I can't have a heart attack now!

And then, as God is my witness, I burped very deeply, felt a rumbling in my guts, and realized that the tearing pain was actually from my upper stomach, a hiatal hernia. The anxiety had produced a bubble of acid that triggered a violent chemical reaction with the bleached white flour and preservative-laden chocolate donut I'd snitched from the faculty room refrigerator—from a box clearly marked 'Lincoln Philbert'. So my gut cleared itself with another rumbling, some more emanations, and my life was given an extension.

I did something very unlike me; I picked up the phone and called Sheila's office. On the third answer she picked up. "Hi, Sheila, it's Peter Dumont."

She had a pleasant, professional tone to her voice. Maybe she had others with her but I couldn't tell. "Peter? Hi. You get my email?"

"That's why I'm calling. What're you doing right now?" It was a test, of sorts, of how serious she felt her problem was. Was she willing to clear the docket for me?

"Yes, actually, if you can give me…fifteen minutes?" She must have had someone there, but she really wanted to talk to me. I felt my stomach acids gurgle.

I have one great mental skill: I can block unpleasant or distressing thoughts. I'm poor at memorization, which is an interesting shortcoming for a history professor. Happily I came up during the era of academic liberalism, where rote instruction was tossed in favor of open book exams. But I could block: I blocked out the sounds of students' protesting outside my Master's oral exams. I blocked out Linda's previous ten thousand entreaties for a closer relationship. So I blocked the fifteen minutes until Sheila's meeting, blocked it so well that I found myself on the pot in the Men's Room reading the *Chronicles of Higher Education*—great want-ads—and realized I was late.

Which was why I arrived at her office door winded—winded from running down one and a half corridors, which reveals too much about my physical condition—and greeted her. "Hi," I gasped. "Sorry I'm late. I got tied up."

"Peter?" she greeted me, rising from her desk chair to get me into a seat. "You didn't have to run. It's only ten after."

She was right. Only students are supposed to run, to show with apologies for tardiness. I shrugged. "So what did you want to talk with me about?"

She got up again, to shut her door until the latch clicked. My pulse jumped ten beats per minute. She sat at her desk again, and reached for a stack of manila folders, fishing out the third—at least it wasn't on top, suggesting she'd just been reading it. "We both have Judith Rosen this semester."

I didn't know that. My pulse jumped up another ten beats.

Sheila smiled, "she's become quite the radical." Sheila was envisioning a young advisee in Judith. Damn. "Between your Modern American Radicals, and our readings in Women of the Post-War World, we're producing quite the outspoken leftist. Hope it doesn't come back to haunt us in our declining years," she joked. I managed to smile. "This is a paper she's written for me. I let them have free reign and, in a tribute to your course, she chose the Women of the Weather Underground."

I nodded dumbly. My ears were roaring.

"Actually, though she did a really good job, she really did a paper on the Weathermen, gender neutral. Normally that would make this a 'B' paper tops," she picked up the paper, a neatly word-processed fifteen pager, spell-checked, with some modest graphics for titles. Sheila had written comments in the margins, mostly positive. "Please take this and read it, at your earliest convenience."

"Okay," I agreed, taking the paper.

"Now," Sheila was not making eye contact with me anymore, "this is the draft you emailed me the other day, the draft of your review paper. Tentative outline for your book, I believe?" She picked up a copy of my paper and gave it to me. "Peter, I don't quite know how to broach this topic." She turned sideways, and now I understand that academics go to silhouettes when they have to deliver hard news. "You may not know that I'm on the Professional Ethics Committee for the college. The Chair rotates, and I am currently serving."

I knew we had a Professional Ethics Committee; I had no idea she was on it. "How long have you done that?"

"Two years," Sheila said, still in silhouette. She sighed. "Before you read those papers, or actually read Judith's paper, I have to give you my first impression. I thought there was one excellent paper, and one that was long-winded and alluded to the point without stating it as clearly as did the first one." She paused, perhaps for dramatic purposes but more,

I think, because she was clearly uncomfortable. "One looks like a student's paper, one like a well-read academic."

Remember, most academics spend their professional lives avoiding confrontations—I think it's the 'we hang together or we shall surely hang separately' mindset. "Let me say first that this has been shared just between you and I. As a member of the Professional Ethics committee, I need to hear your explanation as to why your paper sounds like a wordy, inferior copy of Judith's." There, the words had been spoken. "If I sound harsh, forgive me. Please look at the papers, in your office, and we can talk some more later."

I released the breath I'd been holding. Saying nothing was my only option. "Okay," I agreed, tucking both papers into the manila folder. "I'll look at them. When do you need to hear back from me?"

Sheila looked qualified to be a traffic court judge just then—'I know you didn't mean to go ninety, you poor imbecile, but you broke the law all the same'. "Soon, Peter. Monday, at the latest. I've got to give Judith her paper back by then."

I left her office as though we'd been discussing the appalling condition of the college's parking lot. When I reached my office I shut the door and pulled out Judith's paper and scanned it quickly. She had read the article psychoanalyzing dead Weathermen and had digested it, related it to the landmark Martin Luther study, and her text was nearly perfect. I can't actually remember any of it verbatim—mental block?—but the psychohistorian had gone digging into the medical histories of two of three dead Weathermen. He found stark evidence of depression and treatment with one, examples of poor mental health and an abusive home environment with the second. The third, Sandy Wegman of Salt Lake City, had had no history of mental illness, just an upbringing in the Mormon Church. Judith had used that evidence to pursue the romantic, suicidal nature of the Weathermen, and she had done it beautifully.

It was a damn good paper. It was a paper I wish I had written. And, still in my lap, sadly, was the paper I had written. And what I had written was better than Art's work only because I'd kept it to eighteen pages.

Rose nicked herself three times with the potato peeler. "We don't want any blood in with the taters," Abby directed her, peering over her shoulder at the basin filled with potato peelings. "You ain't got AIDS or anything, do you?"

"No," Rose said. She was concentrating on her peeling.

Carl was doing much better, leaving more potato after the peeling than Rose. "You can stay here as long as you want," Abby said, grinning. "Only damn man who seems to know how to peel a potato."

Emily came inside, saying nothing. Rose and Carl both looked at the machine pistol she set on the coffee table. "Did you kill Leon?" Rose asked; she was simply curious.

"I quieted him down," Emily said with a Cheshire-cat smile. "He ain't dead. We still have a trial to hold." She asked Abby, "they finished?"

Abby checked. "Pretty much. Just scoop up them peelings and toss them into the garbage and put the taters in that pot. It's already full of water."

The Weathermen busied themselves and in five minutes the potatoes were in the water, the peelings had gone into the garbage—Rose muttered something about composting but Carl easily silenced her with a glare—all under the distant but always within eye-shot supervision of Abby and her .30 hunting rifle. When they returned to the kitchen Leon was sitting on a stool. He hadn't been shot but he'd been rolled in the dirt and some of it was still in his hair and clinging to his shirt. He was bound tightly with coarse rope.

"Did a mere woman kick your ass, Leon?" Rose teased, almost before she thought about it. Carl froze a moment, but Emily heard her and laughed.

"He ain't much as husbands go," Emily assessed him, and she and Abby returned to the kitchen. She got out a battered copy of the Bible and set her left hand on it, raising her right. "Swear me in, Abby."

"Okay, Sis." Abby read off the vow of loyalty to the militia and to God, and Emily said, "I do."

Then she put the Bible back in the drawer and hefted her machine pistol. "This is a duly constituted court to try Leon Michelin for breaking the rules of the militia, gambling on Sunday. I might add that he skedaddled on me, and showed up bringing strangers, and I do mean strangers," she added with a look at Rose, "and now our men are out defending the property against the lawmen come up looking for you."

Abby prodded Carl and Rose to stand against the wall by Leon. "Leon, you swore an oath to this militia. You've heard the charge. How do you plead?"

Leon, with some grass stuck in his hair and a shiner developing on his right eye, looked quite desperate. "I plead guilty and throw myself on the mercy of the court."

Emily rolled her eyes. "That's not gonna happen." She addressed the Weathermen. "You two claim you've come up here for a hunting trip. You want to stick with that story or do you feel like telling the truth, that you're government agents?"

Rose and Carl looked at each other and Carl barely shook his head. "We're not government agents," Carl said, "and if we were, what would you do about it? You seem too sane to be shooting FBI agents. That's a whole other world of trouble."

"Base?" It was Walsh, calling in. Emily picked up the two-way radio from its base by the telephone. "Perimeter, this is Base. What's happening?"

"We had a Maine State Police car with three state boys in it. We sent a couple rounds their way and they hauled ass out of here. Otherwise quiet. Dinner ready?"

"See?" Rose interrupted, "it's just the state police. And given the weapons you've got up here I'd say you're—"

"Taters are boiling. Did you want the moose steaks?" Walsh did. "Okay, I'm concluding Leon's trial. You want to see him before we pronounce the sentence?"

"No, he's all yours," Walsh answered.

Emily set the radio back on its base. "So you still don't want to admit you're government agents, eh?"

Leon, looking more anxious now that his fate was clearly in the hands of his estranged wife, said, "Emily, remember I told you when I met you that I, uh, hung around with some protestors when I came back from Viet Nam?"

Rose and Carl turned pale: Leon was about to inform. "I was actually in the Weathermen for awhile."

"The who?" Emily was only in her early thirties. Rose couldn't suppress a giggle.

Leon sighed; this was much worse than her not knowing or caring who played at Woodstock. "The Weathermen. They were terrorists. Left-wingers. They bombed a lot of police stations and labs, took over college campuses, that kind of stuff. These two," he nodded to them, "robbed an armored car in Ohio, and killed a cop."

Emily looked at them with new respect, but Abby's face hardened. "My father is a retired cop," she said, anger growing. "How did it happen?" she asked like a cop checking the license of a suspect.

"I just helped them get the guns," Leon said quickly. Abby nodded, and then, in one swift motion, swung the barrel of her rifle as hard as she could and cracked it against the side of Leon's head. He went over, and dark blood began to trickle from a gash in his scalp.

"How did it happen?" Abby asked Carl.

"It was unintentional," Carl said, saying words he'd coined decades ago, "I wish to God it hadn't happened."

Emily knelt to feel Leon's pulse. Leon was alive. "Abby," Emily said, looking at them with the eyes she used to stare down drivers who cut her off, "you okay?"

Abby was looking Carl in the eye. "Did you shoot him this close, or were you a way's off?"

Carl went pale. Abby's finger was curled tightly around the trigger. She might not simply club him. "He was a way's off," he borrowed her words, his eyes watching the tip of the barrel, "and I shot him as he came at me," he added, almost whispering.

Abby was absorbing the story. "So you two ain't FBI after all. Weathermen, eh? You probably wish you were FBI now." She stepped back from Carl, brought down the barrel of her rifle to Carl's chest, and shouldered the stock.

Rose was the quickest. She shoved Abby and wrenched the rifle from her hands just as the rifle fired, and shot a hole in the ceiling. A moment later Rose had the rifle, barrel smoking, tucked under Emily's chin, and quickly worked the pump action to chamber a shell as Carl took her machine pistol.

Abby had gone to the floor and was rubbing her sore rump. "You won't get far," she vowed. "There's nobody around here except for us."

Carl's hand, and the gun, were shaking, and he was short of breath, making his chest heave. "You okay?" Rose asked.

"Yeah." Carl said to Abby, "I'm sorry a cop was killed, but it was self-defense. Not like what you tried to do." Abby flipped her middle finger at him.

"Carl, I'm afraid we have to tie up these women," Rose said. "Start with her." He grabbed the duct tape and went to work on Abby. "Leon," she said, "I really should kill you, you...pig, you informer. We were part of the same cell, for thirty years. Thirty fucking years."

Leon looked up at her, one eye swollen shut and a welt on the other side of his face. He blinked blood from his vision. "You still don't get it, do you? I wasn't in a cell with you. I wasn't in anything with you." He felt a wave of pain throb in his temple. "I thought when Carl called me it was going to be like a college reunion. Thought we'd maybe drive to New York, drink a lot of beer, raise some hell. This dumb-ass plan of yours was fucking doomed from the start. Like everything you guys did." He sat up, working his jaw, rotating his shoulder, checking out the damage. "You guys didn't stop the war, you didn't turn the country socialist, you didn't do shit. You just killed a few people and pissed your lives away. Losers. Freaks."

Carl watched Rose's finger curl around the trigger of her weapon, but he knew she'd never shoot for her own sake. "Yea, well, fuck you Leon," he said. "You know you weren't the first one we called. Let's haul ass," he said to Rose.

She paused, let the barrel of her weapon fall, but then wound up her foot and landed a hard kick in Leon's ribs. Carl failed to suppress a smile. "Let's haul it," she agreed as Leon curled up in pain, curse words hissing from his clenched teeth.

The coast, as they say, was clear. Floating in the shallow water near the shore, tethered to the end of the pier, were the seaplanes, one a Duck and the other a Seagull. Both looked ancient, with dual wings over and under the fuselage and pontoons under the ends of the wings with a larger float under the plane itself. "Neither one looks particularly new," Carl said.

"Which one will fly the furthest?" Rose asked.

"Well, our destination being Boston, either one will probably do the job," Carl said. "Just a matter of which one has the most fuel."

"You look," Rose said. "I'm going to find some more goodies." Carl headed for the Duck, and Rose jogged to the first Quonset hut, the toy shed where the men had appeared with the weapons. Inside was a modest arsenal, though overstocked with rifles for Rose's taste; she was partial to explosives. The walls were lined with coarse pine plank shelves. Smokeless gunpowder, ignition caps, cotton wadding, shot canisters...they were into hand-loading their shells. Then, in a dark corner where a big oil drum seemed the only item, Rose found something she could use. "Hand grenades?" she announced with delight. A metal canister with about twenty grenades. Someone had been monkeying with them and left twisted newspaper tucked where the pins should be. She carried a woven bag for a purse, and dropped a few grenades in. On her way out she saw something else to grab. A gallon jug with red paint drips down its side.

A piston fired loudly in the clearing, two more fired, echoing in the air, and exhaust streamed from the Seagull. Good, Rose sighed, the plane is started, I've got the explosives, and we're ready to rock and roll.

"Stop right there you BITCH!" Rose heard Abby coming out of the house, unarmed but angry.

Rose aimed the machine pistol at Abby, safety on, and Abby froze. "I definitely don't want to hurt you, Abby. Let us go, and you'll read about it in the papers," she said. Abby didn't seem impressed. Rose did her best to trot across the clearing, swinging the paint in her right hand and keeping the pistol on target with her left. When she reached the dock, and was well past Abby, she dropped the pistol into the water and huffed out to the plane.

Emily got out, and she and Abby ran off to the toy shed.

"Can you fly this?" Rose yelled at Carl over the roar of the engine.

Carl had been trying to figure that out himself. In his early days with the Air Force Reserve he'd had to get qualified on take-off and landing planes, then helicopters, as part of flight-testing repaired aircraft. "This plane is really old," he said, his voice uncertain. He worked one lever and looked out to his right, and smiled as a wing flap moved. He found the throttle. "That's air speed," he tapped one gauge, "that's altitude," he tapped another, "and that's fuel." The fuel was past 'F'.

"Can we get out of here?" Rose asked, anxious. She pointed. Abby and Emily had emerged from the toy shed with some kind of shoulder-mounted rocket. "Get out of here!" she screamed.

Carl decided he knew enough. He revved up the engine and the plane pulled away from the pier, moving slowly out into the middle of the lake. Abby and Emily were toting another prized weapon of small armies called the rocket-propelled-grenade, which fired like a rifle, launching a grenade at the target. They dropped it once, and picked it up the wrong way; apparently they were struggling as hard to work their equipment as was Carl.

Carl got the seaplane positioned at the end of the lake, pointing into the wind, and throttled up. The plane began gaining speed, and halfway across the lake it lifted out of the water. Abby had mastered her weapon, aimed and fired it. The impact knocked her on her rump for the second time that day. Emily stood too close and her ears would ring for a week.

The grenade shot across the surface of the water, towards the seaplane, hitting a half-submerged tree close to the plane. It exploded, and bits of shrapnel peppered the plane. The impact made the Seagull bank to the right, then bank to the left, drop a few feet in altitude, but then regain its climb and rise into the sky. In a minute they were out of range, as Abby struggled in vain to reload. Inside the Seagull, the Weathermen screamed in joy and relief as they climbed into the Maine sky and headed south. "And I hope Leon has a concussion," Rose said.

The drone of the plane became a calming hum as the lake receded behind them. "I'm really hungry," Carl said. "Is there anything in here to eat?" Rose found half an old chocolate bar and they split it. Checking his watch, "we need to find a place to land this, stay hidden until tomorrow." Rose rummaged in a pile of charts and found a topographical map of the state, standard hunting issue. She pointed out their current position, as best she could tell, and they pointed out alternative hiding places until they settled on one.

"Dumont!" My office line was drowning in engine noise. "It's Rose!"

"Yeah!" I yelled into my phone. "What?"

"We've got the plane!" Rose yelled. "We're going to be at the wharf at six tomorrow. You better be there!"

And then the phone line went dead.

If there was any question left as to my motivations, I answered them to my own satisfaction when Jimmy called ten minutes later. He and the

Maine State Troopers had been forced to retreat from the hunting camp, and the Maine troopers were still discussing whether to call for massive backup and storm the camp or whether to call for massive backup and besiege the camp. There were references to Waco and Ruby Ridge, and nobody wanted that kind of trouble. "Have you heard from them?" Jimmy asked me on the phone, from up in Maine. I was amazed he could get through, though I heard later that the Maine Detached Militia had set up a very nice relay tower, as well as satellite TV.

"No, nothing," I lied.

"Nothing, huh?" he said, clearly disappointed, clearly suspicious, "well, keep me posted. You got my cellular number?" I did. He hung up abruptly.

Rose and Carl flew the seaplane inland, presuming the police would be looking for them on the coast. Thanks, in part, to me, the police weren't yet looking for them.

At dawn, Rose called, and Linda answered. I heard Rose's voice, and then Linda turned to me, "it's them. You keep them talking and I'll call Jimmy from my cellular phone."

"Hello?" I answered, groggy, as Linda tiptoed out of the room. She needn't have bothered, the connection was so bad the Weathermen wouldn't have heard a siren on my end.

"Listen," Rose said, "Leon is out of the plan. You have to go to the Park Plaza tonight and wait for Westmoreland. We'll be in the harbor. When he gets in the limo, you call us, then get out onto the Common with the camera. Okay?" I mumbled. "Repeat my instructions," she ordered. I did so. Before I could then ask what transgression of Leon's had finally crossed the line she hung up.

The conversation had lasted less than a minute. I didn't worry about Linda reaching her brother in time to put a trace on the call but I was certain my home phone was already tapped. So whether I'd told Jimmy the truth last night or not, he knew where and when he could find the Weathermen now. I lay back in bed, but sleep was impossible. Linda came back a minute later. "I had to leave a message on Jimmy's answering machine," she said, defeated.

"Don't worry," I comforted her. "He's a smart cop." It was a little early for work, so Linda began to seduce me, successfully. It was actually our first time making love since she'd moved in. There went about a half-hour, which meant living together had neither magnified nor minimized our love life. I almost managed to forget that damn phone call.

When Linda got up to shower for work, I remembered the two Horrors of My Life: the first was that seaplane and the second was Judith's paper on my kitchen table.

I waited until Linda had left for work.

When I got up I made coffee and sat at the kitchen table and read Judith Rosen's paper again. On my second reading it was less perfect. She couldn't distinguish between its and it's, and she was of the generation that had merged two words into alot. She had a penchant for run-on sentences, and most maddening, she kept calling them 'Wethermen'. But, after habituating myself to her grammar, I could see she had thought out a good paper. 'Ultimately,' she wrote, 'the romantic Wethermen point of view requires two elements. First, the Wethermen had to discipline themselves to strictly political confrontations. Second, the government had to be, and remain, evil. Neither of these lasted. When Nixon left office there was a period of reconciliation, including the election of Jimmy Carter (Sheila had written out a lengthy note on Carter that I ignored) who gave amnesty to the draft dodgers. And the hard-core Wethermen joined with the hard-core Black Panthers in the robbery/shoot-out in Nyack, which could not claim a political target. Consequently it would be difficult, if not personally and professionally risky, for anyone to raise up the Wethermen as romantic revolutionaries after that. Che Guevara had the good sense to die in the jungle while pursuing his political goals. That's why Che is still an icon, and the Wethermen are not just forgotten, but impossible to romanticize, except perhaps in a hundred years, as sometimes happens when real people's exploits become mythic legends.' Sheila had asked her for examples of this, but we all knew examples existed, i.e the James Gang.

Damn good. Even without the lousy 'a' in Weathermen. I finished my coffee, poured another cup—two in the morning is my limit—and, with a powerful sense of trepidation, looked at my own paper. It hurt to read it; not only was it plagiarized, it was bad writing. I won't quote from it. I argued that the Weathermen (spelled correctly) were 'difficult to romanticize'. I suggested that while the Weathermen 'claimed martyrs, none existed in popular culture' (don't ask why, I certainly didn't). I wondered if 'possibly the Weathermen might have been romanticized if they had been better revolutionaries', and then I blathered on for five pages about lost opportunities.

Well, it was plain to me, and to Sheila, that Judith's paper was better. If Lincoln Philbert's name had been on the paper, I would have been demanding the college dismiss him just as soon as we could find someone to take over his courses. Given the gallows mentality rampant on campus, with legitimate if not brilliant scholars struggling to survive the cuts, this sort of gaffe would almost certainly put me first in line for the guillotine. I sat there for a moment, waiting for the walls of my secure life to crumble, for the first cracks to appear, and was surprised at how relaxed this made me feel. No anxiety attack. No sense of desperation. I wasn't creating an alibi to feed Sheila to make this all just an embarrassing misunderstanding. I actually scribbled out a practice resignation, lengthened it, cut it, polished it, edited it, then crumpled it up.

A powerful sense of freedom was sweeping through me, freedom from the luggage of my life. I felt like I was a young lecturer again. And where I really, really wanted to be, in the worst way, was on that damn seaplane. What I did, after fantasizing about driving around the country on the highways, not the thruways, trying to find the old Weather Underground, old SDS, old Vietnam Vets Against the War, seek out former members, old sympathizers, embittered Vietnam vets and aging hippies living in seclusion in the Oregon woods and the Arizona desert, finding folks who remembered what the movement was trying for before time and age and life eroded it all, what I did was to tell Linda about the paper.

She came home for lunch pretty chipper; I fixed that. "Got a minute?" I started talking about the paper. First I explained to Linda how bright Judith was. Then I reminded her of my career crisis, and how Winfield had paired us up. Then I told her what I had done.

"Why did you copy Judith's paper?" Linda asked. She wanted to know if there was even one good reason why a professor would copy a student's paper. "Technically it's plagiarism, isn't it? Were you asking Sheila to read it and comment, and you…forgot to mention that part?" God, Linda loved me. She was doing a better job of cooking up an excuse than I.

"I told myself at the time, which was a few days ago, that with the Weathermen in Boston and me reporting to Jimmy every hour, plus teaching, that I just didn't have time to write this review paper," I said. "I'd need at least a month in solitary confinement to write the paper. I've been procrastinating for ten years. And then," and I was, for the first time since my parents passed on, sort of crying, "then Judith writes the paper I wish I had written. I've been carrying this idea around with me for ten years, but she got it on paper better than I could. I swear I'd get a job pumping gas now, but I couldn't cover my mortgage. I have no business in front of that class. Certainly not pretending I'm teaching Judith Rosen anything."

I slumped onto the couch and Linda sat down next to me, and she gently stroked my head as I tried to exorcise an aching, a self-loathing, sense of shame that crowded out my happy fantasies of the previous hour, my growing love for Linda, overwhelmed even my powerful sense of self-preservation. "You'll get it straightened out," she said, repeating the phrase and versions of it, in a calming voice.

I knew only one possible thing I could do, and it wouldn't straighten out this mess with Judith's paper, but it might help me walk away from this day with a shred of dignity. The lapped race car crashes into the retaining wall. I needed to create a distraction to draw attention away from the stupid thing I'd done. There was one hell of a distraction available to me, tomorrow, at six o'clock, on Common. I could save the life of a retired Army general. That ought to cancel out a little plagiarism, no?

I got a white canvas windbreaker from the coat closet. "You're going into Boston?" Linda asked. I nodded. "Did Jimmy call?"

I shrugged. "No, nobody's called."

"Let me try him again." A moment later she was dictating a message to his voice-mail. "This is Linda. In case you didn't get the earlier message, Peter may or may not have remembered to tell you that the Weathermen have a seaplane and plan to fly over the Common tonight and…do something to the general's car." She hesitated, then said goodbye and hung up. "What will you do after you videotape them?" she asked. "I assume you can't just come home."

"After I tape them I have to copy the tape, and then I have a list of addresses to which I send copies."

"CNN?" she asked.

"Among others. After taping, I come home." Linda looked at me as though I were piloting a dinghy into a hurricane. "Will you be here when I get back?"

She nodded. "Can I call you for a ride, like from Riverside?" She gave me an irritated glare. I thanked God. And then I went out the door.

I parked my Toyota in the Common underground garage, and checked it for anything I'd need in the coming days. I figured that if I were lucky I could escape the scene and get to the 'T'. I might get the car back, but not until the police were done analyzing every hair and crumb in it. I had enough evidence in that car to bide them over the next millenium. Just being sure, I searched it. There was nothing in the glove compartment except old car maintenance receipts and maps to New Hampshire and New York City.

Collecting the video camera, and the extra tape I'd bought on my own initiative, I crossed Boylston Street—in and of itself a life-threatening activity—and got to the main entrance of the Park Plaza, and saw three State Police cars parked in handicapped spots, their lights flashing. They were young cops and Westmoreland would mean much less to them than Schwartzkopf. The video camera was good camouflage, I suddenly realized, as I looked like the quintessential tourists that invade Boston each spring. All that was missing was a harassed-looking wife and a teen-ager. "Officers?" I asked, and two of them paused in their talk. "Is this where General Westmoreland is going to be speaking? I'm hoping to get a shot of him. See," I started babbling, "I was in Vietnam while he was there," and what? I was hoping he'd remember my name? Once again, the Man Who Did Not Go was passing for a vet.

"Aw, well," the first cop said sympathetically, "that's too bad, sir. He's not coming."

I must have looked pole-axed. "He isn't?"

"Got some librarian or someone coming instead. And he's running late. If you want a shot of the librarian you'll be able to tell because he wanted a ride in a Hummer," the other cop grinned. "So wait for the Hummer and you'll see Westmoreland's librarian." Hummer is jargon for the Humvee, which is jargon for the Army's replacement for its venerated Jeep. I'm certain they'd made a crude joke of those terms because they both blushed and giggled far more than the sentence merited.

"Aw, shit," I said, rather lifelessly. It was something we should have foreseen and hadn't. I thanked them and walked back to the Common, and hoping against hope, turned on the cell phone and called Rose. "Du—"..."Dumont?"

"Rose?" I yelled into the phone, "he's not coming! Westmoreland's not coming! Copy that?"

Suddenly they reached a good relay tower and the line cleared up. "Westmoreland's not coming. Is that what you just said?" Rose asked.

"That's correct. He's not coming. Two cops just told me he was not coming. There's some Army librarian coming instead. And he's running late," I added.

"FUCK-FUCK-FUCK—" Rose broke the connection. It wasn't her voice swearing.

A minute later my phone chirped. "Hi," I answered.

"We're coming anyway. You sure it's an *Army* librarian?" Rose asked.

"That's what the cop said. And he's riding in a Hummer," I added.

"Well, at least that makes a better picture than a limo," Rose sighed, "we're in the harbor now, out by some deserted island. Call us as soon as the librarian shows up."

"Will do." She hung up.

There's a small cemetery tucked into the Common on the Boylston Street side. With road building and other modern changes, the natural slope of the ground began threatening the cemetery and it had to be shored up on one side. From the iron grate fence around the cemetery I had a good angle from which I could see the Arlington Street intersection the Hummer would drive through, and the entrance of the Park Plaza where it would stop. So I pretended to be a tourist shooting old gravesites in Boston. There are a lot of them. Tourists, that is. And old grave sites in Boston. Six o'clock passed, and I imagined that banquet room of old men and some old women tucking into their prime rib or baked scrod, and maybe two or three with the vegetarian choice. They were the Directors of the Veteran's Association of Boston, and from what Rose had found on the Internet there were bank presidents and corporation presidents in there, the Mayor of Boston, possibly the Governor, and eventually an Army librarian.

And then, in the last bits of sunlight I saw two police cars driving slowly through the traffic with lights flashing, followed by a big, camouflage-green, Army Hummer. I pulled out the phone and called up Rose. "The Hummer's here," I reported.

"Okay," said Rose, "we're going to taxi in a little closer. Do you think you can get in by the banquet room without any trouble?"

"Yea," I explained my tourist disguise.

"I guess we haven't tapped all your talents," Rose said dryly. "Okay, if you can call us when the librarian is leaving the room, then get your ass out to the Common. You should have just enough time to get there. You'll know us when you see us."

I could feel my heart thudding in my chest as I walked in the failing light. The air was chilly and I zipped my jacket up, feeling chills where nervous sweat met the cold air. The camera started feeling heavy. Inside the hotel was the usual crowd of people around dinner time, waiting for seating to begin in the banquet room, so the lobby was a little crowded. There were state troopers in one corner, and that's how I found the right banquet room. They didn't challenge me when I entered the hallway, making me wonder what they would challenge. There were a lot of old men in Army uniforms, but they all looked retired. As I approached the banquet room, I tried my innocuous tourist grin again. The cops recognized me. I held up my video camera and looked hopeful.

"If you want, real fast, aim your camera up at the front table," said a kindly Officer Kraft, according to his badge, "the old guy in the Army uniform with six rows of braids is Army Archivist Walter Saunders. And the Governor is sitting two seats away from him."

"Thanks," I said with a grin, and briefly stepped into the doorway and started filming. At least now I knew for sure who our target was.

"Hey—" someone said, touching my arm, and I dropped the camera in shock. "Take off the lens cap," advised the other officer with a grin.

"Thanks again," I said, blushing. Popping off the cap, this time I actually saw Army Librarian Walter Saunders. He was about five-eight, about a hundred and seventy, maybe eighty pounds, filling his uniform without embarrassing himself in it. He was mostly bald, with a white comb-over across the front of his forehead. Under his arm he was carrying a wall plaque. I shot for a minute and exited out of the doorway, thanking the cops again, and then retreated with a copy of the agenda I'd picked up.

Army Librarian Walter Saunders was filling in for Retired General William Westmoreland. Westmoreland sent his regrets. Saunders had brought two identical plaques. One was to be presented to the Boston Veterans Association in grateful acknowledgement of…something. The other plaque Saunders would be showing had the names of several of the people attending the dinner engraved on it; it would be displayed somewhere in Washington. Like anyone would find it there. The agenda noted that the speech would follow the dinner. My stomach grumbled. I hoped the librarian was a man of few words.

A Protest to Remember

Major Walter Saunders had done a hitch in Nam, from '63 to '65, "and I was en-listed," he added pointedly in a drawl he picked up in Tennessee. "I served in support of the Second Logistics Division," he went on, and I think the upshot was that he was a clerk-typist in Army Intelligence, transferred to the Quartermaster Corps, and somewhere in there he either transferred to, or at least attended, the USO tour. "I can still see Mister Bob Hope on that stage," he chuckled, "and Miss Jill Saint-John and all the other wonderful performers." Though my eyelids were dipping, Saunders was actually doing a good job of entertaining the room. He and his audience were in the same age bracket, if not income, and they were smiling and nodding at his memories, chuckling at his old jokes. I guess he was a good choice. Probably did a better job than Westmoreland would have.

I found a couch in the lobby, and bought the Boston Globe and was scanning the EMPLOYMENT listings. At nine forty-five Saunders' applause woke me up. Guests were streaming down the hallway towards the rest rooms. I could hear the amplified speaker's voice. "I want to thank Major Saunders for the wonderful, wonderful talk he gave," the Assistant Vice President of Boston Commercial Properties was saying. I dialed Rose.

It rang, and rang. I almost disconnected to retry when Rose answered. "Hullo?" she answered in a sleepy voice.

"He's done. Finally," I said. "You guys ready?"

In the time it took me to say that, she was awake and I could hear a motor firing up. "Get to the Common," she said, and disconnected.

My heart began pounding alarmingly hard. This was it. My hands began to tremble. I tried to refold the Globe back to the front page, but I'd creased it and it was rustling and resisting folding. "Fuggit!" I hissed, glanced left and right and decided to walk away from it. I picked up the camera from my lap, held it in both hands and walked quickly out the doors.

Outside, the crisp autumn air woke me completely up. Chilly, I zipped up the windbreaker, and wished I'd worn a sweater instead of a just a dress shirt. "They must be freezing out there," I remembered thinking of Carl and Rose. I had to cross the street, a triangular block, then across Boylston Street to the Common. I walked fast without thinking, and only when I was on the Common did I realized that Army Librarian Saunders was having a great evening and was taking his time leaving the room.

The engine started fine, but the plane was listing to the left. Apparently the grenade back in Maine had punctured the floats and water had seeped in. Carl was struggling to get the plane to taxi. Fortunately the sea was very calm that night or they'd have flipped or foundered. But Carl got it moving across the water and increased the throttle to takeoff. At that point the engine was going close to full-tilt. Rose was sorting through her purse, digging out the grenades and examining them more critically in the cabin's dim light. Instead of firing pins there were twists of paper jammed into the holes. "What's with the paper," she wondered. She picked up the can of red paint and found a small screwdriver and, bracing herself as the cabin rocked, she pried up the lid; there was paint. "Okay," she said over the roar of the engine, "we're ready for violent or non-violent. Can this thing fly?"

Carl's muscles bulged in his sweatshirt as he wrestled with the stick and what was clearly an unbalanced craft. "I'm trying. I think the floats are full of water." And after a long taxi, past one island and past another, well after the plane should have risen into the sky, CR-A-A-A-C-K! The left side of the plane rose oddly. Then again on the right. Sounded like something was tearing into the plane from underneath.

And then they shot into the sky like a missile. "What the hell?" Carl said, working the stick and throttle to even their flight, then banking back to look down at the water; then they understood. "Our floats," Carl pointed them out still in the water, half-submerged. "We've lost our landing gear. Good news is we've got an hour's worth of fuel."

They said nothing after that, so Rose told me. How they ignored or avoided Air Traffic Control at Logan I don't know, but maybe Carl knew a little about that, having flight-tested for the Air Force. They reached the city skyline in a few minutes and Carl flew up to go over the Customs House tower, and a few skyscrapers ahead was the vast, darker space of the Common. In a minute they were over the top and dropped down to about a hundred feet.

The plane was camouflage-green, so I heard it before I saw the lights at the wing tips as they moved through the night sky too near to be stars. "It's really happening," I said, then got the camera up, lens cap off, and focused, realizing then that my hands were trembling. I saw a garbage can stand, and knelt to steady the camera on the black iron lip. I was also panting, and sweating worse than that dark day in Winfield's office. I filmed them buzzing Charles Street; traffic was light. There were only a dozen or so people on the Common, and only gradually did they all recognize that a plane was flying low overhead.

Then I saw the flashing lights of the Boston Police escort as they started out onto Charles Street with the Hummer snug behind. The seaplane had disappeared for the moment up Newbury Street. As the escort vehicles and the Hummer cleared the Boylston Street intersection and proceeded down Charles Street, I saw the flying lights of the seaplane appear over the Public Gardens, dropping like a Stuka steamrolling Poland.

I worked around, filming continuously, to catch both the Hummer and the plane in the frame. This is going to make for a wobbly film, I remember thinking, especially when the camera slipped off its rest and I almost dropped it. Through the viewfinder the REC light flashed with the digital time readout—9:23 PM. The police stopped dead, which stopped the Hummer dead, which was precisely what the Weathermen needed to nail their target. When the seaplane was about fifty feet up and away, it dipped its wings and a rock, or something that size, flopped out the window. Rose had dropped two of the homemade grenades.

"I thought we were going for symbolism," I yelled.

They landed like rocks. I held the camera tight on the Hummer. No explosion. The seaplane flew over and climbed into the night sky over Park Street. "Thank God," I heard myself pray. A minute later the Boston Police were gunning their cars to get under cover, but the Hummer had stalled, and the seaplane returned and dove. Watching through the camera lens, I saw the seaplane return. It dipped its wings again, and this time I saw red paint pour out the window. Feeling sturdier, I held the camera and began running, still with my eye to the lens—again making for more very wobbly footage—and saw that Army Librarian Walter Saunders had gotten out of the Hummer on the driver's side. Apparently they'd let him drive, and he'd hit a wrong pedal and the vehicle stalled. When he saw the plane making its second dive he looked left or right for cover, then froze there in the street, arms outstretched like he was trying to make himself a better target. The red paint came down. I filmed his august looking self in his perfect uniform as he was drenched in symbolic blood.

It reminded me immediately of the old 'Laugh-In' skits where comedienne Judy Carne would yell "sock it to me!" and get drenched in water, paint, whatever. Walter Saunders just stood there, much like Judy used to, raising his arms now to examine himself. Is this the usual

Boston welcome, he must have wondered? The seaplane had risen into the night sky again. It made a third pass, but this time the Boston Police were firing their revolvers at it and it aborted its dive.

It flew directly over me for the first time and I looked up and saw the twisted legs of metal and realized that it couldn't land. "Carl!" I screamed, "your gear is gone!" Carl couldn't hear me but the Boston Police did, and that's when I set the camera down, popped out the video, and started my own escape plan.

Such as it was. I started walking, quickly, briskly, to the Boylston 'T' Station. My original plan had been to hot-foot it to the Arlington 'T' Stop, but now it was a million miles away, with lots of cops in between. With the video in my hand I heard cars behind me, heard the loudspeaker from a police cruiser, "in the white windbreaker! Stop! This is the Boston Police ordering you to STOP!" Peripherally I saw a cruiser race down Boylston, pass me with its lights flashing, then hurl itself onto the pavement and come to a screeching halt directly in my path, blocking my way to the 'T' station. The driver's door flew open and a burly looking cop jumped out with his pistol drawn. "STOP!" he ordered.

I stopped, and looked startled. "Oh," I said, pretty unconvincingly, "were you yelling at me?"

Our attention was drawn by a crashing sound. Looking back across the Common, the trees obliterated the view, but I heard the seaplane hit the pond in the Public Gardens. A wave of smoke and steam curled up, backlit by street lights, then an explosion echoed across the Common, reverberating off the fronts of the buildings around us.

"Oh God," I said, more of a call, a warning to the Almighty, than a cry of anguish. Flames rose briefly above the trees. According to the many photographs published later, the plane's tail rose out of the water at a shallow angle. "Carl?" I called, "Rose?"

The officer attended to business. I was cuffed, tucked into the cruiser, and driven to Area A station where I was, with a minimum of discussion, searched down to my skin, fingerprinted, and photographed. I had been 'booked'. Then I was led to a room the size of my classroom with but three chairs and one table. And that's when the night got quiet again. I was left alone, cuffed, to relive it all again, and again.

I was happy to sit for a while as my mind absorbed the events, but time passed and I got up to look around. The walls felt like metal. Bits of graffiti had mysteriously gotten in, though they certainly hadn't let me keep a pen. There were no windows. Two long, humming fluorescent bulbs lit the room. Initially the humming was comforting. After a while it was more like tinnitus. One wall had a mirror the size of a picture window. "Hi," I tried to smile at the window. Who was back there, I wondered? Jim Falcone?

I pictured the plane in the night sky again, wondered what would have happened if the grenades had exploded. I'd be facing some sort of murder charge then. The lights hummed. It was about ten-thirty, I guessed; they'd taken my watch. I was tired. Normally at that hour I would be parked in front of my television or reading on my couch. I'd be enjoying a glass of red wine, and with Linda there I could only speculate on other more lively possibilities. In any case I was usually bedded down by eleven. I yawned and guessed it was closing on eleven. I tried to find a position where I could doze, but the back of the chair seemed perversely designed to dig into the back no matter how one contorted, and the floor looked just dirty enough that I wouldn't lie down. I closed my eyes, felt myself drifting near sleep. Occasionally I heard footsteps pass by outside, and I opened my eyes to the painful glare of the lights. I got very thirsty.

The door flew open and I jumped. Jim Falcone came in first, followed by another man and a woman. "Peter," Jim brusquely acknowledged me, "this is Detective Terry," he introduced Terry, a sixtyish man with a round gut and drinker's face, "and Detective Klees." Klees was a sturdily built Hispanic woman half Terry's age. Then Jim got my full attention by slapping his hands on the table in front of me. I jumped again. "Why didn't you tell me as soon as you knew about the seaplane?"

"Sorry," I said meekly.

"'Sorry' gets you charged with accessory," Terry weighed in, dropping into one of the chairs. Already I didn't like him. "What the hell were you doing on the Common shooting home movies?" he asked. I wondered how much I should tell him. Before I could answer, he added, "Detective Falcone has already told us your connection with this plane attack. Speak," he barked. Treating suspects like dogs either worked well or just made him like his job, because he smiled in an ugly way.

As though Terry hadn't spoken, Jim asked me, "where is Rose?"

"I was hoping you could tell me," I answered very sincerely. "How is Carl?" I asked without much hope.

"Carl's dead," Jim answered, his tone more subdued, "probably died instantly in the crash. But Rose was not in the plane when we reached it. Was she in the plane?"

Hesitating just a moment, I nodded. "Yes. She called me on her cell phone from the plane." Klees started taking notes.

Carl was dead. I remembered his voice over the phone when I told them they'd missed Westmoreland again…"FUCK-FUCK-FUCK…" and when I thought I would laugh, I softly cried. The detectives ignored me.

Since Jim already knew my history with the Weathermen I sat there not saying anything for almost an hour while he talked to Terry and Klees. "You're a college professor?" Terry asked rhetorically, bloodshot-eyes wide; I would have to guess from that that Terry hadn't attended college (see Chapter 2).

Klees was better at absorbing information, filling in her notebook and asking Jim questions, "if Rose is missing, is she likely to recontact him?" as though I wasn't in the room.

"My sister lives with him," Jim said, somewhat reluctantly, "so if Rose shows up I can count on her contacting me." I blushed. Whether because Jim considered me unreliable or because, at my age I was cohabiting, even I don't know.

By twelve-thirty, cuffs removed, the detectives had wrung a signed seven page initial statement from me. I was, with Jim's intervention, released on my own recognizance. "Call me tomorrow, be back here by Sunday. Bring a lawyer if you want," Jim said.

"Am I under arrest?" I asked, as I'd never heard the tell-tale, 'you have the right to remain silent…'

"Not yet, but probably soon," Klees said in mock excitement that, much as I didn't want to, made me smile. My wallet and watch and car keys were given back to me and Jim led me through a heavy door with sturdy iron mesh on it. On the other side was a public area and, rising from a hard looking bench, was Linda. She had been sleeping. Or crying.

"Linda," Jim said, irritated, "I told you could go back to my desk and wait there."

"It's okay," she said softly, hugging her brother, then holding me.

"Hi," I said with obvious relief. "I'm so glad you're here. You didn't have to wait for me here."

"Shhh," she hushed me with a hug and a kiss. Oh God, I don't deserve her, I remember thinking. She walked me to her car—mine had been impounded—and on the way home at one-thirty in the morning I sniffled a little as I explained that Carl was dead and Rose was missing. "And all to throw paint on an Army librarian?" she asked softly, not cruel, not sarcastic, just bewildered.

"That wasn't the original plan," I said. "The original plan was…much worse."

And Rose? As the seaplane went down she was able, somehow, to escape a few seconds before impact. She landed hard in a tree and fell from it, hitting a couple of thick limbs on the way to the ground. She broke her right arm between the elbow and the wrist, broke or turned her right ankle, her knee as well, and broke her nose. She also broke several ribs. She also had a scalp wound that bled badly, and the police followed a trail of her blood as far as Newbury Street. It was blotted by traffic after that. They brought in dogs but couldn't track her. How she got herself moving is, I guess, testament to her will power.

What a tough soul she was. She reached an alley, found a dumpster behind a restaurant and scavenged some kind of paper or linen to blot her head wound enough to slow the bleeding. She passed out and slept in the dumpster until the next morning, when the sun woke her. She had lost her huge handbag in the plane, which is why I didn't get a call from her. Finding a half-empty bottle of something alcoholic in the dumpster, she gargled some of it, used the rest to anoint herself, and climbed out, limping to the street, hoping to pass as a drunken street-person, and looked for a woman she could approach and beg for help.

As it happens, the first woman was a Boston Police Officer, and she helped Rose into her back seat and drove her to Mass General. Although the police sent alerts to the hospitals with a good physical description of Rose, the vision of a terrorist jarred so badly with the battered woman reeking of wine and garbage that she raised no suspicions. Repeating 'he tried to rape me', the staff treated her without question. They put her arm and her leg in casts, wrapped her ribs, stitched her scalp wound, gave her some Percodan and admitted her into a public ward. Thirty minutes later Rose was out the door, getting used to the crutch she'd been lent.

The morning after my booking I woke up next to Linda, which I was becoming very fond of. As I woke, so did she. "I screwed up," I said softly. She looked at me, her hair tangled around her neck. "I told Rose I'd mail copies of the tape to the media," I said, sighing with disappointment. The tape, of course, had been seized as evidence well before I could do anything with it. Then I got up and tottered out to the kitchen and heard a rapping knock on my front door. It was seven-fifteen. I was trying to focus on coffee making. Instead I had to find pants. Couldn't find pants. Found bathrobe, put it on, tied it around and went barefoot but clad to the front door. Opened front door. Big, big mistake.

“Professor Peter Dumont!”

“Professor Dumont?”

“Peter Dumont?”

“Are you the Weatherman?”

Five or six men and women, three with camera-guys in tow, were on my sidewalk and lawn. At the curb I saw three vans parked with garish CHANNEL 7 WGRU and CHANNEL 38 WUTV and FOX adorning them. My mouth hung open. I still had the screen door between the media and me. “Professor Dumont!” a woman screamed, and made my ear ring.

I shut the door, tight. Linda was up now. “Oh, crap,” she said. A few seconds later the phone rang. Linda answered, mumbled a hello, and then said, “he’ll have a statement in an hour. Pass the word.”

She set the phone down. “That was one of the jackals on the front lawn. I bought us an hour to find you a lawyer. Incidentally,” she said, turning on the television, “let’s see if the media is up to speed.” She turned the channel to CNN and within three minutes my video was playing. Actually it was an edited video, using some of my footage and some from one of the police car’s cameras. No wobble, no muffled vocals, the point of view shifted twice. “I remember thinking while I was waiting at the police station,” Linda said, watching the TV,” and thinking about you videotaping last night.” Looking at me, she was enjoying some irony. “In 1969 you might have needed to arrange publicity, but now the reporters have scanners and everybody’s got video cameras.” Linda mused, “I was thinking, Rose seems so smart, but you really weren’t needed out there last night. Not for publicity.”

“She’s not so smart,” I realized, “but she’s tough.”

That wasn’t even the worst of it; not only was I not needed, but the crappy video I shot was inferior to the ones the networks were using. “Kind of ironic,” Linda said. I felt so unredeemably stupid that I covered my hands with my eyes to give myself a sense of privacy to find what was left of my self-esteem.

Linda made coffee. Sipping coffee, Linda and I did a quick scan of the yellow pages under 'LAWYER'. It's like picking one chip from a jumbo bag. "We don't have an accident claim, we aren't selling property," Linda crossed out ads with a pencil; thanks be to God Linda is a morning person. "Oh, this guy's name I recognize. L. Joseph Schmidt."

"L. Joseph Schmidt? What is that first initial crap about anyway?" I asked. "He was born Larry and wants to be called Joey?"

"Maybe he was born Llewellyn. Who told me about him?" Linda was trying to remember. "Jim mentioned him. I don't remember why, but if Jim had anything good to say about him he must be good." I let that judgement pass untouched. I needed help. Linda dialed his number, and had to wait through an automated answering system. Then the call was transferred to his home number, and I heard Linda introduce herself and briefly explain our predicament. "He's on his way," she said with a smile two minutes later.

"How much does he charge?" I asked, mostly out of habit. I hadn't remembered yet to thank her for being quick thinking and resourceful and supportive…what the hell did she see in me?

"He knew your name immediately," Linda answered, "said 'the Weatherman' and said he'd take you on for five percent of the eventual book sales."

Yet another crises predicated on publishing.

L. Joseph Schmidt showed up fifteen minutes before Statement Deadline. He pulled up to the curb in a battered blue 1992 Taurus wagon. I wasn't impressed until I saw him blow past the media like they weren't there, then tap on my door. I should note that, in the interim, Linda and I had quickly showered and dressed, so that the second time I opened the door I was wearing a button-down Oxford shirt, my most professorial.

"Peter Dumont? Joe Schmidt," he introduced himself. Joe was a husky fellow, possibly once an athlete, a few years older than I. "Don't mind my car, I really am successful," he said, "I'm also putting three kids through college. None of them inexpensive state colleges."

I snagged that comment for a moment, then decided he was being matter-of-fact and that there was no reason to be defensive, and let it go.

He listened to both Linda and I simultaneously for five minutes, nodding at both of us as he dug a legal pad out of his briefcase. "Okay," he announced, "Professor—what is your exact title, Peter?"

"Associate Professor."

"Okay, Professor Peter Dumont," I got brevetted by Joe, "of Hawthorne College by the Boston Police and the Massachusetts State Police last night in regards to the incident on Charles Street. Dumont has taught history at Hawthorne for thirty years. Two suspects in last night's incident were former students who were members of the Weatherman, uh, Weathermen," he looked at me quizzically.

"Their last version was 'Weather Underground'," I answered.

Nodding thanks, he returned to his statement. "Professor Dumont has not been charged in connection with this incident and is cooperating fully with the investigation." He glanced up at me. "You weren't charged last night, right?" I nodded. He added some other folderol, and both Linda and I held each other and hugged with relief.

The phone rang again. "Hello?" Linda let me go and answered. "Jim? Yea, the media's here. Three channels. I didn't notice. Jim? We hired a lawyer. Joe Schmidt?" She was listening then, but smiling. "You want to talk to him?" I got up to take the phone but Linda shook her head and handed it to Joe.

"Jim Falcone?" Joe asked, "hey, how the hell are ya? Yea, I'm here, with your charming sister and the professor—" doesn't that sound like a line from 'Gilligan's Island'? "—and we've put together a statement. Sure, just a second," and Joe read it to Jim. "Yes, 'questioned'." He listened for a long minute, then said, "okay," and handed the phone back to Linda.

"Y'know, it's my frigging head we're talking about here," I griped. "Anyone want to share the details with me?"

Linda hung up. "Jim says the D.A. is antsy and wants you to come in today, aye-ess-aye-pee to finish your statement."

Joe said, "and I just wanted to be sure he agreed on the terms. See," and for the first time I was getting legal advice, "you aren't a criminal, Peter, you're a fellow traveler. As a history professor, I'm sure you understand my meaning."

"Yea," I said, "of course, the fellow travelers in the fifties got blacklisted."

"Well, yeah," he conceded, "but this is the nineties. What they'll want is anything you can give them to lead them to," he checked his notes, "Rose. If you can give them Rose they'll drop your file in the shredder." He looked at me hopefully. "Can you give them Rose?"

"No more than I can give you Jim Hoffa, except to suggest mid-field at the Meadowlands," I said.

We stepped outside on time, and Joe read the statement. They filmed him reading it, then began peppering me with questions that Joe had warned me to completely ignore. I thanked them and went back inside. Then they peppered Joe with questions, and he spent ten minutes answering them with no information.

And about half an hour later we all heard from Rose.

It paid to leave the TV on CNN. "—this just in, a statement has been received by CNN, issued by the 'Reconstituted Weathermen', claiming responsibility for the bizarre seaplane paint-bombing on the Common last night." The newscaster was replaced by a shot from the video while the audio went to a low-timbre female voice I recognized, rasping a little on a bad phone connection. "The Reconstituted Weather Underground claims responsibility for the paint bombing of the Army Hummer, and Army Major Walter Saunders." Her voice was monotone and tired. She must have been badly hurt, I realized, having no idea at that time. "The planned target was Retired General William Westmoreland, who was largely responsible for the genocidal war in

Vietnam. We regret the inconvenience to Major Saunders, but want all pigs to know that the genocidal war in Vietnam and the racist politics practiced in this society will never be forgotten, nor forgiven."

I hoped Carl could hear it. I wondered where he was. I wondered where she was.

I was charged with conspiracy to assault, which was the only charge the evidence could support. Lawyer Joe had me plead 'not guilty', though he had no illusions. "Given your record," he advised me, "you'll get probation. You weren't in the plane. You probably wouldn't have been charged, but they're really irritated about the video." The video I need not have shot. Looking at it, at the Boston Police on the periphery, they seemed to be running in both directions at the same time. Some clever soul had created a version of the video on the Web with them running to the theme of Bugs Bunny.

Hawthorne was two weeks from finals, so after I gave Jim and the detectives my full statement, Judge Caroline Hunter, whom Lawyer Joe was very pleased with, agreed to release me again on personal recognizance and set the next court date for a week after finals. The media had besieged my home since the morning after. Joe wrote me a short list of facts I could speak from. "You were on the Common, you were in telephone contact with Carl Krajewski and Rose Thomas, and you shot a video," Joe told me as though I hadn't been there. "You are not now, nor have you ever been, in the Weather Underground. You were involved in this plot through duress, and you were the one that alerted the police to the plan. You have been charged with conspiracy to assault, and not with actual assault. And don't say a goddamn word more, okay?"

My first morning after the court appearance I tried to be civil to the reporters by answering their questions in a gathering at the foot of my driveway, keeping them away from my door, sticking to my list. I even took it out and held it out for them. "This is what I can say, folks. See it?" The cameras closed in like it was the Shroud of Turin. "Let's let the print media see it," I held it higher for the Globe and Herald and the Metrowest fish wrapper. Still, they seemed to have a contest amongst themselves to try prying some confession from me. Next day, on my way to the mailbox, I got ambushed. The fastest one to reach me, Lori Bogart, a young woman with a local cable station, asked, "Professor Dumont, have you seen today's news on Leon Michelin?" I hadn't. She had her tech run the tape and I watched it on the monitor in her van, with three other media folks calling out to me for comment.

"Leon Michelin, identified as the third Weatherman involved in the attack on the Army vehicle (that was the only way to describe it straight-facedly) was extradited to Massachusetts yesterday from Maine to answer charges of wire fraud," the voice-over narrated, and the video showed Leon, trussed in handcuffs, being led from the back of a van through the open doors of the Charles Street Jail. "After questioning by Boston Police, more charges are pending on possible wire fraud in Washington, D.C." I smiled; one less thief at large.

The newsman directly behind me, Jasper Kill, some-damn-news-service, asked, "were you aware of this during your activity with the Weathermen?"

"I told the police about this before the incident," I said in self-defense. So then he asked the predictable question, "did you receive reduced charges by cooperating with the state?"

Was I a stoolie? "I cooperated," I clarified, "in part to try to…" the judge had warned me, really warned me, not to discuss the case, any of it, with anyone, and I'm sure her first concerns were the newshounds yapping at my elbow. I sighed, "no comment."

"To try to stop something? Do you know where ROSE IS?" Jasper asked, jamming the mike almost in my mouth.

I recoiled and hit my head on the too-close camera of Lori's cameraman. "Ouch. I can't talk to you guys," I said, and held my head where I'd hit the camera, "and I now have a headache." I went inside, without the mail, shut the door tightly behind me, and sank to the floor, where I sat for a while reminding myself that it could be worse, I could be sitting in jail.

Thanksgiving came and went, and I talked Linda into eating out, but only by promising the next Thanksgiving would be with her family in Detroit.

The next morning returning to campus I was followed by two TV cameramen and, as a result, at least a hundred students. Lawyer Joe had carefully warned me again to say nothing to the cameramen. "You slipped-up yesterday. You took a breath in front of a camera. You cannot afford a slip-up. Especially if they ask you about Rose. If you actually know where Rose is, and don't tell the police first, they'll hang your ass." The fact that I had not a clue where Rose was didn't mean much to anyone.

My office door had been adorned with a photocopy of an upright black fist. "Wrong group," I announced to the crowd. "Obviously didn't take my class. My students know the Weathermen from the Black Panthers." I shut the door behind me. My voice-mail was flashing. I dialed in: thirty messages, which was the system's maximum. I saw a handwritten note in Winfield's almost indecipherable script, 'Peter—see me as soon as you can—'. It was my first civilized request of the week.

I called him. "Winfield? It's Peter."

He held the phone for a moment, and I heard a door shut over the phone. "Peter? How are you? What a show!" Winfield also used that phrase to describe the Gulf War, the Brookline abortion clinic shootings, and the Atlanta Olympics bombing.

"Not much of a show," I said. "I'm really sorry for any embarrassment I've caused to you and the department—"

"Peter," Winfield interrupted in his gruff, friendly tone, "don't bother. Admissions will probably spike as a result of this. And they'll all want to take your course. It's the old actor's adage, there is no such thing as bad publicity. Listen, I know you've got a pile of trouble with finals and the police, but can we pencil in a time to talk this week?" He wasn't usually so urgent, so I promised to see him later that day.

My office became the site of a pilgrimage. Students started roaming up and down the halls, pausing to look at my door. My Woodstock poster seemed for the first time to be in the right place at the right time. Art spent almost the entire day hanging around my door, even when I was gone. He spent most of the time scribbling in a notebook. "I'm writing a paper on this," he said excitedly, and that was almost the straw that broke my back. My trips across the campus to the bookstore to see Linda brought in so many students at once that campus security posted a guard. "It's probably good for business," Linda said, hugging me, which she was doing practically every time we saw each other. I was never a hugger, and I'm not sure I'll ever be a hugger, but I tried to fake it. And that's as far as I'll discuss that.

"So, Leon got booked for bank fraud," I told her.

Linda nodded. At her desk was a computer with a nineteen-inch screen, and she was on the Boston Globe's website. "This just got posted. Read it."

The defenders of Camp Freedom had, after exchanging brief gunfire with one Maine State police contingent—the guys Jim had gone with—expected the state to then send in a force that would dwarf Operation Desert Storm, and had booked. When three Maine State police cars showed up the next day the camp was totally deserted, except for a few weapons that probably wouldn't fit in the trucks. But the boys hadn't gone far, because Emily and her sister Abby and Major Walsh were found in the woods about a mile away. Emily and Abby were questioned and released. Major Walsh was sitting in the Gilead lockup on assorted charges of unlicensed vehicles and writing bad checks. The story finished with a one paragraph reminder of the Common' incident and finished as all the stories finished that month…"the whereabouts of one of the Weathermen, a female possibly named Rose Thomas, are still unknown."

Linda and I shared a bowl of pasta salad. Then I kissed her good-bye and reluctantly left the sanctity of her office to cross the campus, run the gauntlet, and get back to the History Department and my pending appointment with Winfield.

Winfield greeted me like I'd been at war. "Good to see you, Peter," he clapped me on the back and shook my hand and guided me to the seat across from his desk. "I can't imagine what it's been like for you, but I want you to put it all on paper."

I smiled. "What?"

"I've been on the phone with Tony, " Hawthorne's president, "and we're going to leverage your experience to save your job and probably the entire history department!" Winfield looked like he'd been delivered from a dark place. I looked as clueless as I felt. "It's politics," Winfield explained, "you've been initiated into the Weathermen, and that's a credential no one in the eastern University community can claim. In Tony's opinion we'll be lucky if Yale or Brown doesn't recruit you. But I told him you were a team player, and I think I'm right, aren't I?" Winfield asked, a touch of concern in his voice.

"You think that my adventure will make Hawthorne," I searched for the word, "a stop on the tourist trail?"

"Academically speaking," Winfield corrected me. He looked happy, his second chin framed in his deep grin. "Tourists show up for a day and a meal and spend maybe a hundred bucks. Students stay longer and spend a lot more." I must have looked dismayed at hearing such cold financial calculations issuing from Winfield's mouth. "Peter, it's history to us. To them," he indicated with a toss of his mane towards the administration building, "it's numbers. You teach a good course," he reminded me. He didn't say 'great', he said 'good'. "With this experience, your course will be a stronger draw. Tony needs to make cuts, but now he'll do it evenly, the way they should have tried in the first place. We had a funded seat in Middle Eastern studies we never filled, and that's all we'll lose."

I nodded understanding. "That's good." Except, I thought later, for those of our students with any interest in Iraq, Iran, Israel, the Gulf, oil economics, the Islamic revolution, etc. I sat in silence for a moment. "So why am I here?"

Winfield was trying to look clever, like a used car salesman trying to slide past the nasty financial fine print. "I told Tony you were a team player. You have tenure here, and you'll stay, and Tony said, that's great, and that's the end of our budget nightmare." He posed it with just a hint of a question. My eyebrows rose, as I understood.

"The articles? Our writing projects?" I asked, for after all that had happened, my sudden fame could be eclipsed by the tale of the purloined paper.

Winfield smirked. "Not necessary, not now. I mean, you should write this. This is an important book and you have to write it. But you don't have to write it to save your job. You've just saved all of our jobs."

"Even Lincoln Philbert's?" I asked with obvious distaste. Winfield and I shared a nasty chuckle as he shrugged and nodded.

"I'm not going anywhere," I promised Winfield, "especially since I have court dates as soon as finals are over."

Winfield clapped me on the back again at his door. He looked relieved of a burden. He had been—he'd been on the verge of discovering through our attempts at scholarly writing what a bunch of 4-Fs filled this department. He was much happier not knowing.

Oh, I should add that Lincoln Philbert sent me a draft of a paper he'd been writing for a few years. It had to do with fossilized stool samples from Macedonia compared to turds from Rome, and I think his point was that there were similarities previously unmentioned in the diets of the two cultures. It was a painstaking effort, and he defended each point with extensive if not scholarly footnoting—in one case a cite from 'Healthy Living'. This went on for fifty-seven pages. I made a mental note to strongly recommend his course to Art. They'd love each other.

Let me compress a little.

The fame, or notoriety, eased by. It passed quickly on campus, in part because it was finals week. By my third day back I had no entourage to speak of. Even Art left me alone.

I had daily telephone discussions with the police and, consequently, with Lawyer Joe. Their questions could all be traced to "where is Rose?"; "had I heard from Rose?"; "had Rose ever mentioned a contact from the underground?"; "did Rose ever tell you where she lived with Carl when they were underground?"; and back to, "where is Rose?" They dug up a high school photo of Tom Rose. First they digitized it and did age-progression, and it looked a little like his father in Boca Raton. When they had it switch genders the software hung for fifteen minutes. What it finally produced looked like Kurt Russell in 'To Wong Ho, thanks for everything, Julie Newmar'. I tried to help with a sketch and the result resembled Rose in bad lighting.

Five normal days later I was in my office, truly working my butt off, grading essay tests, when I heard a knock on my door. "It's open," I said.

Judith Rosen opened the door. "Hi, Professor Dumont," she said, not smiling. She was in her customary denim jeans, a t-shirt with DED SEAL SCRAWLS imprinted in stenciled letters, with their concert dates. Her eyes were bloodshot, a common sight here during finals week. She looked tired and sad, perhaps a touch of anger. She was holding some papers she'd rolled up in her hand. "Got a minute?"

"Sure." My pulse picked up, but I wasn't truly scared anymore.

I had neglected to get back to Sheila. I had called her to tell her how busy I was—getting arrested, getting questioned, getting charged, getting a lawyer, getting in and out of jail, getting in and out of my house via the media gauntlet—but I'd had to leave a message on her machine and I hadn't tried to contact her since. My own message machine fried after logging a hundred messages in one day. With Judith in my office I wished I'd called Sheila and spoken to her. But I was wishing I'd told different people a lot of different things then.

So, I had to assume Sheila had done what she had told me she would do, take my plagiarism to the university committee. I expected my first visit to be from Sheila, or Winfield, or whoever else sat on the committee. It would have been easier that way. Instead, I had to speak with the victim. "Please have a seat," I offered Judith.

She sat. She slumped, actually, and she tucked one sneakered foot under her rump on the chair, which only made her look more frail. She gazed at my desk for a long minute.

"Finals over?"

She nodded, and yawned. It was a deep yawn, deeper than she'd intended, and she tried to rein it in. "Sorry," she said, almost in a whisper, rubbing her right eye. "Um…I take 'Women's Issues' with Professor Medeiros," she began, looking at my desk all the time. I nodded. She drew in her breath with an effort and said, "I had a paper to do for her."

I was bleeding inside. This was punishing the victim. Why was she here? Sheila held her students' hands more than most around there. She would have told Judith to take a hot soak, sip hot tea, read a book, pet a cat, watch Lifetime, and leave it all to Aunt Sheila to make right. But none of that struck me as Judith's style.

"Judith," I interjected, "you wrote a paper on Weatherman for her course, and it was excellent." I reached for the far stack of papers on my paper-strewn desk, and found my copy of it. I'd written nothing on it. "Here it is," I held it out to her, "Professor Medeiros gave me a copy." She took it, but she was still looking at the paper she'd brought with her. "I'm going to confess something to you," I said, "first, please shut the door."

Leaning back in her chair, she gave the wooden door a too-hearty shove. It shook the doorframe when it latched and I flinched. "Professor Medeiros showed me your paper and," I sighed, for it was time to tell the truth or to tell a beautiful fiction. "You wrote a paper that I've been trying to write for ten years." I let that hang in the air for a minute. At any other time that confession would have ripped my rib cage out. But in the context of the Weathermen and the week I was having, it seemed no more painful than a mistake in my Chinese take-out. "I wrote a draft of a paper for Professor Medeiros to read. It's a faculty project. She read my paper and, naturally, it reminded her of your paper because...I had used your paper for my outline."

God, I remember thinking, why did I tell her the truth? Sometimes the victims have been victimized enough, and the truth victimizes them further. I could have avoided this in a dozen sleazy ways. I could see she was at a loss as to how to deal with it.

"So, it was pretty good, huh?" she asked, a wisp of life in her voice. "She doesn't know I'm here. She just told me you'd used a...significant portion in your paper." She smiled. "I'm flattered."

I nodded. "Your paper was better than 'pretty good.'" She let her smile bloom. "I hear you've been accepted for that semester in Oxford. Are you going?" I'd wanted her as an advisee, but if I had to lose her I wanted to lose her to the big time.

She looked away. Oops, I'd touched a nerve. I'd heard that news from the department secretary. "Have I said..." my mouth hung open.

Her eyes teared up. She bit her lower lip and turned away from me as tears spilled from her tightly shut eyes. Tissues! Tissues, dammit! I found some in a lower desk drawer, yanked out a bunch and handed them to her. She gurgled 'thanks' as she dabbed at her eyes. I remember thinking, good thing she doesn't wear mascara. I looked helpless and concerned, trying to hand her unnecessary tissues as she composed herself, asking if she wanted a glass of water; she didn't.

"Sorry, Professor Dumont," she said raggedly when she got her voice back, "I, uh, got accepted for the semester at Oxford, but," she shook her head.

Heard about the food? Heard about the weather? Heard about the coffee?

"I'm going to have a baby." It frightened her to say it, but once it was out she brightened.

My jaw dropped. I only pulled it back up through conscious effort. Now I had information I didn't know how to deal with. "That's...wonderful," I said, very hesitantly. Was it? She needed more tissues, but at least she was smiling. I wanted to ask inappropriate questions, like who was the father, how had a bright, promising young woman gotten knocked-up, etc. That young women now deliberately *plan* single pregnancies is a message still seeping its way up the WASP ivory tower. Life has pleated itself into levels of complications my generation still can't fully grasp.

She sniffed again. This wasn't the Judith I knew from class. "I'm pregnant. It's okay, I didn't plan it. And my boyfriend and me both know what birth control is." Somehow hearing True Left Rosen saying 'boyfriend' jarred me. "We just got careless and now I'm pregnant." She beamed through the tears. "And I'm going to keep it."

I was so far out of my depth I didn't know which way was sky, which way ocean-bottom. "You...could still go to Oxford," I said, making it a question, and realized that I was back in the professorial, parental role, rather than being the Second Man to Screw Her.

She shook her head. "You know why I was applying to go to Oxford?" I knew any answer I came up with was probably far off the mark. "I was going to join the Green Party. They're pretty active in Oxford. See, this semester, between your course and Professor Medeiros, I've really come to appreciate the power of protest, and I thought, there isn't a Weather Underground anymore," she smiled as her dreams surfaced again, "and Greenpeace is cool but I get seasick, so I was planning to go over and join the Green Party. They take the fight to the street," she said admiringly.

I had come dangerously close to igniting another protestor. What the hell was I saying in those lectures?

"Instead, my boyfriend wants to get married," she glanced at me with a ferocious, pure True Left Rosen look, "which is *totally* bourgeois and outdated," but the fire faded then, "but it's important to him, so I'll do it."

True Left Rosen was going to be a pregnant bride. With all that I had experienced in the previous month, this topped everything for sheer surprise. "You might know him," she was saying, "he's in our class. Dan?"

"Dan?" Conservative, dumb Dan? My jaw dropped again. "Oh," I got out. I would have believed Judith had emasculated Dan with a cat food can before suspecting they'd coupled.

My office was dead quiet as I tried to figure out which of the many things I was thinking of saying were acceptable or useful. Judith's life taking sharp, sharp right turns. Judith pregnant. Judith married. "Forgive me for however this sounds, but does Dan have a job?"

"His father owns a fuel oil distribution company," Judith said, unoffended, "I think he's doing pretty well, and Dan's been working there since he was sixteen. He's got a really cool car." The baby? "His father is overjoyed. His mother?" she shook her head. "But I'll be doing day-care and getting back to school, like twelve hours after I birth this critter," she smiled confidently.

There was still this paper. "Judith, about this paper," I brought the topic back. "It still needs to be addressed. Professor Medeiros will presumably put this before the faculty senate. If you wish to take part in the process, I encourage you to—"

"No offense," she interrupted me, raising her hand, "Professor Dumont, but I really, really don't care." She stopped, her eyes tearing up again. "Fucking mood swings," she cursed, pulling out another tissue. She blew her nose, wiped, then struck out of the blue. "What would you have done if you hadn't become a history professor?"

"Huh?"

"There must've been some point where you were thinking of doing something else, right?" she asked, searching for signs of intelligent life. She was clearly discouraged by what she found. "Like, I wanted to go for a graduate degree in history, up until about this semester."

Is that my fault? I wondered.

"It's not because of you," she said, so I must have telegraphed that one. "I'll tell you why. I have a roommate who's really cool. We like books, we like the same music, she's very intelligent, she was thinking of coming with me to Oxford. She was going to major in French, but last summer she took some programming classes in C+ and Java." I knew that those were names for programming languages, just as I know some Latin names for plants. "She's not going to finish her degree," Judith went on, "because she's already been offered a job as a contractor, programming web sites. She's starting at roughly sixty thousand, though that doesn't include benefits, and she can work from home on snowy days, which would be perfect for me, with the little monster." Judith searched my face. "How long did it take you to earn sixty thousand a year?"

I was hoping to reach that with my next raise. I cleared my throat. "What's your point?" I asked, a little brusquely.

"I know what you did," Judith said bluntly, looking at the paper on the desk.

"I'm sorry," I said. I was hoping that would make me feel better, but it didn't. "It's incidents like this that cost teachers the respect of their students."

"Oh, I didn't really lose respect for you," she said reassuringly. "I feel sorry for you." If her first line stuck the knife in, that line twisted it. "You guys are in danger of losing your jobs, right?" I shrugged. "Well, you were trying to survive, and I can understand that. It *is* kind of sleazy," she said, with a hint of disdain that made me blush, "but put it all in perspective," she said. "You wanted this," she said, indicating our surroundings, and she looked at it as though it was a small, battered apartment in a bad neighborhood, "that badly, and that paper could do it for you? So be it."

In my own defense I wanted to tell her that it was my irresponsibility with the Weathermen that had saved my job, not my irresponsibility with her paper, but I was being granted absolution so I shut up. I thought of her pregnancy, of Dan working the dispatch desk during the

January cold, which was actually a good place for Dan. Judith at home in front of some souped-up computer, doing all kinds of odd programming, the money rolling in and her little girl sitting in a playpen, wearing a Greenpeace t-shirt. Then I thought of Carl dead, of Rose injured and in hiding, of my own legal problems. I thought of the History Department's unjust deliverance based on my misadventure. If only I hadn't panicked and plagiarized, the innocent would have escaped and only the guilty face trial. "And you?" I asked.

"I'll finish my degree next term, before my water breaks. And when I come back, I won't need that term paper to get where I'm going," she assured me with a touch of True Left. Neither of us tried to say where she was going.

I thought, you're going to have this baby, and within about five years you'll go to graduate school, probably in Massachusetts. You'll learn programming, but you'll earn a degree in Sociology, maybe something more political, concentration in Women's Studies. You'll probably write a great book and it might be on women or it might be on raising children. But you'll do something wonderful, Judith, because it's in you and it's got to come out.

"No," she said, "history is really entertaining," and the word shot through me like a bullet, "but I'm going to try a couple of business courses. Maybe someday own my own company."

"I said that out loud?" I knew my mind could be porous, but not transparent.

"S'okay," she said, smiling, "it was nice. Chauvinistic, but a sweet chauvinistic. What you need, Professor Dumont, is to get a life." She got up, kissed me on my cheek, and strode purposefully out of my office.

When I'd snapped out of my shock I emailed Sheila that Judith and I had spoken, and I wanted the plagiarism issue put before the senate. Five minutes later Sheila emailed me back. 'Peter, let's wait and see how the courts deal with you before you submit to the lions of Hawthorne. I don't want you gone, for what that's worth. Sheila. P.S. Judith stopped by earlier and told me she intended to 'give you' her paper. Want to go halfies on a nice baby shower gift????'

When the Term Ended

Mrs. Krajewski arranged a private burial ceremony for Carl, and called me the day before the funeral, three days before the end of the term. "I know he listened to you, Professor," she said, in a voice both tired and heavily accented, "and that's why he's dead." She paused, primarily to let me squirm, then went on, "but he respected you, and I think he'd like you to be at the funeral. If you wants to come, you can come." She gave me the location and time then, assuming I'd come.

I went. I was buried in final papers and tests and grading, but I could hardly not go. I wished Rose would show, not to take the heat off me but because I wasn't sure she was still alive. The police had trailed her blood, and that disembodied voice I heard was drugged or exhausted. So I wanted to see her, and thought if anything drew her out it would be Carl's funeral, but I knew she was far too smart for that. She was still the subject of a manhunt. And when the Weather Underground went underground, they went deep. No contact with family or friends. No letters, no phone calls. No visits. No birthday cards. No marriages, baby showers, graduations, funerals, absolutely no contact. It was too much for most of the Weathermen back in 1970, and most surfaced within months. Rose endured it for thirty years; this sad day was just another hash mark. I knew she wasn't in the crowd, but I still looked, in vain, for clues of her presence.

We had a warning of snow, it having become December, and the air was freezing but we were spared a snowstorm. The radio was playing Christmas carols on the way, and I stopped in a drugstore for aspirin and the Christmas promotional stuff was blocking the aisles. It made the funeral seem that much sadder.

The police didn't send anyone in uniform, but I know they had plain-clothes around. The ceremony was in a flat, suburban lawn of a cemetery near Stoughton. The lawn was smooth and featureless, with recently planted saplings dispersed evenly across the landscape. The groundskeeper's building could've passed for a dowdy brick house. We've become dull, even in death, I realized. Only a fraction of the land was in use, and the graves were marked only with metal plates; Carl was an atheist but his mother was burying him Catholic. He was in the military reserve, and while the circumstances of his death and what the military now knew about him ruled out a military funeral, three men in uniform did attend; they were probably pals of Carl from Westover. They kept to themselves and left after the service without speaking to anyone. I guess they had a lot of questions too, and no one to answer them.

Linda came with me, and I was relieved that she did. She was quiet, looking beautiful, a little disconnected, but then she'd never met Carl. She was elegant in her black dress, and she made me proud to have her by my side. We skipped the service—actually I was so damn late getting ready we missed it—but were in the second row at the gravesite. The casket was closed, as Carl's crash had marred his face. His mother, accompanied by a man her age I didn't know, walked slowly with the aid of a cane from the funeral director's black limousine to the grave, where she settled slowly and heavily into the reserved seat.

"I'm Father Graca," the priest introduced himself to the gathering. He was closer to my age, mostly bald, heavily dressed in his black robes of office, which swayed gently when the cold wind pushed. "I'm sorry to say I never met Carl, and I know that his life was a hard one. His death was premature. Maria Krajewski has asked me to say a prayer for Carl. Let us join in the Lord's Prayer."

Linda remembered the Lord's Prayer, so I lip-synched. I could see her breath frosting in the cold air, and we squeezed each other's hands through our gloves. There were maybe twenty people there, most of them friends of Mrs. Krajewski. The Weathermen, for reasons already disclosed, did not send representatives to their members' funerals, and in 1999 I wasn't sure there were any left anyway. And, as I said, the only one I knew of didn't show.

Father Graca said a long benediction, then sprinkled holy water over Carl's casket, stepped back and bade us go in peace. Then the three soldiers lined up in front of the casket and, without speaking, all stiffened, smartly saluted Carl's casket, turned parade-perfect on their polished black heels, and marched off. Remembering Carl's wistful wish of a second turn around that he might have spent in uniform, I felt myself slide into a deep hole of sadness. There's something terribly sad about a military uniform at a funeral. Especially at that one.

Mrs. Krajewski didn't cry; I imagine she'd done a lot of crying over the years, and maybe this one day was less sad because at least she knew where her son was, and would remain. I stood in line to set a rose on Carl's casket, and passed by Mrs. Krajewski quickly with just a murmur by way of condolence, as I suspect we both preferred. Linda squeezed my hand again as I walked away, and I realized my eyes were streaming tears. "He pulled choking kids out of the tear gas. He protected Rose and he never cashed in. I think I'd rather be cremated," I whispered as we got into the old Toyota and slowly drove away, "and scattered somewhere nice."

Back to the living: we drove slowly back to Framingham. We stopped for lunch at a great diner just down the road from the college. I was composed again by the time I got out of my suit and into my khakis, and headed up the hill to continue the end of the term ritual. The walk felt shorter, as though time had become compressed. Death had just touched me, refreshed my sense of priorities, and the important and the trivial were reorganizing. Then I saw Winfield, and he smiled and asked, "get your cards?" Oh Christ, I thought, the punch cards.

To fully appreciate this ritual, a little history lesson. Hawthorne computerized its records decades back, which was a wonderful thing. They invested heavily, very, very heavily, in a state of the art (1978) 'mini' computer that sits like a fat beetle in the subbasement of the Computer Operations department. It needs a constant temperature with constant humidity, and the closer to the bowels of the earth the better. In 1978 this made Hawthorne look very technologically sophisticated, and we won some awards from some technology councils.

The machine—labeled 'the Thing' by computer science students who had to maintain it—has been kept running every semester since. Like a 1956 Chevy cruising the streets of a provincial town in Latin America, its parts periodically wear out and are replaced (with greater and greater difficulty, because, to continue the metaphor, it's hard in 1999 to get parts for a 1956 Chevy). Unfortunately, it runs, though the tasks it takes a minute to execute are now performed in microseconds by laptops. It also takes data only in the form of punch cards. We have many modern computers around here, with keyboards. For a reason heavily dependent on the original contract and the state bureaucracy, we are expected to use the Thing until it gets completely amortized, i.e. paid off. Erich, our guru, says the repayment plan called for very low payments for a very long time. Using the amortization table of Simon Legree, payout is finished in roughly five more years. Could we do the grades on our current machines? Of course. But the cost to use the Thing is now down to something like .005 cents/grade, and some damn bureaucrat insists that the Thing, which has actually been quite durable over the decades, be used because it is now more cost effective than a laptop. I think another factor might be that the college has an entrenched staff dedicated to punch card operation and that they will be pensioned off about a day after the Thing has its plug pulled. In the mean time, we fill out student's grades on punch cards.

So, on the last day of the term I collected my punch cards from the Registrar, imprinted with the name of a student on each card, and I was returning to my office with a brand new No. 2 pencil to punch out the hole for the corresponding letter grade. It wasn't really a hardship to make up the punch cards, it was just silly and antiquated. It gave us fuel for jokes, suggestions that we go to electric light soon, that the college's next investment be in nuclear power, etc. I was trying to come up with a fresh one for the faculty lounge when, in my left ear, I heard, "Professor Dumont!"

Now, if you think I got off easy with Judith, this will renew your faith in blind justice. In the waning hours of the grading period we hear many desperate calls, and this one sounded quite familiar. I turned, and saw Art jogging across the Faculty Parking Lot, book bag on his back. He was too far away to hear me swear, "oh shit." I really had no choice, once eye contact had been made, but to wait for him.

"Professor Dumont," he gasped when he reached me, "I need you to sign this form." He heaved the book bag off his back and unzipped a pocket, fished in it and pulled out a sheet of paper that had been folded into matching trapezoids. I took it and glanced at it. CHANGE OF MAJOR was boldly printed across the top.

My whole day took on a fresh, bright sheen. "Change of major, huh?" I asked, trying to sound neutral, neither exultant nor pretending disappointment.

Art nodded quickly. He was nervous. "I…" he was studying the form, "decided that the field…that history is really cool but…" he looked me in the eye finally, "there's a lot of competition. For jobs. In history."

I met his look with a sympathetic, serious smile. "Yea," I said, "a degree in History, outside of public school teaching," and I saw him shudder, "is a tough degree to market." And with Judith's memory still fresh, I tried to picture Art in five years, a couple years after he would earn his Bachelor's. History degrees don't translate to high-paying jobs, not like programming or business or the potential pay-off of pre-med. Almost the only employment path a history degree creates is teaching; in that respect we're perpetuating our existences. I've run across former students as retail management trainees, UPS deliverymen, bartenders and so many jobs we both knew didn't require a college degree. Art was on the fast road to student loan payment crises. "Do you have another major in mind?" I asked, to be polite.

He nodded, looking very serious. "Journalism." I nodded. Another low paying career. Frank Giramonte was one of our two full-time journalism professors. I owed him a warning call. "Journalism?" I said, respectfully, "that's very interesting stuff. And your coursework is good preparation. When do you plan to start the courses?"

"I'm starting the spring session," Art said, his conversation taking on suspicious new life, "and I'm hoping to transfer some of my history coursework. That's the other thing I needed to talk to you about." I tensed; he'd said nothing about 'another thing'. "See, since some of my history courses are transferable I am getting some credit. But Professor Giramonte suggested I start with an independent study with him." It was already too late for Frank, I realized. "And his first suggestion was that I do an in-depth interview with someone. He suggested," and I felt rapidly rising in me the soul-withering dismay Art has triggered in the past, "you."

Frank rapidly plummeted from my Pity List to my Fecal Scroll. "You probably have had the most significant," he heavily stressed it, "experience of anyone in this college this year. Is there a time I could interview you?"

I certainly couldn't say no, though I stood there a moment, breathing deeply, hoping for a...traffic accident, perhaps. Then, "o-o-okay." I looked off at the distant tree line, then glanced at my watch; Art was still there, looking expectant, and there I was, now looking foolish. Finally I thought of one more delaying tactic. "Let's do this...not now," I emphasized, looking thoughtfully at the tree line—trees are very relaxing to look at—"but like, a week after the trial, so that the story has a clear ending." It was the longest postponement I could think of. Waiting for the next holiday season would make no sense to him. He nodded agreeably, disappointed at my unwillingness to draw up a tree stump and spin my yarn.

"I'll really miss your classes," he said, almost with a straight face.

"Art," I began and realized I was going to try actually speaking to him, "can I give you a little advice on writing?" He nodded dumbly, as would any student, though he hadn't come looking for advice, just a lousy signature. But after my first successful writing experience of the decade I had begun thinking about my teaching. "You and I have the same problem in writing. We want to be funny and still get the point across." He looked a little insulted. "I haven't been able to write anything worth reading for the past ten years." His look became more sympathetic. "I think the trick is to try skipping the jokes. Brevity is the soul of wit." Was that my best advice? "One good joke on a page that flows with the story will have more punch than the five you struggle to plant. I'm trying to take that advice to heart. I wanted to pass it on. Good luck," I said, and offered my hand.

"Thanks, Professor," he said, and a light went on where I would have bet my pension one wasn't even wired.

"And drop by my office in a month or so, my legal headaches may have minimized by then, and we can do an interview," I promised. And then I half-heartedly considered calling Lawyer Joe and asking him how many delays and continuances were available.

Actually, when the term ended, my life went into limbo. The day after Carl's funeral I was formally charged with conspiracy to assault, which was a felony, barely, and some lesser charges the police would drop the moment I produced Rose. Joe plead me 'not guilty'. "I'm assuming we can get them down to no jail time," he said, "but right now they'll try to make this sound like it deserves the death penalty to get good press."

Normally I taught the first summer semester, but that was out of the question as I prepared for the trial

Jim Falcone stepped away from the case, as it was now in the District Attorney's hands, but he talked to me every couple of days, sometimes calling Linda first, then asking to speak to me. Usually he was looking at some part of our adventure and had a question to ask; "where did you buy the laptop?" and "did anyone other than Leon use the wire-transfer software?" "If you can deliver Rose, all charges will be dropped," he reminded me every time. "Otherwise, you're our only live body."

Leon had been a tasty morsel for the states in which he'd committed wire fraud, but he hadn't actually been in the plane or on the Common, so he was, so to speak, not a target. By December he was already starting his first stretch as a guest of the state of Maine, which would be followed with tours of Massachusetts and then D.C.

From the outset the trial seem less than real, less than threatening, given what had actually happened. We wanted to blow up General Westmoreland's statue, then the man himself. What we actually managed to do was dump paint on a librarian in uniform and a stalled Hummer. It was hard to believe I was going to do anything but stab litter with a pointed stick for a few weekends over that. As the tabloids had more and more fun with it, it began to be embarrassing. Like it or not, Carl's photo and mine, if not Rose's, would be on the same page with Squeaky Fromme's. It was more of a footnote in history than I would have voluntarily left; sometimes there's more dignity in anonymity.

What worried me more than Joe was when the Army filed charges against me. They made a show of appearing in court to file for a change of venue, to request that I be tried under military law, and talked to any reporter who would listen about Leavenworth in the summer. "They're full of shit," Joe reassured me, "the judge will dismiss this as soon as they get finished signing off on the forms." He was right, the judge did, but I was a miserable soul for that four days.

Army down, Federal government up. Lawyer Joe and I spent a couple of days in my home as a few inches of snow fell, going over the facts. "This is called 'discovery,'" Joe explained, "which means we get to see any evidence the government has on you." The government had pulled data by the giga-byte from my computer and the college's, zip drives of downloaded email, ten cardboard boxes crammed with photocopies. "It could've been worse," Joe said, "I was defense counsel on a patent violation lawsuit, civil suit between two companies, and they filled a room this size with paper. That's a common tactic, to bury you in paperwork." As it was they filled the corner of my dining room.

He had done a cursory review already. "So far the most interesting reading I've found," he said that first day as he opened Box #35 and pulled out a bulging manila folder, "is this file on Hawthorne's SDS activities. Your name came up quite a few times."

I blushed. It was, before this, the closest to fame I'd come. "What do they say?" I asked, in the same gushing voice anxious starlets use on Opening Night waiting for their theatrical reviews. He fished out a couple of clippings, and I was disappointed to see they were all from the student newspaper, circa 1975. I was a lowly lecturer then, and a damp sort of firebrand.

The first clipping was from a rally—I remembered it—being held for a draft-dodging student who had returned from Canada under President Carter's clemency program. "Someone actually came back?" Joe asked. I had been one of about twenty people who'd spoken that day. The student was actually from UMass Boston. "Why did you hold a rally for another college's returning draft dodger?" Joe asked. "It was college, it was Opening Day, and Hawthorne had no baseball team," I explained. The other clippings were articles about other people connected to the Weathermen or Vietnam or the Sixties, and there were obligatory calls to me for comments that, in retrospect, could have been deleted to spare the paper. In one case the Peter Dumont in the story was wanted in connection with a Peeping Tom incident. "This one's wrong," I indicated.

"Good," Joe said.

"What other sort of evidence do you think they have?" I asked.

"Well, they caught Leon so they have his telephone records. And you've been pretty cooperative, right?" I nodded. "So anyone you mentioned was questioned, and we'll have a record of that. The real heart of this investigation, and of your defense, is Rose." I nodded wearily. "When did Rose first contact you?" Joe asked, and I sighed, because Joe was starting to sound like the FBI, asking me the same question repeatedly, listening for changes and inconsistencies.

"In my classroom." I repeated the story in poorly controlled singsong boredom. "She and Carl were together. They asked a question about my book, I was taking them to my office, and when we passed their van they gassed me with ether and, I assume, threw me in the van. I woke up strapped to my own kitchen chair."

The next day Joe came by with a Fedex package. "Where do you think Rose and Carl have been living for the past ten years?" he asked with a mischievous grin.

"I don't know," I said defensively. "I think they said they'd been living in the Northeast."

Joe nodded. "Easy, cowboy. Let me help. She was a beautician?"

"And Carl was a mechanic," I added.

Joe continued, pulling a thick envelope from the FedEx box, "I finally got copies of his records from the Reserve. His home base was Westover." I nodded. He retrieved a photocopy with the Air Force seal on top. "The Reserve had three addresses for him. The first two were apartment buildings in Springfield and in Westfield, but there are no tenants now that remembered them. The third address was a P.O. box."

I nodded dumbly. "Oh."

He set the box on the table and popped open his briefcase. "The college's record keeping isn't very good if you need to go back more than ten years. This morning I was finally able to get Thomas Rose's records from Hawthorne. His family's last known address was on Salem End Road."

Salem End Road was just down the street from the college; it was so named centuries ago when refugees from the Salem Witch trials fled to Framingham. I was stunned, that Tom Rose, who had grown so large in my life, had grown up literally down the road. Somehow that had never come up. "Did you call them?" I asked, suddenly anxious, for no reason I could pinpoint.

"Yea," Joe said, "there've been two owners since. Nobody knew much about Thomas. Neighborhoods change fast these days." I guess he hoped that the news would jog some dormant memory of mine. It didn't. And he left me hanging on that revelation, damn him. He flipped over page two of his legal pad. "The police called the state licensing bureau for beauticians. There were two Rose Thomas'."

"Two? Well, it isn't that odd a name."

Joe nodded. "First one works for a Blaine Beauty Academy in Waltham. Second one listed a Framingham P.O. Box." My eyebrows rose.

"Really," I responded. "Post office boxes were standard procedure for the Underground. I'm surprised it was in her name, though."

"It wasn't," Joe noted, flipping through a thick sheaf of photocopies from the state police file. "It was to 'Carla Tortelli' who, if memory serves, was the barmaid in 'Cheers' but the police got Rose's name on some mail when they opened the box."

"Still sloppy of her," I criticized, "probably got tired of coming up with new birth certificates and social security numbers just to get her monthly allocation of junk mail. Doesn't mean she actually lived in Framingham," I noted. "In fact, I would guess she did not live in Framingham."

Joe nodded. "Police apparently agree with you," he mumbled, his eyes, assisted with half-lens reading glasses, roamed quickly down a page. "They tried a door-to-door with her picture," he said. "Cops had some surveillance photos from the Plaza Hotel. Nobody remembered her. Though that could be the gender change." Another dead-end.

At the end of that day we had completed reading the police files on Carl and Rose. They had little beyond her license for cosmetology and her application for the P.O. Box, the contents of the PO box for the past month, which was, indeed, mostly junk mail. "Anyway, no utility bills, and I guess," he flipped another page in the report, "they ran a check on her name with the utilities. Wherever she lived she either didn't pay the bill directly or paid under another name." I nodded, a little proud. Rose wasn't going to be caught by a slip-up so elementary as a name on an electric bill.

Otherwise, they had her file from Hawthorne, which was also slim. She had completed three years, paid for by her parents by check, then dropped out. "Did you find her parents?" I asked. Joe nodded. "Her—his—mother's dead, when she was a teen. This," he handed me two pages, "is from her father. Thomas Rose, practicing attorney, now semi-retired to Boca Raton, remarried to a widow."

"So Rose was originally Thomas Rose, Junior," I deduced. "How'd the father take the information that he's a she?"

"Badly. Father disowned him or her decades back and wasn't feeling any more paternal," Joe summarized.

Chronologically, the state police file picked up then, with additions from the FBI. Most of their entries were actually newspaper clippings, with 'Thomas Rose' underlined or touched with hi-lighter, his name one of several. Then there were some internal FBI reports, detailing attendance and discussions at SDS meetings. In the last meeting, in Carl's dorm room, there were four reports, all by different informants, all reporting that Tom and Carl had announced they were joining the Weathermen.

"Y'know," I said, glancing over the report, "it looks like there were maybe ten people in this meeting."

"And four of them were informants," Joe said. "So there was Tom, and Carl, and Leon. Couple others whose names never showed up again. The other four, including David, their cell leader, were FBI informants."

"And that was just little Hawthorne College," I said. I wondered what legions of informants the government must have wielded. "Their security sucked," Joe noted. "You'd think the spies might've compared notes afterwards to avoid repetition."

"None of them knew each other. The Panthers were right," I said sadly, and Joe, confused, smiled politely. After Carl and Rose dropped out of Hawthorne to join the Weathermen, the FBI had more clippings and reports of their attendance at demonstrations, and then reams of paper on the armored car heist and cop killing, concluding that 'Rose and Krajewski would likely be apprehended near the Canadian border', finishing the file. Then the air was suddenly still, like we'd run through a cave that turned and twisted, and we had turned a corner and found the end, a wall of stone. It was anti-climactic, and we were on a trail turned cold.

Joe discussed various strategies we could consider, but ultimately if the FBI didn't find Rose by the time I went to trial he advised me to change my plea. "D.A. said he'd go with three years, suspend all but three months. And you'll do that in one of those upscale joints, probably nicer than this neighborhood."

I nodded. Joe packed up and said goodnight.

She'd grown up down the road, I remember thinking that night, and I put on boots and coat and hat and stepped outside. Linda was working late, doing an inventory. The media had left me in peace by then. I walked carefully down my unshovelled driveway, the snow crunching underfoot. Looking into the night sky, seeing the fat flakes dropping gently around me and into my face, I smiled. There was nobody out, so I cleared a pathway on the sidewalk and walked down the road to the address. I started to feel the cold, but it has long been a point of pride to me to belittle New England winter compared to the Buffalo winters I cut my teeth on. I found Rose's childhood address. It was a condo building now. There was a supermarket encroaching on its backyard. Cars were lined up on the side street, waiting for a difficult left turn. I turned around and walked back.

I'm going to compress some more here, which just reinforces my fundamental laziness in writing. I never went to trial. We found a flaw in the state's case. Actually, my wonderful, beautiful, sexually desirable fiancée Linda found it.

My trial was scheduled to begin on April 15th. With Rose's whereabouts still a mystery, Lawyer Joe had gone back to focus on my files amongst Mt Paper, which now made a stack four foot, seven and three-quarter's inches tall. "Most of it is from your days as a lecturer at Hawthorne, when Tom and Carl were in your classes," Joe summarized to us the Wednesday evening before the trial. "Today they also provided, very tardily, their judicial permissions for the wiretaps they've been running on your phones."

"It's about time," I said, angry, "did they think we couldn't tell? They must have done the tapping with paper clips. I almost asked them how they liked their coffee. If I learned anything from the Weather Underground, it was paranoia. Assume they are listening." I was getting a case of jailhouse blues. Although I'd been assured by Jim and Joe that my worst-case scenario would be three months in a very nice correctional facility, jail was jail. What would send me up the river was a stack of paperwork ten feet tall and eighteen years old that itemized my radical teaching, my calls for the overthrow of capitalism, for youth to rise in violent revolution, i.e. my desperate and successful struggle for tenure. I would go to jail for doing my job, so to speak. "I may have asked this before," I asked that night of Linda and Joe, "but is the fact that there isn't a scintilla of originality in any of that," I indicated the pile, "a defense?"

Linda was supportive throughout, following Joe's discussions as though her own butt was on the line. That evening she was leafing through one of the thick folders labeled SURVEILLANCE—PETER

DUMONT. I had leafed through it and had abandoned it in favor of another file I'd found of news clippings, which were more interesting. She was reading one stapled sheaf in detail, flipping back and forth from the second to the first, then to the third page, then back to the first. Then she studied the date stamp and got up and came back with the calendar, which she flipped back to October. Then, each word an announcement, she carefully said, "this is not right."

Joe and I both put down our readings, as Linda hadn't said much, which made her words very noticeable. "What is it?" I asked.

Linda frowned. "This is a conversation between my mother and I."

Joe set down the papers he was holding, rubbed his tired eyes and said, philosophically, "it's an unpleasant side-effect of police work, Linda, but they invade privacy in the course of their investigations."

She frowned and nodded. "I know. But this list," she picked up the page that listed all the judicially approved phone taps, "lists all the phones that were tapped, on which days, for this case." We listened and she displayed the papers in her hands as she spoke. "They've got the house phone, they've got Peter's phone at the college. They had my phone, though I was living here for the most part. They've got the phones at the Park Plaza that the Weathermen used. They triangulated most of the cellular calls. There's a couple here I don't recognize. But they don't have a tap listed for the bookstore phone. And that's where I was when I had this talk with my mother," she indicated the transcript in her hand, "at work. In my teeny tiny office."

Joe's eyes narrowed, as they seemed to see a bright light. "Let me see that," he said. "It's," his eyes flashed through the text, flipping the first page back, and then the second, "it says you," he looked at me, "have house guests, and that that's really unusual." He smiled, glanced at Linda, who blushed, then at me, "I'm paraphrasing. You have house guests, and Linda is also very surprised by your sudden trip to Washington. This," he checked the calendar again, "took place the day after she came back and first spoke to you after the Weathermen had contacted you," he summarized. "That means..." he was lost in thought for a long time. He got up and sorted through other piles, through two of his well-used legal pads, checked the calendar twice, and seemed to gain speed at each step. Then, after reading through the transcript of Linda's call to her mother, he smiled the biggest smile I'd seen from him. "That means we've GOT them!"

The short version, which is the only version I understood, is that if the police improperly gather evidence, then any information they learn and whatever comes of it, is known as 'poisonous fruits'. They cannot use as evidence anything that proceeds from evidence obtained illegally. And, in the list of judicially approved wiretaps, the police clearly neglected to ask permission to tap the bookstore's phone that day.

Joe carefully prepared a case for dismissal, based on the illegal telephone wiretap. There was an element of poetic justice. When the Weathermen went underground in 1970, many of them were facing charges from dozens of courts. Almost all these charges were eventually dropped in the following decades as Weathermen resurfaced. A lot of the more important charges—conspiracy being a big one—were based on information learned from illegally tapped telephone conversations. Illegally obtained evidence freed almost as many Weathermen as did bail bondsmen. So getting my own ass free on a 'technicality' was, in fact, a very poignant homage.

It was almost certainly a typing error, a clerical glitch. If the police had asked the judge to tap the bookstore phone, I expect the judge would have consented. He consented to all their requests. But they forgot to ask. The police struggled, of course, and Joe did go to a half-day lawyers' meeting and he came home that night cursing the Boston and State police up, down, and sideways. "They should drop the case." Instead, they postponed my trial until August.

We did overdue Christmas shopping. Linda visited her mother back in Detroit for a week, and the night before she left I gave her the diamond engagement ring I should have given her years ago and formally asked her if she would stay with me forever. Linda flew off with a smile and when she landed her Mom called me to ask, "when?" I got Linda back on the phone and we agreed to wait on a date until my legal problems cleared up. Christmas came, usually a pretty downbeat day for me, but much happier with Linda. Jim came over, we watched some TV, and I listened to cop stories until Jim and I began to be friends.

On December 29th the state postponed until October. Since I'd already arranged to take the spring term off to prepare for my trial I asked Joe, "how long do they expect me to put my life on hold?"

"They don't give a shit," he said, "but I smell a rat." Two days later they asked the judge to continue it until January of 2001. And that was when the judge insisted on knowing the problem with the case. Since so little had actually happened, since my role had been so peripheral, the momentum to try me was waning. Other crimes had occurred since then that people were now angry about. When she was told about the 'clerical error' the judge banged her gavel twice, and on New Years Eve I was a free man who had to start writing a book or face a $45 thousand dollar legal bill. I called Winfield and said, "I can do two classes after all. I need the money."

"Good, because I never cancelled the American Radical history course," Winfield admitted. When I asked why, he said, "to tell you the truth, Lincoln Philbert came up and begged me for the chance to teach your Weatherman class. Even he can tell it's hot stuff. I'd rather you taught it. Now don't get upset," he heard me struggling for a good epithet, "I wouldn't actually let him teach it. Hell, with everybody watching, I was going to teach it."

I read the transcript of Linda's talk to her mother. At the time Mom was convalescing at home and mother and daughter had a long—hour and a half on the company phone—heart-to-heart. I'd not met Linda's mother, since she lived in Michigan, and I guess after eight years she suspected I was a bum, so when the question 'where's the relationship going' came up, probably not for the first time, Linda did her usual hedging. Mom, having had a dose of the ICU, used her new leverage—"I want to live to see my grandchildren". (It's there. It's in the transcript.) Linda defended me pretty well. She was also wondering where the relationship was headed. Nowhere, it was clear to Mom. Thanks Mom; your suspicions got me off on a technicality.

It was January 4th when I received formal notification that all charges pertaining to the 'incident' had been dismissed. Linda and I were married on January 10th, in a very private ceremony, and Winfield was my best man, and our honeymoon was my long overdue visit to meet her family in Detroit. I had a week before the semester started. The plane ride to Detroit was quiet, the plane half-empty, and I asked her a question I probably should have posed prior to our vows. "Can I ask you a question I should have asked prior to now?" I began. She looked at me, and before she could answer I asked, "what do you see in me? Why have you stuck around with me? I just don't deserve someone like you." I really had my heart in my hands, where it had never before been.

She smiled, and her eyes teared up, and then she started to shake with suppressed chuckles. A few escaped. "You are so funny," she said, chuckling some more as she hugged me.

"But it can't just be that," I pressed my point. "Can it?"

She pursed her lips, and then whispered in my ear, "I also happen to think you look like Richard Dreyfuss, and he is the sexiest man alive. Okay?"

I nodded. "Let's rent JAWS when we get back. Maybe I'll see the resemblance."

"No, hon," she said, gently, "not Richard Dreyfuss at twenty…"

Her mother stood four feet three, and was slightly hunched over, and I wanted to call her 'Yoda'. Blue hair styled in waves and piercing dark eyes, she looked at me for at least a minute after our introduction before she spoke. Now I know what 'being examined' is all about. I could read her mind: my daughter could have done better, and I agreed. I was grateful she hadn't. Linda cued me in advance when Mom offered me a glass of homemade wine. I was to compliment it, for Mom was very proud of her vintage.

It was sterno, liquid fire. I couldn't breathe enough to compliment it, it was all I could accomplish to clear my throat and draw a laboring breath. "Smo-o-o-oth," I got out, and Mom was still howling with laughter ten minutes later. After that we were cool. It was a long weekend, during which I met most of Linda's hundred and forty-three thousand cousins, all named Jill and Stan. Detroit in the winter reminded me of Buffalo, the rust belt under snow, and even Linda sighed with relief when we rolled back East.

In the week before our marriage I got three recruitment calls, one from the Chair of the History Department at Brown University, in Providence, another from the History Chair at Berkeley, in California, and one from my alma mater, the University of Buffalo. I was offered an interview for a tenure track job at Berkeley, I was promised immediate tenure as an Associate Professor at Brown, and Buffalo dangled a grant in front of me. I could become their first Winslow Chair in Modern American History, which immediately doubled my salary and allowed me to do things like sabbaticals and conferences and less teaching.

I was being 'courted' for the first time in my life. I knew at the outset I would disappoint everyone, but it was a nice week. A damn nice week. Winfield called me seven times, and would have called me seven more if I hadn't promised him that none of the kind offers was going to be taken seriously. I knew quite well that taking any of those jobs would mean I had to become a real scholar, and a real teacher.

In my early days of job-hunting we A.B.Ds (all-but-dissertation) were like hungry ferrets sniffing the air for telltale traces of employment. Having the phone ring, rather than dialing and trying to get past the secretary, was a true rush to my ego. I talked on a conference call with the Chair in Berkeley and two members of their Search Committee. I drove down to Providence and spent a very pleasant day shaking hands and hearing compliments from the hoi polloi at Brown. But Berkeley wasn't that interested, and when Brown heard Berkeley wasn't really interested they lost their interest. That left my alma mater.

The job in Buffalo was tempting, and Linda got a little anxious, but she swore it was my decision to make. I flew up there for a day, we got down to dollar signs and were discussing sabbaticals and they were talking about all the great research they knew I would do (!), and the Dean of the History Department presented me with a nameplate, presumably to be affixed to my new door, there. "That's very…" I never finished that sentence. Doctor Philip Lawrence was the Chair at Buffalo. He had earned his doctorate at the University of Florida, had taught in some other warm climates, and during both of my visits made endless comments about the winters. "You're from around here, aren't you?" he asked at least three times in his Southern accent, "so you're already prepared for the winter."

I sensed the minute I walked on the old Main Street campus that I couldn't go home again. The tall snow banks didn't bother me, but I had grown soft in my fifties and didn't want to shovel a lot of snow. I tired of hearing Lawrence go on about last winter's snowfall. "Y'know, Watertown gets twice as much," I mentioned offhandedly. Linda winced on the phone when I compared Buffalo's offer to my current take at Hawthorne; Buffalo would be giving me ten thousand over Hawthorne, but I had to earn tenure again, and I knew that meant more publishing.

"But you don't really like to write, do you?" Linda reminded me. She knew damn well writing felt to me like passing a bowling ball, but like a sixth toe or third nipple it wasn't usually discussed; that's when I knew how much she wanted to stay at Hawthorne. And I wasn't going to become a scholar again. Even if another renegade student from my early days showed up at my doorstep I couldn't repeat the experience. I'd just send him to Lincoln Philbert. Lawrence invited me to a partial-faculty meeting (the ones he could scare up before their semester started) and it made Winfield's faculty meetings seem like meetings of the Algonquin Round Table.

So I called Lawrence to thank him the day after I returned. "But we made you a name plate," he jested, "in New York that'll earn you palimony." He was good about it. "It's the weather, isn't it?" he kept asking. Where do you get faculty from, I wondered, Hudson's Bay? I have since been monitoring CHRONICLES IN HIGHER EDUCATION so I'll know when Lawrence cracks and makes a break for the Deep South.

I finally explained to them that I had to write the damn book—which was how it was now referred to, 'Damn Book'—to pay my legal fees. Depending on how the book came out, they could call me after it was published. That made Buffalo content. It made Winfield very happy, as Winfield had read my writing.

Rose

The Damn Book took just three weeks to write. I only had to teach one course and I threw all my spare time into the word processor. I worked late and rose early. I was a man possessed. I've never written anything so fast, or so easily. I just knew that I needed to write it all down before it left my memory. Scribbling notes to myself for a year and a half meant I would dissipate my thoughts and never recapture the ideas or the energy. And I wrote from my memory, not from a pile of books or a stack of index cards (I had, after all been reading for this for over a decade). Instead of struggling to tuck in quotations from the voices of the sixties, I wrote instead of voices from the nineties. They spoke for over three hundred pages.

But I had some blank spaces over what happened to the Weathermen in the Maine woods. So I went up to the minimum-security lockup in Maine Leon was doing time in to interview him. I called him first, and he sounded happy to have a visitor besides his wife. When I showed up the next day, I was escorted into a room with a long table with a Plexiglas divider in the middle, telephones on either side, pretty much as seen in modern movies. Leon had grown a beard and lost weight. He smiled and waved at me when I entered the room. "Leon, thanks for seeing me," I said, and got out my tape recorder.

"Twenty bucks," he said, still with the smile, "twenty bucks a question."

"What?" I said. "I'm not CNN. Are you serious?"

"Am I going to get any royalties from this?" he asked. "Twenty bucks a question."

If he'd been truly smart, instead of a twerp, he'd have gotten an agent and negotiated for real money, and without Rose or Carl available as sources I'd have given him more, but Leon hadn't gotten to his current station in life through an excess of foresight. Although historians, by nature of their usually deceased subjects, rarely have to pay in cash for information, I should have seen it coming. "You might have warned me," I complained. Digging out my wallet, I already knew I was carrying just twenty-two dollars in cash. I opened it wide for him to see. "Take a check?" I asked. He shook his head. And I knew we were half an hour from any town that might have an ATM. "You might have mentioned this before I got up here. I could have brought more cash." I held out the lonely twenty. "This is it."

He shrugged. He probably would have been happier if I'd only brought ten. "How do I get the money to you?" I asked. He waved at the guard.

"Give him the money," he said. "He'll get it to me. Ask your question."

The guard probably wasn't supposed to do any such thing, but he did. I set my briefcase on the chair next to me and pulled out my legal pad of questions. I'd written up about eight questions to fill in gaps I had in my chronology of the adventure, as well as getting Leon's version of Tom and Rose's antics in the sixties. "Give me a minute," I asked, rewriting a question, scratching two others out.

"Don't bother," Leon said, "you want to know what happened in the camp, because you weren't there, right? And you never got to ask the other two." He told me his version. I took his account and added a big grain of salt. It certainly made him seem heroic, but when I asked if he really had grabbed a shotgun and fought off the entire militia while Carl and Rose ran for the seaplane, he had a little temper tantrum, hung up his phone and indicated the interview was over. Fortunately I was able, some weeks and lots of paperwork later, to see portions of statements the Maine State Police got from Leon, from Walsh, and others they questioned. When I got the full picture I figured Leon owed me change, but I never tried to collect it.

The only part of the story for which I had no first-person account was the actual attack; it would have helped the book if I could've interviewed Rose.

The typical scholarly, historical book has hundreds of footnotes. At the end of the book are citations for all the books the author read to write the book; usually this bibliography goes on for a quarter of the book. My book had fewer citations than a celebrity biography. It wasn't, after all, a historical study. It was first person, autobiographical in parts, and more journalism than history. I did cite the police records I had to dig through, though they aren't readily available to the public. Altogether my entire book had the shortest bibliography of any scholarly text I've seen in years. I added a dozen that I considered repetitive, because Winfield read the final draft and worried that, without fifty books, I'd be considered shallow.

Some thought so anyway. When it was finally published, RETURN OF THE WEATHER UNDERGROUND was modestly successful on the East Coast, where the New York Review of Books deigned to mention it but didn't review it. When it was published in August, the Boston Globe sent out a young man to interview me in my office. He was in his twenties, and apparently barely knew the distinction between 'Weatherman' and meteorology. He photographed me in front of my Woodstock poster. I tried to smile, but I might have been cringing. I also got interviewed via telephone on Public Radio in Seattle, Washington, where the Weathermen had been legendary, and that summer I attended a dozen book-signings in Boston and New York. It would sell thirty-five thousand copies in hardcover, more than Winfield's best book! (and probably another hundred copies when Barnes and Noble remaindered it for 75% off the cover price), and with the advance, for the first time in my life, I would actually have enough money to buy a new car and not finance it. We would put most of the money into some modest mutual funds and I knew I could afford to retire a little sooner than my department chairman.

But I'm getting ahead of myself.

On a Sunday night two weeks after Christmas, freezing, with a gentle snow flurry falling, Linda was on the computer trying to upgrade our Windows software and I was reading an old FBI file on the Weathermen for possible class reading, when the doorbell rang. After the stream of media and others, I prepared to deal with another irritation. Opening the storm door, I flipped on the porch light and saw a fellow in his late twenties, early thirties, thin and maybe six feet tall, a little taller than I am, and both pate and jaw sporting several days of stubble. I remember thinking 'he must be chilly' without even a ball cap on that bald head. He wore jeans, a hunting jacket, sturdy shit-kicker boots, and he had his hands tucked into his coat pockets. His eyes were red rimmed, as though he hadn't slept well. "Can I help you?" I asked through the door.

I could see a pickup truck at the curb, but I couldn't see its license plates. "You Professor Dumont?" he asked, with a Midwestern twang.

I glanced to my right, where I'd come to leave my cordless phone. "Yes, what can I do for you?" I asked, testily.

"Do you know Rose Thomas?" he asked, and still I couldn't get a reading from his face. He didn't sound angry, didn't seem obviously disturbed, yet he wasn't delivering flowers.

"I knew Rose Thomas," I emphasized the past tense.

He looked left, right, then down at his boots, and we were at an impasse. "Can I come in? I'm Walter Schneidel, Junior. D'you know who I am?"

Within the blink of an eye I remembered the name: the cop Carl killed in Ohio. Junior? "What do you want?" I asked, shifting to the right and grabbing the cordless; my thumb was on the first function button, to call 911.

"I'm not going to cause any trouble," he said, "I just need to see Rose Thomas."

"Well she's not here," I said, letting him hear my exasperation. "If you've been following the story in the papers," I said, keeping my voice as officious and neutral as possible, "you know she's missing. Nobody knows where she is." He stood there, as though he didn't speak English. "I know who you are and I can," I paused to pick my words, "guess why you want to see her, but she's not here."

"Can I come in?" he asked, this time somewhat plaintive.

Linda had certainly endured some strange encounters in this marriage already, I thought; one more won't hurt. "Sure, come in," I said, and opened the door for him. "Can I get you something? Some hot coffee?" He nodded and thanked me. Linda having the habit of keeping a pot available at all hours, like a good convenience store, I led him into the kitchen and poured him a cup and he held the mug in his winter-dried hands. Linda came out at the sound of a strange voice and I introduced them. "Walter's father was the officer killed during the hold-up Rose and Carl pulled."

"Oh," Linda said softly. She looked at him as though he was ten. "I'm so sorry," she said. He blushed as he probably had for much of his life, said it was okay, thanks. She said to me, "I just got the computer working again. I'll be, uh, in there," she finished and left us.

"Walter, you may or may not know that I'm a history professor—:

He smiled. "I know all about you. It was in the papers. You're the one got those kids all angry about the government." He was taking it pretty well. "I wanted to talk to you, too." I sat across from him and waited. He took a swallow of coffee, licked his lips, and set the mug on the table. "I'm the only son," he started. "I was only eight when Dad was killed." He was looking into the cup as he spoke. "I've grown up with stories about how the hippies killed my dad, and how the hippies were robbing, stealing credit cards, hitting up their rich Commie friends, and dealing drugs to pay for their drugs and shit." He looked at me. "Were they stoned when they killed him? Were they getting drug money?"

"No," I answered. "The Weathermen did abuse LSD a lot, but I've asked Rose what they did with the money, and they sent most of it to the lawyers to pay for court expenses, bail," I said. "They weren't stoned. The money wasn't just to live off and get high."

He nodded. "So this was a kind of a fund raiser?" He wasn't making a joke, near as I could tell.

I made sure not to smile or show any mirth. Yes, Walter, instead of holding a bake sale, they robbed a bank. "I guess you could say that," I said.

He leaned back in the chair. "The police department had insurance, and a lot of people donated money and stuff, so we weren't pressed too hard growing up. And I kind of got extra slack, still do, because of what happened." He was clearly tired of that extra slack. "I'd trade every speeding ticket, every bad night I've gotten away with to have a normal life," he confessed. "My dad was not a bad guy." Those weren't glowing words from an orphaned son. "But I remember he came home sometimes pretty," Walter pursed his lips, touching sensitive memories, "he used to beat up my mom. And me, too. Once he used a belt on me, the buckle, because I lied about playing when I should've been doing homework." Walter sipped some more coffee. The wall clock ticked from the dining room. "We didn't even see much of Dad's family after he was killed. I think they blamed my mother somehow. My Uncle Sal, my mother's brother, taught me about hunting, and how to drive." Smiling, "bought me my first beer."

I smiled, grateful eternally that there are Uncle Sal's out there.

"But when I saw in the paper that these hippies had showed up again," he returned to the topic at hand, still not visibly angry, "I kind of felt like people expected me to come and," he looked at the refrigerator, then at a picture Linda had hung of two cats sitting in the sun, "set accounts right." Closing his eyes, rubbing them, he added, "but I'm not sure I know how to do that. How would you do that?"

It was my turn to lean back in the chair. How to set matters right so he could go back to Ohio and continue to life among friends and family, without whispers that his father's killers had surfaced and he'd done nothing. I whistled gently. "That's a tough question, Walter. Carl is dead, there's nothing else you can do to him," I said. "And Rose is wanted by the police for the murder, so if—when she's caught, she'll be behind bars for the rest of her life. Wouldn't that be the right ending for a cop's family? The law prevails."

"Sure," Walter smirked, "if the cops could find her. She's been free for thirty years. I got a feeling she can outsmart the cops. But if someone she knew, like you, were to help her get caught?"

I hadn't seen it coming, hadn't even guessed at Walter's intent. And I was trapped in my sympathy. I must have looked shocked, perhaps offended. "Help her get caught?"

"I'm sorry," he said, seeing my reaction, "I'm out of line. I appreciate your time. Maybe you could just…think about that." He stood. "Thanks for the coffee. I'll just see myself out." He left, pulling the door shut behind him, and his truck started a minute later out front, all the while I sat in my chair, looking at my own winter-dried hands, thinking.

Just before the semester began I panicked and asked to skip American Radical History. "But it's going to be a huge draw," Winfield begged, "it's already filled. It's got a waiting list." None of us had ever had a waiting list. That honor was reserved for the computer programming courses and our certificate program in HVAC (Heating, Ventilating, & Air Conditioning), whose teachings the students could actually earn money with.

"I need to rethink the course outline, Winfield." I was talking to him on the phone. "I have stuff I have to cut, and I'm not sure what to use in its place. I need a semester to tinker with it." In truth I didn't want to teach the course again. I'd been looking for more balanced material in current literature but I'd struck out. In the end, Winfield prevailed, and I agreed to stick with it and teach it, somehow.

I did enjoy my moment of celebrity; all of my courses filled, with waiting lists. I lingered for an hour on the first day in the Faculty Lounge to make sure as many of my cohort as I could arrange saw my enrollment list. Sheila gave me a smile and a pat on the back, Winfield teased me a little, and I had a little more bounce in my step than usual.

I still remember, vividly, that first meeting of American Radical History, that cold Tuesday in late January. Every seat was filled. That had never happened before. I ran out of handouts somehow, though I'd made ten extra copies. "I'll get more, uh," I struggled to concentrate on the basics, "you can come to my office later or," I never finished that sentence. The room had a little more noise when I stepped to the podium and clearing my throat didn't silence everyone. "Good afternoon," I announced, my nervous stomach gurgling aloud like bad plumbing. The room fell silent. "This is American Radical History." No one blushed, rose and headed for the door. "Four, eight, twelve," I tried to count them, but I was rattled and in the back of the class the seats weren't aligned in rows and I lost count in the thirties. My roster said forty-two, but they were notoriously inaccurate. I'd expected thirty-two. I must have had fifty in there. It looked crowded. I scanned the names and, as in past semesters, saw familiar last names; sometimes these were the younger siblings of students I'd taught. Well, this semester the course would be at least a little different.

What were they all expecting? They had signed up for the course taught by the professor that hung out with the Weathermen who were wanted for dive-bombing the Common. Were they expecting me to denounce Amerika? Were they expecting me to champion downtrodden minorities and call for the Socialist Party to take over the White House? Were they hoping I'd howl like Jerry Rubin or Abbie Hoffman, leading them in a march on the administration building?

If I did, would they follow?

I decided the answer to all the questions was probably 'no'.

Getting my wind back, I started again. "On the handout I have listed my office hours and my phone number, and my email," I said, surprised by the quaver that made my voice sound scared. Clearing my throat helped, a little. "I do respond a little faster to email just…because." I looked at the list of lecture topics and the readings assigned. "The topics are pretty much accurate. There isn't a textbook for this course, which should save you all some money. I do put a lot of articles on Reserved Reading at the library." I looked at them again; they were attentive and waiting for something. "As I understand the new Copyright Law you can each make a copy of the articles for your own reading. But if I catch you selling them on the street corner the Copyright Clearance Center will have your hides." That got some polite smiles and a few chuckles, which helped me ease up.

How much utter confusion should I confess to? The handout was last semester's. I was changing the course on the fly. The first half was almost the same, but when I got to the Weathermen I was going to have to scrap everything. I'd adopted some shrill material and I had to go back and look at the primary sources again. "The readings for the first three sections, up through McCarthyism, are correct. The ones for the Sixties will change." And why hadn't I updated the syllabus? "I haven't updated the syllabus because I had some…extenuating circumstances of late—"

A student in the second row giggled, then started clapping. And then the entire room was clapping. "Yeah extenuating circumstances!" someone cheered. I stood there with my mouth open, preparing to say 'but I promise to get them to you in adequate time for class preparation'. Never got to it. I endured their applause for a few moments. I held out my hands to quiet them. "Thank you for your understanding," I said, and knew I was beet red all over.

"This course begins with America in 1918," I began the first lecture, and they obediently started taking notes, "and finishes with…" Oops. My old lecture dropped out from under me like a California highway in an earthquake. "We are going to explore the roots of modern radical politics in this country," I tried again. "Who knows where it will end?"

I always left a minute—and only a minute—at the end of each lecture for questions. Ordinarily there were none and I cut them loose. That day I got up to the Palmer Raids, "under the presidency of Woodrow Wilson, Attorney General Palmer directed FBI raids on hundreds of American immigrants on January 2nd, 1920. Homes were entered, people were arrested, all without warrants. The FBI was out to nip the Communist Party in the bud, and since trade unions were considered Communism, they went out with the bath water. Two hundred and forty people were deported." I paused. "Questions?"

The girl who had laughed, then initiated the applause, raised her hand. "Your name?" I asked in my most professorial tone.

She had short black hair and a pleasant, common Irish face atop a mature but somewhat tomboyish body. Perhaps because overalls were 'in' that semester. "I'm Midge Costello, Professor Dumont. I'd like to ask you about your own experiences last fall. Why did the police drop their charges against you?"

I started to answer, rejected my first choice, rejected my second choice, and then just stood there. "My…I had a good attorney," I answered, feeling apologetic for my flippancy. Midge looked disappointed, and I saw something of Judith Rosen in her, and that stirred me to a better answer. "I got off on a technicality," I said. Joe had advised me to say nothing about the boo-boo for fear of further attention from the parties that had committed the boo-boo. "Which is really all I can say about it. Not that I was guilty of doing anything except holding a video camera."

"Were you a Weatherman in college?" asked a young man in the third row. Finally, finally, *finally*, someone asked that question. And he looked like a radical-in-training. He was trying to grow a beard, wore John Lennon-style glasses, Doc Martens black boots with yellow thread, and his t-shirt said something about 'Smash—' something.

And now was time for me to be more honest with an American Radical History class than I had ever been. "No, I wasn't a Weatherman." He looked a little disappointed. You ain't seen nothin' yet, I thought. "I also wasn't in SDS." I saw some glances exchanged as to what 'SDS' was. "I didn't march on Washington, either for civil rights or to end the draft. I visited it last spring, with three former Weathermen, but as a student I was never active in radical causes." I let the raw honesty float through their minds; it was a little more than they wanted to hear.

He looked aghast. "Did you *support* the government during the war?"

"No, I certainly didn't support the government's war in Vietnam," I answered. "Like most young men in the Sixties, I was scared of being drafted, but I didn't do anything about it, besides pray my college deferment held." That admission took thirty years of accumulated guilt off my soul. I felt better that day in class than I ever remember feeling. By joining the revolution in late innings, I could admit I walked by it when it was just begun. "I hope by the end of this course you will have more facts and fewer illusions about America and radical history." I knew then that I had popped whatever illusion I'd allowed or encouraged to grow about my life in the Sixties. "Any other questions?" None; that was more like it. I walked out of the class feeling a thousand per cent better than I'd expected.

And I'd like to add that, while the enrollment dropped by a record fifty-two per cent that semester, the drop-outs didn't leave the first week, they stayed until the first major test; and since it was over-enrolled, the course simply found its usual level at twenty-three students. It also reminded me that I hadn't changed that much Detective Klees called me on Martin Luther King, Jr. day. I'd had no contact with the police for over a month and my guard was down. "Detective Klees?" I said, as though she was a telemarketer at dinner-time; I sounded rude because I was panicked. "You must be low in seniority to be making calls on a holiday," I joked to ease the stress she'd triggered.

"Well, as you know, the case is closed," Klees said, sounding neither frustrated nor relieved, "but I was wondering if I could ask you some questions anyway?"

I'd gotten off in part by being cooperative. They could still charge me with something, so cooperating was still my best policy. I took a long swallow of beer. "Sure," I said, closing the People magazine, "what questions do you have?"

"What recent contacts did you have with Rose, prior to your abduction?" Klees asked.

I listened to that question for a moment. Was there a trick there? Some double negative phrasing that I might stumble over? Cautiously I said, "I didn't have any recent contact with Rose until she abducted me."

"That's right," Klees answered, as though discovering that very fact in her own notes. "Have you had any sort of contact with Rose or other Weathermen since the abduction?"

'The abduction', which irresistibly reminded me of anal probes. "No, I've had no other contact with anyone associated with the Weathermen."

"To the best of your knowledge, are the Weathermen still organized in cells?"

Ah-ha, I understood. She was fishing. With no bait, on a bent straight pin, in a swimming pool. "They organized in cells thirty years ago," I answered, treating her now like the student newspaper writers that called me for commentary on Sixties stuff. "I don't know of any active Weather Underground cells today."

"What did you think Rose was referring to when she announced the 'Reconstituted Weather Underground'?" Klees asked. "Is she recruiting more radicals?"

Now that was a damn good question. "Honestly, I have no idea," I answered. "Are you concerned that she'll try something else?"

She turned the question back on me. "Have any of your students approached you asking about how to join the Weathermen?"

"Uh…" I'd answered a lot of questions from students, some from Art's interview (yes, I finally had that interview, and Art just might have found his niche) that got published as a feature in the student paper, some emails, some from students loitering around my office. There were some young potential radicals who clearly admired the Weathermen, who made banners and hung them in the student union, who gathered to protest racism and raise the campus' consciousness about political prisoners in our penitentiaries and U.S. policy wrongs elsewhere in the world. But Hawthorne's newest crop of radicals were, like their predecessors since the mid-seventies, deprived of the kind of immediate, frightening monster that Vietnam had been to the Weathermen. Without a good enemy, without something that upset people, radicals have a hell of a time converting the comfortable and the complacent. So I'd gotten some questions on how the Weathermen first organized on campus. Big deal. Perhaps I could spare Mike Kennedy of the Doc Martens, and his cohort, the indignity of surveillance until they were at least sure they wanted to be radicals. "No, nothing of that nature," I lied.

"Have any other former Weathermen contacted you since?"

"No," I said, for the second time; I was used to the repetition. "Who were you expecting?"

"Well," Klees sighed, "I did a little digging, and the only member of the Weather Underground I could find still at large is Joanne Chesimard. Is that your understanding?"

"Chesimard was not a Weatherman," I corrected her.

"She wasn't?" Klees asked.

Chesimard had had a very high profile career with the Black Liberation Army, heirs to the Black Panther movement. Wounded in a 1973 shoot-out with New Jersey troopers, convicted of killing one, she was sprung from jail in what was described as a 'daring, well planned raid'. The Weathermen did spring Timothy Leary, but they probably didn't spring Chesimard. She may have received aid from Weathermen en route to her current life in Cuba. I considered her the last true living radical. "No, I don't know of any, certainly none that were felons. Why do you ask?" Was Klees looking for a career-advancing bust?

"Did Rose ever have any contact with Joanne Chesimard?" Klees was pleading.

"Not to my knowledge. Her name never came up." Klee's fishing had, by then, eased my panic and turned it to sympathy. "They complained early on that their old contacts had declined to join them," I said. "Most of them settled down and didn't want any more trouble. I don't think Leon Michelin was Rose's first choice in digging up help, he was just the only one they could find." I tried again to take control of the conversation, "why do you ask?"

"Why do I ask," Klees repeated, sniffled a little, and for the first time I realized she might be a little drunk. "They were about political change, weren't they?" I agreed. "I mean, they were trying to change a system that was racist and…and there was Vietnam too." I felt better about Klees then. "Just between you and me, Professor Dumont, I kind of miss the Sixties."

I didn't. The Sixties were scary. Picture Hawthorne's students demonstrating against the Iraqi embargo and National Guardsmen show up and shoot live ammunition, leaving dead students on the grass; Hawthorne students try to build bombs to blow up the Army recruiting office in Framingham. Picture angry, wounded veterans of Desert Storm in long beards and wheelchairs throwing medals at the Pentagon; picture last season's presidential conventions struggling to maintain order with pitched battles in the streets. The Sixties were scary. "I understand," I said to Detective Klees, because I knew she didn't.

On a warm, pleasant Saturday afternoon in late March my phone rang, and it was Jim. "Peter? Rose Thomas was filmed by a bank camera trying to withdraw seven thousand dollars from Commerce Trust in Worcester." Oh shit. "She was using the same software Leon Michelin had. That's how we knew she'd be there. I guess the software is dated. The banks have been watching for it, and she must have run short of money and used it. Has she contacted you?" he asked.

"No," I said, checking my answering machine, "not yet."

The laptop was destroyed in the plane crash, but Rose was a competent computerphile and apparently had copies of the software and access codes. In a rare mistake, she got sloppy and used the same codes. Leon having spilled his beans, the police had warned the regional banks. Then the police had a burst of cleverness and asked the bankers not to block access, but to alert them when it was used.

Rose penny-looted three banks just as Leon had. When she picked up her winnings, the bank camera zoomed in. Despite the rotten quality film, Rose was identifiable.

I expected to see her again, but not in my basement.

Actually, she could have been down there for weeks if she'd been fairly quiet. I forget sometimes about the basement. The washer/dryer is down there, but in a small, enclosed room at the bottom of some steps off the back door. The biggest part, last visited by a plumber a year ago, is hard to reach. I've accumulated a stack of boxes of Christmas ornaments and some old boxes of books and old clothes I intend to donate to someone someday, all up against the inside wall, covering the door to the rest of the basement. Otherwise the basement is only accessible by going through the outside bulkhead doors. They aren't locked, and that's always been my backup in case I lose my house key: go through the bulkhead doors and somehow shove my way through that wall of boxes. Anyway, Rose got in through the bulkhead doors.

Linda found her first, and I'm grateful I wasn't present for that, because the sight of Rose hog-tying my wife would have tested my sympathy for Rose. When I came home Rose had her tied up and gagged with duct tape in my kitchen chair; deja vu. Linda had heard a noise, one I would have dismissed as squirrels (in the basement?), then made her first, abortive trip through the bulkhead. Linda is a healthy woman, but Rose had been a man, and I guess that extra muscle kicked in. I untied my wife, gently pulled the duct tape from her mouth and introduced them. I was, for the first time since my doctoral advisor insisted on me retyping the bibliography for my thesis, intensely furious. "I'm sure each of you has heard about each other, through me," I said, "Rose, what the fuck are you doing here?" Without waiting for her answer I continued, "this is my house. This is my wife. You have just committed felonious breaking and entering." Then I remembered Rose's rap sheet: murder, assault, etc. "Whatever."

Rose was sitting in a dining room chair when I came in, her right leg rigidly straight. Linda, standing and easing muscle strain, looked at her captor and said, "Rose? You are so dead." Linda was nursing her shoulder. "She grabbed my wrist, put me in a hammer-lock," she hissed at Rose, "and pushed me to the ground!"

Rose spoke, in a very tired voice, "actually you tripped. But I did kidnap you, and tied you up. I'm very, very sorry. I got the strong impression you would have called your brother the cop and I had to talk to your husband first. I'm really sorry." She looked to be holding back tears as she apologized to Linda, and it took a little of the edge off Linda's temper. "Dumont, can I speak to you in private?"

"No," I answered, still angry, "speak here and now."

She nodded. Her hair was died blonde, the gray roots clearly visible, and her hair was dirty and disheveled. Her dark sockets and eyelids barely half-open, together with her dirty clothes and some cuts and bruises reminded me that Rose had been on the run. She noticed my examination. "You know the story, Peter. You get older and the cuts and bruises don't heal so quickly," she said in a distant voice. She was about forty-eight, but that day she looked at least ten years older. "Peter," she started, her voice anxious, "Peter, could you and Linda possibly let me stay here for a day or two? I made a stupid mistake and I really have to go far away, but my leg hasn't worked right since the crash. They gave me a crutch but I can move faster without it. Just hurts like hell." Her hand was nursing her right kneecap. I saw she couldn't bend it. "Just a day to sleep and not walk? Please?"

Linda had gone into the kitchen for a drink of water, and when Rose was done, Linda set down her glass and said, from the kitchen, clearly and firmly, "hell, no." I looked at Rose apologetically. If Linda had been visiting her mother in Detroit, I might have ignored my own shaky legal status and aided a felon. Linda knew better.

"I thought as much." That's when Rose reached into her bag and pulled out the handgun. It wasn't a very lethal looking one, not with the rich array of firepower we see every week in the movies. "It's a twenty-two caliber," Rose said, "and, yes, it does fit in the palm of my hand. And it does shoot," she said. "Although it jammed once, at a bad time." Her eyes misted up again.

Linda came back to the living room. She was pale. "You bitch," she said, but she said it softly.

Rose apologized again, for holding us at gunpoint. "You know," I told her, "at some point, and this is one, apologies are bullshit." I had almost pissed my pants when she aimed that thing at me. "So now what?" Linda returned to the kitchen and began making coffee.

Rose said, "I just want some time to sit and rest." So we sat. And, given our respective personalities, we started going at it.

"Rose, what's it like?" I asked, "the gender switch?"

"I prefer not to be addressed as 'it'," she answered with her customary hauteur. Lame and exhausted, she could still summon indignation.

"Was Carl able to live with you for twenty years and never offend you?" I asked, my own exasperation surfacing.

"Carl was a gentleman," Rose answered, her voice dimming. She blinked away tears but more appeared. "For thirty years, with everyone we met and knew, he was the only one who knew I'd been born a man and...yet he never forgot I was a woman. He knew me so well." Her voice choked, tears spilling on her cheeks. Then she let the gun fall from her hand and she leaned forward, resting her head in her hands and her hands in her lap, and keened, tearing sounds that brought tears to my eyes, trembling in her spasms, a woman who had lost not her lover but her best friend. "God, I miss him!" she gasped between sobs, shaking.

She cried a while, then the sobs ebbed and left her looking sedate, glazed. I still hadn't gotten a straight answer to my question. When she thought to pick up the gun again I decided she was alert enough to continue our discussion. "Rose," I asked in my gentlest voice, "what was your first public experience as a woman like?"

"It was uneventful," she answered. "I didn't leave work Friday as a man and come back Monday as a woman. Carl and I were living anonymously in Europe. The first day I put on a bra was just an incremental step towards the change. You take hormone pills to begin the chemical changes. You wear women's clothing for months before any physical changes, to determine whether you simply wish to cross-dress, or if you need to change your gender. It takes months. The day I first walked outside after the major surgery I just felt the way anyone feels after major surgery. Weak, out of sorts. No one except the surgical staff and Carl knew who I was." She made eye contact with me, her puffy, bloodshot eyes still swimming in tears, "the person who could really answer your question is Carl. My turn?"

"Are we taking turns?"

"When did you sell out?" she asked, as though she were asking for the correct time.

"Do you ever lighten up?" I asked. She shrugged. It was an insulting question, certainly, but after the day I'd had it didn't sting as it would have just a month earlier. Still warming me was the memory of the best class I ever taught, my great moment of honesty. "If you mean, when did I stop accusing the government of lies and cover-ups, and warning my students not to trust anyone over thirty, it was also incremental," I said. I thought about it for a minute. "It started in 1975, '76. The college started getting a lot of Vietnam vets. They weren't your typical eighteen-year-old kids. They were older and they'd been away from home, and in the Army, and in a war. They knew enough to ask for what they expected, demand it if necessary." I hadn't thought of Donny Rizzo for over twenty years, but suddenly I could see him in detail, his shoulder-length black hair, his persistent stubble, the fatigue jacket he wore to class. "The most difficult one was Donny, Donny Rizzo. He was a grunt, and about twenty-eight when I got him in class. He took my American history survey class, and since I'm not a terribly demanding grader he took my American Radical history class." Linda was standing in the entryway to the kitchen, sipping coffee, and listening. "It was an odd time to be teaching college. We had students then we've never had before or since, because college is harder to pay for today and Donny was really just waiting to get into the union at Raytheon. But these guys had GI benefits and they could get a paycheck for coming to school, so some attended that probably wouldn't bother today."

"Do you know what happened to him?" Linda asked.

"I heard him say something about getting a carpenter's union card. Or plumber's. Some trade. Anyway, the political mood was in limbo. We'd bailed out of Saigon and nobody wanted to talk about it, except me, of course. I think I called the Weathermen 'Don Quixotes' at the time—"

"Which is a little kinder than 'failed revolutionaries'," Rose kibitzed.

"Yes," I agreed, nodding slightly. "Donny raised his hand and asked who 'Don Quixote' was. That was another difference between traditional students and these guys. Kids would sit there, silent and anxious, afraid of sounding stupid, then run to the library or ask their friends after class. The vets were much more laid back. Donny just asked. So I took a minute or two to explain 'Man of La Mancha', tilting at windmills, idealism flying in the face of realism, etcetera. Then he started tearing into the Weathermen and the draft dodgers and anyone who had ever done anything to a flag other than salute it. And what do I say in response?"

"Nothing?" Linda asked, smiling.

"Precisely," I answered. Shaking my head twenty-five years later, "Donny had an opinion, I did try to pull out the facts that supported it, and some of it was based on anecdotal evidence. The eternal 'friend of mine heard about this guy who…' whatever. I started picking on these 'unfounded sources' and Donny started getting really mad. Really mad. He worked up to personal insults. His buddy, Rudy, finally gave me a hand signal to shut up for my own sake. Which I did."

"Did you think he'd attack you?" asked Linda, frowning.

"No 'think' about it," I responded. "Donny had been in combat, and I heard some references to him having PTSD. The other guys had a buddy system to keep Donny from going too ballistic. He'd seen men die, and slugging a teacher was pretty trivial to him."

"But not to you," Rose said. She seemed almost understanding.

"He wasn't interested in hearing praise of any sort about the people who had been fighting against the war. Jane Fonda, for example, was a bitch who should die of festering boils."

"So you started changing your political stance to suit the mood of your class?" Rose prodded. "Was it fear of being beaten up by your students?"

"You may not respect Peter, and even though you're holding a gun, keep in mind you're in his house," Linda said, glaring angrily at Rose. I was surprised; more interestingly, Rose was surprised. She blushed and looked uncomfortable for a moment.

"It wasn't my courage," I pressed on. "And it wasn't just Donny. I admit I chose my words more carefully that semester and…did Donny drop out that year? I don't remember seeing him after that class." My focus drifted. "This is a pretty liberal state as a rule, and even here people were closing ranks behind the veterans, and the protestors just went quietly away. Trying to support the anti-war movement after the war, I felt like the Last Man Left Alive. I finally got tired of arguing with people. Some of them smarter than me. It became easier to teach the class if I cast the Weathermen in a harsher light. Fewer arguments."

"Fewer arguments means less learning," Rose lectured me; she had clearly recovered her emotional energy.

"My turn," I said, and Rose looked at me like a game show contestant facing the tough, big money question. Remembering my visitor of a January night, whose face and truck I hadn't seen since, I said, "Walter Schneidel."

Her lips pursed, her brows joined in a frown, and one moment she looked furious, like she was going to empty that little gun into me, and the next moment she looked utterly bereft, like she was going to empty that little gun into herself.

Linda looked at me. "Walter Schneidel was the cop killed during the armored car robbery," Rose said. She picked up her huge bag and pulled out an oddly stitched wallet of some material I didn't recognize. "It's a Brazilian leaf," she said, "save the rainforest, Dumont." Carefully extracting a piece of newsprint, she unfolded it. 'Officer Killed in Shootout with Robbers'. "He was thirty-eight years old, had been on the Conneaut, Ohio, police force for twelve years, and left a wife and child." She looked at it like it was her license, a familiar sight, then refolded it and carefully tucked it back inside her wallet. "We stopped the armored car in the plaza's parking lot. It was a Tuesday evening."

"Did you have a reason for robbing them on a Tuesday?" I asked.

"We needed money and it was no longer Monday," Rose said. "We waited for the truck, the bank was the last pickup. They picked up deposits from ten other businesses before, so we knew they'd have some money. We picked that spot to hit them because it was the most remote. There were only three shops in the plaza and traffic was minimal."

"Did you rob them coming or going?" I asked.

"Coming," Rose said, looking irritated. "We knew they'd have more money after picking up the bank's cash, but it seemed safer somehow not to try for all of it," she remembered, "we talked big but we were so scared. The truck pulled up to the bank, almost on time. We parked right on the curb, and the truck pulled around us, and, incredibly, the guy in the back opened the back door, right in front of us." Rose smiled sadly at the memory. "So we jumped out. We both had pistols, I had this," she indicated her .22 handgun, "Carl had a forty-four, which he stuck in the guard's chest and he dropped his pistol. A woman with a child walked by just as Carl and I got out, with our guns. She froze, she screamed this long, horrible scream, and then dragged her kid back to her car. I think that's what Schneidel heard, her scream. I got in the truck, found several canvas bags with currency, and as I was getting out, here came Officer Schneidel." Her face lost any warmth from the memory. "It was around sunset. He came from the southwest like a silhouette. He was yelling. We couldn't make out exactly what, undoubtedly something like 'drop your weapons' or 'police officer'. I shot first, a warning shot, well over his head." She sank back into the chair, sinking into it as though the memory had gained terrible weight over the years and was now all but crushing her. "He ducked behind a car when I fired, but then he got up and kept coming. Crazy thing is, all that time the driver was still up front. If he'd just gunned it and took off, I don't know what we would've done."

"Would you have shot the driver?" I asked.

"I have no idea," she whispered. "In retrospect, we didn't plan it well. Anyway, I was carrying three or four little canvas bags of money, Carl had a hand free," she added, in a softer, more distant tone. "According to the paper, Schneidel was on a paid detail, for a road crew down the road. They were just finishing up. In ten minutes he probably would've been heading home." She looked at me with a wry smile. "It's the ifs that give me the worst dreams. If the truck was on time the road crew would've been finishing up and he would've been busy directing traffic and might not have heard that woman scream. If the truck was on time we'd have robbed it and been gone before the woman came by. I dreamt once that he got into his Plymouth and was driving home, listening to country music when it started. If we'd robbed a place closer to the hospital, the ambulance probably would've arrived in time to save his life."

"If you hadn't staged the robbery, none of it would've happened," I said.

Rose gave me the bored look of a teen-ager. "When Schneidel was close enough that his pistol was accurate he fired twice, hitting the wall next to me. I don't think he saw Carl. Carl was behind me. My gun jammed, Carl jumped in to protect me. He fired."

"Fired six times," I recalled. "Emptied the revolver. Four of the bullets hit Schneidel."

Rose's eyes filled again, and the drops spilled down her cheek, leaving trails on her tired, hollowed-out face. "Carl was scared. His first shot hit the cop right in the heart," Rose shuddered. "But I guess it was momentum, the cop kept coming. I mean, he must have been clinically dead and still he was running at us. Carl was scared. He fired until the cop finally fell, then he fired once more." She covered her eyes and shook her head slowly, fingertips rubbing her eyes, squeezing out the tears. "You think of the odd things, over the years. I remember seeing that cop running. He was a big guy. Didn't look all that fat, but he was big. How hard his heart must have been pounding, how short of wind he must have been after running at least a thousand yards and yelling non-stop. He must have been out of wind by the time we…"

A school bus drove by outside, a couple of kids got off, laughing. The diesel motor roared as the bus moved on, and the sound echoed in the room.

Rose spoke again, her voice stronger, more assured. "Weatherman had declared war on the police, so in that sense Walter Schneidel was just a casualty of war like every dead Viet Cong soldier U.S. forces butchered. However," she said, "I sent a letter to Evelyn Schneidel, from Paris. I explained our reasons for the robbery, telling her how sorry we were that her husband had been killed."

"'Had been killed'?" I repeated. "It wasn't accidental. Roving dogs didn't attack him. He wasn't the victim of a meteor." Linda gave me an anxious look; Rose still had the pistol. "You guys killed him. If I were Evelyn Schneidel, given the tone of that letter, I'd have burned it." Up until that moment I not only respected Rose but also thought she was the better person of the two of us. Since then I've come to understand we are both just flawed humans. "Rose, some day you have to take responsibility for that man's death." Her eyebrows went up in surprise; this idea was new to her. "When you take responsibility for it, you're innocent. Until then, you're guilty."

"Are you volunteering to be my confessor?" she asked. "If so, I should warn you that, in the course of living underground for all these years, I've told a million lies, used many people, stolen money and property, illegally crossed borders, and lobbed a few grenades. And if I had to, I'd do it all again."

"Fine," I said. "If you still believe in your cause, then you're innocent, and the bad dreams will never end. Everything is political until you allow it to become personal. If you drop your banner, then you are guilty of everything, and your conscience can rest. Are you innocent?"

She nodded. "But I'm not without remorse."

"Well, someday you'll die," I reminded her. "If you never achieve your cause, you'll end up dying sad and bitter, to say nothing of sleeping badly, which probably isn't the punishment Evelyn Schneidel has in mind for you, but it's punishment, and if Shakespeare is to be believed, you'll come to wish that cop had killed you."

"Been there," she said.

We moved to the kitchen for coffee and Oreo cookies. Then the phone rang, and it was Linda's mother, and she took the cordless into the bedroom to talk.

"All of this leads me to something I intended to ask you," I said after Linda left the room. "I'd like you to speak to my class, to introduce the Weathermen section. Nobody can set the record straight enough to please you, except you," I said, and then I enjoyed watching her squirm, just a little bit.

"Speak to your class?" she said, surprised, "aren't you worried I'll contradict everything you've taught them?"

"I'm prepared for that risk," I answered; for the first time in many years, I was.

"You should be holding the gun on me," Rose said, and she smiled, blinking away the last of the tears. The idea appealed to her. In the first days of the Weathermen, when they believed simply announcing the revolution would make it happen, they invaded school classrooms to incite the students, minority students in particular, to revolt. Now she had an invitation. "If I do, can I put this damn gun away and get some rest?"

"Absolutely."

"What about her?" Rose indicated Linda.

"I think I can persuade her," I promised boldly.

"Okay," Rose said, "if you'll do one more thing for me. Take me to Carl's grave. I never got to say good-bye."

It was a major break with procedure for a Weatherman to risk identification by visiting a grave, but Rose was tired and, I think, less afraid of capture. Neither of us said a word on the ride down. Not sure I could find the grave, I drove through the cemetery once, trying to find the right section in my headlights. It was in the twenties, with a couple inches of old snow on the broad, barren lawn of the Stoughton cemetery. It was a sterile, desolate sight, not a place I wanted to be. Recognizing a section, I stopped. "I think it's around here. I wish they'd use headstones," I said. "Or some sort of sign listing who's where, something for these late night visits in the snow." Rose was sitting in the back so she could stretch her right leg out. "It's cold. Stay in the car," I said. "I'll find his grave." She whispered thanks.

I got out into the crisp air, pulled on my fleece-lined gloves and thought again of using my fading fame to land a teaching job in the Deep South. It was enticing, palm trees, four seasons of warmth. But it wouldn't save me from having to find Carl's grave in the dark, so I tabled it. By sweeping the snow from a lot of plates with my foot, and using the flashlight I keep in the car, I found Carl's plate.

Rose could have used help but she refused it. She opened the door and held it tightly as she shifted her rump off the seat, her leg straight out. As she was getting her good leg under her we saw headlights coming from the entrance gate. Both of us froze; the headlights rolled slowly towards us and we waited, motionless, as they rolled up to us, I saw an Ohio license plate. Young Walter got out. "Oh shit," I said. Rose held her pistol out of sight in her right hand.

"Good evening, Walter," I greeted him as he got out and came around the passenger side of my car. Walter was carrying a shotgun.

"Professor," he greeted me. "Are you Rose Thomas?"

"Yes," Rose said. Her color was bad, for any number of reasons. "Walter who?"

"Schneidel," Walter answered, "Junior. Did the professor tell you I came by once, couple months ago?" I hadn't. Rose gave me an angry, surprised look. "Yeah, I asked him to consider helping to bring you to justice. Is that what we're doing tonight, Professor?"

"Not what I was planning," I said, looking at Walter's rifle and Rose's pistol and my unarmed self. "We're here to visit a friend's grave. Can you give us a couple minutes?"

"Why not?" he said. And he shouldered the shotgun and got back in his truck. Rose tucked the pistol away. Together, slowly, we got to Carl's grave.

"Is he telling the truth?" she asked en route, out of ear shot, "you going to turn me in?"

"No," I said. "He came by in January, and I felt sorry for him, but not that sorry. I don't know what to do now."

"We'll visit Carl's grave," she said. The featureless patch of ground covered with icy snow in the dark got Rose crying again. She managed to sit on the frozen ground in front of the plate. "Carl," she said softly, "we never knew what to expect after death. I hope you can hear me." Thus does the seed of Methodism planted as a child confront the Marxism embraced as an adult. "It's been a tough time for me, but I'm hanging in there. I hope you weren't in any pain." She was quiet for a bit, perhaps speaking to herself; someone else might think she was praying.

As I was thinking of how warm my car's heater was, I heard her. "You were right," she said, and I didn't know to whom she spoke. "We made our statement, but if we've ignited something it will be years before we know the result. We have to have faith, I guess. You said not to expect anything soon, maybe not in our lifetime. Yours is over now, so I guess it's up to me now." She kissed her fingertips, then touched the plate, and in the glare of the flashlight I saw the veins and tendons and sunken flesh on her hand and thought, Rose is old. I knew what that made me. A minute later she struggled to her feet, grunted in pain, and said, "thanks, Professor. I'm starting to stiffen up. Let's go face the music."

He'd sat in his pickup to stay warm, getting out when we returned. "That's Carl, right?"

"That's right," I said. He saw that Rose's face was streaked with tears.

"So which one of you shot my dad?" he asked. "You or him?" he looked out at the grave.

"What difference does it make?" Rose asked. She was hardly able to stand. "We both fired at him. Not sure which one of us killed him."

"That's not quite true," I said. "Rose's gun jammed. Carl was the better shot. I'm sure he did it."

Walter looked bored. "That's kind of convenient, isn't it," he said. "But you're the one here." He had been holding his rifle by the barrel, resting the stock on his boot.

"And it's a cemetery," Rose said, "I guess this is a fitting place for you to exact revenge. Do you like to hit your game running, or should I stand still?"

Walter picked up his rifle, shouldered the stock, barrel pointed to the ground. He pushed two shells into the magazine, worked the slide to load one. I had, until that moment, somehow separated myself from Rose's plight. "Is that how you want to end up, Walter?" I asked, "in jail for murder?" Walter was poker-faced. "This isn't something you'll get slack on. Murder is still murder." I was then so tired of the trouble the Weathermen had landed me in I swore I'd go back to Colonial American history if I got out alive. Walter just stood there, holding the rifle, his finger resting on the trigger guard, not the trigger. "Walter, what would your father want you to do?"

"Blow your fucking heads off." He looked at me with the eyes of an angry child. "I'm not my father," he said. "I told you what he was like."

"So what are you like?" I asked; it was like using a Ouija board. I thought I could influence him but there was no accounting for the impulsive action of a stray spirit. "Did you grow up dreaming of revenge? Or did your friends and family talk about it for you? Is the goal to see Rose in police custody or to blow her head off somewhere in the dark?"

"Dad's family all wanted to blow her head off," Walter said, "but they were just stupid drunks most of the time. I dreamed of shooting you, when I was about ten. My Mom said she just wanted one thing." Rose was shaking with the cold. "She wanted you," he looked at Rose, "to come to my Dad's grave and admit your sin, say you're sorry, and ask for God's forgiveness."

For a good Marxist this was either the easiest or the hardest request. Rose nodded. "I'll do that," she said. "Is your father buried in Ohio?"

Walter nodded. "If we start now we'll be there by tomorrow, noon. I can stay up. I'm a truck driver." He saw she was trembling. "Question is, what happens after you ask for God's forgiveness. The graveyard outside Conneaut is out in the fields too. No cops for miles."

Rose shivered. It was in the teens by then and a cruel breeze was building and her coat wasn't lined. "Well, I guess I'll find out, won't I?" she said, then asked, almost meekly, "can we start tomorrow? I owe Peter a favor tomorrow morning."

Walter looked at me suspiciously. "She's going to speak to my class," I said, appreciating the absurdity.

Another chilling breeze swept past us, and we hugged ourselves. "Walter, would you be a good sport?" I begged. "Come home with us tonight and you and Rose can take off tomorrow, after my class?" It kept Rose alive one more night.

Walter wasn't happy with the delay. But I think he was tired from keeping a vigil on my house and after a moment, perhaps, of considering the long drive already short of sleep, nodded. "Sure," he said. "No tricks."

"No tricks," said Rose.

We drove back, Walter's pickup close behind the whole way.

Rose sat in the front row of my class and buried her face in a copy of the student paper, and I stood before the desk, as I always did, with my notes on a narrow podium. The twenty surviving students half-filled the room, and when the clock read a few minutes into the class I stepped to the podium and, suppressing a yawn from just three hour's sleep, cleared my throat. "Good morning," I greeted them with a smile, "today we are going to begin studying a radical group, one that I've had some personal contact with." Their faces went from studiously blank to alert. "The group was initially called 'Weatherman'. The name was taken from a Bob Dylan song, 'Subterranean Homesick Blues', and the line they borrowed from it went, 'you don't need a weatherman to know which way the wind's blowin'. That's for you budding music historians out there," I said, my dry professorial tone pretty much sucking the life out of the joke before it had a chance to bloom.

"My experiences this past fall were given pretty thorough media coverage, and I don't want to waste your tuition by repeating what you already know." Of course, if I'd been that conscientious at any time in the previous decades I shouldn't have bothered showing up half the time, but I was deliberately underplaying my introduction to make Rose's intro that much more dramatic. "I wasn't a Weatherman, or member of the Weather Underground, as it finally was known, or a member of the Weather Bureau, the leadership council." I had planned a joke, something like 'in fact, I don't even watch the Weather Channel', but I cut it.

"In fact," I paused, with a look at Rose, already the object of much surveillance in the room, "I have, in the past, described the Weather Underground in less than flattering terms. I was recently challenged to re-examine my opinions on them. The person who did so was a member of the group. I have asked her to speak to you, and we are very fortunate to have her here today."

It had been in the back of my mind since the day I rode with them to Washington. Were the Weathermen failures? Time is supposed to sharpen one's focus, to settle the murk and leave the water clear. We did pull out of Vietnam, let the Communists take it, and the Weather Underground scared Nixon so badly he directed the FBI to infiltrate them, produce counter-intelligence and otherwise fight them, a level of concern worthy of a true aggressor. But Socialist Revolution was less likely to come to fruition than the world of the Turner Diaries. So they weren't as successful as the Young Republicans or the NRA or the Moral Majority or George Bush…Jesus, has the right wing won *all* the recent fights?

But Weathermen did help stop the war. They rang the bell until people paid attention. The further one got from the war the easier it was to forget that. And after watching Carl give his life in a desperate attempt to make a political statement, I couldn't mock the Weathermen anymore. I had begun looking for a way to refresh that lecture. (It was also when I first realized that a truly awful teacher wouldn't have a conscience pinging him as often as did mine.) Having come to rely on videos and slides and other methods, I thought of how perfect it might be if I might someday get Rose in front of the class.

After giving Walter the couch to sleep on, the only hard part left was getting Linda to agree. We tied up Linda and left her in the bathroom. With the coffee maker and a small, portable TV. Actually, Linda could have broken her bonds—just a little masking tape, symbolic bonds—accidentally if she wasn't careful. After I begged her to let Rose and Walter stay the night so Rose could speak to my class before heading off in the truck with Walter, she agreed on the understanding that the minute Rose was done, all coasts being clear, Rose would run out of my life, forever. So it was a pretty good deal for me. And Jim would want to kill me, but Linda would talk him out of it. I really don't deserve her, but now I've got her, and I'm a much happier man. Rose got a good night's rest and a good meal—on the way back from the cemetery we got some Chinese take-out.

And, unbeknownst to Rose, I was recording her lecture for future educational purposes. The Man Who Did Not Go to Woodstock, Did Not Fight in Vietnam, and Did Not March, had finally learned to write and realized in the end that he did actually know how to teach. He just put too much emphasis on originality. Next step: tougher grades.

"Rose Thomas, who attended this college from 1966 to '69, is with us today as, possibly, the last living member of the Weather Underground. Rose," I surrendered the podium.

She set the paper aside, rose unsteadily, her leg still not bending or supporting her, but I knew better than to offer help; she'd leave me unsteady. "Good morning," she said, more as an announcement. "I am Rose Thomas, and as your professor explained, I was, and am, a member of the Weather Underground." She had debated that statement with me into the night. How do I claim to be the last of something, she agonized. Wouldn't it be interesting, I teased, if anyone else showed up with a membership card? "A few months ago, I took part in a political act of protest. A dear friend of mine, Carl Krajewski, and I flew a seaplane over Common and poured red paint, in lieu of blood, on an Army Hummer. Carl was killed when our plane crashed into the Public Gardens." She paused a moment. Already she had them more riveted than I ever would. "Our intended target was Retired General William Westmoreland. For those of you unfamiliar with his record, Westmoreland engineered the buildup of U.S. forces in the former South Vietnam, between 1964 and '66." She paused again, having done her introduction as an extended burst of energy, almost without taking a breath.

"Westmoreland is still alive?" The heckling came from a new student, Alfred Breiden, an outspoken if not well-informed young man. I suspected Alfred was using heckling in lieu of scholarship, and was waiting until he scored at Open Mike Night at the campus bar to abandon history for the stand-up circuit.

Rose took him at face value. "He is still alive. And, unfortunately, he doesn't travel much." I searched her face for a hint of humor and found…a little. She told them the history of the Weathermen. Rose had been in the Days of Rage and described it as brave soldiers storming the garrison of the evil empire. She also explained Weatherman's group therapy approach to throwing people out, where the chosen one was first criticized for days on end for being bourgeois. Then she explained her and Carl's adventures, their dash to Sweden, and then she skipped like a long-jumper over her sex change operation and I realized she never had mentioned Tom Rose. I guess he was long dead to her. Next thing I knew, she was explaining 'the legacy'. "We intended to target Westmoreland, and we did execute the plan, but instead hit another Army officer, unrelated to the Vietnam conflict," she finished.

Practically every student had a hand raised. Rose took to them like a seasoned press officer, nodding to a young woman, Connie MacCarthy, a fairly conservative young woman who I'd already had a run-in with. Connie was a devout Catholic who confused American Radical History with Right to Life; I had had to tell her explicitly to stop asking questions composed to incite debates about abortion. "Why did you choose to attack an old man with no connection to the Vietnam War?" she asked. I was relieved; I was afraid she'd ask Rose her opinion on you-know-what.

"As I said," Rose repeated, "we were trying to target Westmoreland—"

"But you knew before you attacked that he wasn't in the jeep," Connie pressed; that wasn't very widely known. I was impressed; Connie had followed the story.

Rose pursed her lips. Explaining the importance of symbols wasn't impossible, in fact she was in a good environment for it, but she hesitated. "I would have preferred to drop paint on anything or one with a direct connection to the Vietnam War, but they are harder and harder to come by. We had a brief opportunity, in the plane, and we..." she almost choked on the phrase, "did the best we could."

She called on Mike Wells, who was funny if not smart. "I don't know much about the Vietnam War," Mike conceded, "but, since it's long since over, why do you need to make a political statement about it? Don't most anti-war movements cease to be relevant when the war ends?" he asked, sarcastically.

Rose glanced at me; "no, I did not plant that question," I said. "But I'd love to hear the answer." She smiled.

"It wasn't Vietnam I was after, it was the memory of the Weather Underground," Rose said. "We were pretty much all the children of wealthy white people. We were raised in a time when being white and middle class guaranteed you would be raised comfortably and educated well, and you would have a good job and a comfortable standard of living. Being black or Hispanic meant being raised in poverty, barely taught to read, and being forced to go to a far off land and probably die for a government that had made you a second-class citizen." She smiled; the old dogma was coming back. "I'm afraid that there's not much today that I can point to to compare with that war. There are still slums, there are still enclaves of wealthy white families." She glanced around the room. "In fact, I don't even see anyone of color in this room."

It wasn't something I thought of as much, but Rose was correct; the entire class that semester was Caucasian. It isn't always, but they do dominate the campus.

Diane Heffler, a small girl with a rather soft voice who had been quiet thus far in the term, asked, "maybe the government knows better than to create such a conspicuously racist issue like the war was?"

Rose's eyebrows rose. "That's what I've been thinking since the eighties," she said, smiling at Diane. "Nothing has fundamentally changed. The government just knows better than to stumble into another divisive issue like the war."

"What about abortion rights?" Connie piped up; I gave her a dark look. "It's a fair question," she insisted.

"Abortion rights are a women's issue, and gender is certainly another form of oppression," Rose agreed.

"You mean you're 'pro'?" Connie asked in dismay.

Rose glanced at me again and I saw it coming and shrugged. "Your name?"

"Connie MacCarthy."

"Connie, are you aware of my personal history?" Rose asked in an innocent tone.

"I know about the Common," Connie said. The news had, surprisingly, not made much of Rose's gender change.

"When I attended this college," Rose said carefully, "my name was Thomas Rose." Connie's brow furrowed, then her mouth opened, then her nose wrinkled in distaste. "I've changed my gender. I absolutely believe that every woman should have control of her own body. And every man, too, for what that's worth," she added for the males in the class, who were mostly squirming uncomfortably.

"So abortion rights are pretty...academic for you?" Mike asked, and most of the class snickered, as Rose grinned and nodded. Connie was a furious pink, and I was a little surprised she didn't bolt the class. I already knew I'd get a nasty call from the Dean, and probably from the police, for hosting Rose; now I could probably add the Archbishop to the list. Good thing I had an answering machine.

Marilyn Bundy, a 'non-traditional student', i.e. mother of two, asked, "so what do you do now? Are you still in hiding?"

Rose glanced at the clock. The class met for an hour and fifteen minutes and we had about twenty minutes left. "Yes, I'm still in hiding, though I'm not doing much of a job of it this morning," she admitted. My class was collectively pole-axed; they had no idea a real fugitive was addressing them. "If you remember anything I've said today, I hope it's this," Rose said, setting to conclude. "Society as it exists is exploitative. The wealthy can only stay wealthy while most of us stay poor. That's basic. Karl Marx explained it over a hundred years ago and absolutely nothing has changed. When a country like the United States feels its wealth being threatened they go to war to protect that wealth. It could mean attacking a smaller country, or establishing military colonies. The Philippines used to be our colony, just as Israel is now." Ouch, I thought, add the JDL to the list. "The Weather Underground believed that the only way for everyone to be equal was for capitalism to collapse. We recognized that the major supports of this society were the armed forces, including the police. We attacked them to speed society's collapse."

"Is that why you declared war on the police?" asked Paul Buchanan, one of Winfield's seniors whom I'd scooped. Paul had been doing the suggested supplemental readings!

"Yes," Rose answered, her face stern, still defiant.

"But capitalism hasn't collapsed," Paul responded, his voice a mixture of excitement, at addressing the Last Living Weatherman, and a little hostility, "the Communist governments, most of them, have collapsed. Doesn't that change anything?"

Rose sighed. "It's not that simple," she argued. "Socialism still thrives in some countries, none of them major world powers, and someday if we can equalize power in this world, every society could be Socialist. Communism, albeit an ugly, brutal form, also still exists, in China. But Socialism, as it was originally perceived, is the only form of government that doesn't rely on a few exploiting the rest."

Paul was right on her. "But perhaps Marx was fantasizing. Perhaps he was creating a Utopian form of government that could never really exist?"

Rose snapped back, "that's fascist bullshit! It was fascist bullshit thirty years ago and it's still fascist bullshit!"

Paul blushed, offended. "I don't think you need to use bad language—"

I heard a siren. "Rose, you may want to wrap up. I don't know whether that siren is related to us or not…"

Rose was already halfway to the door. "It's been really wonderful getting a chance to talk to you," she said quickly to my students, "and if you finish this course, you will have gotten a pretty decent exposure to American Radical history. Dumont?" I waved. "Avoir!" And she was out the door.

I vaguely wanted to follow her. I wasn't ready for the adventure to end, but I still had a class to teach, and she'd stirred it up pretty well, so I felt I was obligated to stay put. Besides, following Rose would only put me in more trouble than I was already headed for.

"Questions?"

Time passes, and so did all of my students. Can't quite break the pattern of easy grading.

Five months later, I was still teaching at Hawthorne. I didn't get into quite as much trouble as I had feared. Winfield championed me on the grounds of academic freedom of speech. The police missed catching Rose by about two hours. Walter was parked outside the building, his pickup gassed up and ready.

The History Department did undergo some changes. Michael X did go to BC, but Sheila got tenure. And on a more personal note, when some were calling for my resignation for hosting a wanted fugitive as a guest speaker she was among my loudest defenders.

Linda still manages the bookstore. She asked me the other day to go with her to a realtor. "I'd like to buy a different house," she confessed. "I don't think there's a way to stop what happened, but maybe if you at least move, your next crazed former student might not find you so easily?" It might work. Last week we put an offer in for a colonial in Medfield and they accepted, and now we have to pack up because my little bungalow sold in one day.

Yesterday, in my email, I got a note whose domain of origin appears to have been the University of Berlin. 'Walter and I got to Conneaut in ten hours of non-stop driving. It reminded me of my trip with Carl and Leon in northern Maine, because my butt was aching when we stopped. Walter was much better company than Leon. We talked about a lot of things, including favorite movies. Mine? Grapes of Wrath. His? Apocalypse Now. I told him we might not be so far apart after all. We went to his house and picked up his mother, who kind of reminded me of my mother (maybe all mothers remind us of all mothers?). I went to the cemetery with him and his Mom. I can't quite describe what happened there. It seemed kind of holy. I was raised a Methodist, and they don't do confession, but that's what it was like. Mrs. Schneidel wasn't very angry anymore, and she accepted my apology. Then I put some flowers on Officer Schneidel's grave, and explained to him that even though Weatherman declared war on the police, we wouldn't have shot him except we were so scared. I asked for God's forgiveness for me and for Carl.'

I couldn't tell whether she was being cynical or not, but since she'd posted this from Germany there was no longer any duress.

'Mrs. Schneidel showed me some pictures of Walter as a kid—homely sack of spuds he was—and how hard she worked to raise Walter without his father. She's a heroic woman. I slept on their couch that night. Next day we went out for breakfast, my treat. Walter drove me to the Cleveland airport and I caught a connecting flight to New York and then out of U.S. airspace. I'm writing you from Berlin. The city looks good without a wall. East Germany was a shit hole. Keep your eyes on cyberspace. My leg may never be the same but I can still use a computer. Thanks—belatedly—for all your help. You did a good job, and you're a good teacher. Think of Carl and me from time to time. I think of him all the time. Love, Rose.'

About the Author

Robert Moore lives in Framingham, Massachusetts, with his wife Stephanie and pets Maggie and Mollie, dog and cat. The author grew up in Niagara Falls, New York, an early hot bed of Weatherman activity, though he didn't know it at the time. A librarian by trade, this is his first published novel.

Printed in the United Kingdom
by Lightning Source UK Ltd.
104887UKS00001BB/244

9 780595 196296